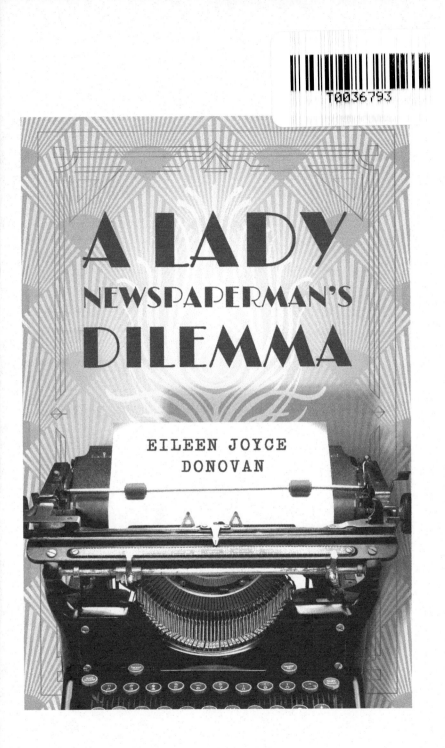

A LADY
NEWSPAPERMAN'S
DILEMMA

EILEEN JOYCE
DONOVAN

A LADY
NEWSPAPERMAN'S
DILEMMA

EILEEN JOYCE
DONOVAN

Woodhall Press | *Norwalk, CT*

woodhall press

Woodhall Press, 81 Old Saugatuck Road, Norwalk, CT 06855
WoodhallPress.com

Cover design: Asha Hossain
Layout artist: LJ Mucci

Library of Congress Cataloging-in-Publication Data available

ISBN 978-1-954907-15-7 (paper: alk paper)
ISBN 978-1-954907-16-4 (electronic)

First Edition

Distributed by Independent Publishers Group
(800) 888-4741

Printed in the United States of America

This is a work of fiction. Names, characters, business, events and incidents are the products of the author's imagination. Any resemblance to actual persons, living or dead, or actual events is purely coincidental.

for Donald, my eternal muse.

CHAPTER 1

Sunset Valley, Montana 1955
Even though I wasn't a soldier, I had the US Army to thank for launching my newspaper career. When I arrived in Sunset Valley, any association with the army seemed about as far-fetched as receiving a coveted journalism award. But both events happened.

However, this wasn't the time to dwell on ancient history. I was here in Maureen's backyard to celebrate the birth of her and Hank's first grandchild.

Shaking my head to clear those old dusty cobwebs, I tried to focus on what the man to my right was saying. As he babbled away about the upcoming rodeo and his prize bulls, I peeked over his head and tried to catch Maureen's eye. Maybe she could rescue me from this blowhard and his bulls, but probably not. Her backyard was filled with friends, gathered here for the celebration.

Although she was my closest friend and I loved her dearly, I found this rural crowd difficult to talk to. I had become too accustomed to my city friends who discussed art exhibits, plays, and current bestsellers. Not bulls. But for Maureen's sake, I'd be polite, listen, and fake an interest in the conversation.

It had been years since I'd seen her, and I was thrilled I could squeeze in a couple of hours for this event. I wished it could be a longer visit, but my awards dinner was scheduled for tomorrow night. As it was, I'd have to drive to Billings tonight to catch my plane to New York early tomorrow morning. But any inconvenience was worth it to see Maureen so happy.

Every time I visited Maureen, memories of my brief time in this Montana town overwhelmed me. The town and people hadn't changed at all, but I had. Funny how things work out. I wouldn't be where I am right now if the army hadn't come to that town under circumstances most people, hopefully, will never have to experience. When I wrote the story for *The Sunset Valley Daily Star*, I didn't think it would go any further than our little paper.

Boy, was I wrong.

Sunset Valley, Montana 1921
As he opened the door, the bus driver called out, "Sunset Valley. There'll be an hour layover here, so take care of your personal needs and get something to eat. We'll go straight on to Billings from here. No stops."

I checked the seams on my stockings, adjusted my cloche hat, and stepped out onto the sidewalk. The Sunset Hotel was directly in front of me. A giant boot spur jutted out from its marquee. Three different saloons took up most of the rest of the block, although now they were all shuttered and dark, thanks to the Prohibition amendment passed six years ago.

As I looked around, I realized Sunset Valley was a lot bigger than I'd imagined. I'd thought it would be a small town where I could get my feet wet. But it was a real city.

What have I done? This may be the worst decision I've ever made.

"Looks like you plan on staying here for a while," the bus driver said, eyeing my valise.

"Yep. I start my job as a reporter for the local paper tomorrow."

I held my purse in front of me like a shield. Ever since I was a little girl, I had wanted to be a journalist. My hometown weekly paper fascinated me, but I knew there were bigger fish to fry, so I'd spent the past four years in college training for this opportunity. I hoped this would be a stepping stone that would launch me into a career with a major metropolitan newspaper.

The sixty-five-mile bus ride from home had left me stiff and achy. No matter what the ads said, the bus was not a luxurious way to travel. But it was about the only way I could have gotten here. I certainly didn't have the money to buy a car.

Am I really ready for this? Maybe I should just take the next bus back home.

"You'll do fine, honey," the bus driver said, winking. "Don't you let these cowboys scare you. They just like to sound tough. They're all pussycats under their ten-gallon hats."

I picked up my valise and walked to the hotel, head held high, ready to conquer anyone or anything that tried to prevent my career from blossoming. But my bravado belied the roller-coaster ride my stomach was on.

Maybe Mom was right. I'll probably never make it here. I'll fall flat on my face and have to go back home disgraced. Then I'll have to listen to her endless tales of people trying to reach above their station in life and where it got them.

When I decided to accept the job offer and move here, I had faced a barrage of questions from everyone back home. It seemed no one could understand why I would want to leave "our nice little town," especially to work as a reporter. Everyone thought I should be content to get married and produce grandchildren for my parents to spoil. Mutterings about what a waste of time and money it was for my parents to have sent me to college were rampant. And now that I was here, I began to have my own doubts.

Stop it, Alex. Now's the time to prove all of them wrong, Mom included.

I knew once I was actually working at the paper everything would work out. I just had to get through tonight.

3

I looked up at the Sunset Hotel, which would be my home for now, and the nondescript building told me this was a no-nonsense town. Windows for the Met Café, the Golden Spur Bar, its shades drawn, and a barbershop interrupted the sterile, white stucco exterior. The second story accents of burgundy-red bricks added some interest, but not much.

I walked into the hotel lobby which had club chairs scattered about, doilies covering the threadbare arms and headrests. The tin ceiling and hanging lights looked like they had been there since the 1800s. The carpets were so worn the pattern had disappeared into the beige canvas backing. And there was a pervasive musty smell, like an attic room that hadn't been aired out in years. At one time, the hotel must have been elegant. Now it was just old, faded, and worn-out.

An elderly clerk stood behind the battered wooden check-in desk at the back of the lobby. On the left was an entrance to the Met Café. *Great—a convenient place to get breakfast, and maybe even dinner.*

On the right, the lobby door to the Golden Spur was closed with a padlock through the handles. A quick glance into the café showed it was crowded. I licked my lips, already tasting an ice-cold lemonade. I checked in, and asked the clerk if he would watch my suitcase. I knew if I went up to my room and kicked my high heels off, I'd never get them back on. And I really wanted that lemonade.

Ah well, the price we women pay to look our best.

"Where you headed, miss?"

"Thought I'd have a lemonade after that long bus ride. I'm awfully thirsty."

He looked at my bright red suit and tan cloche, and shook his head. "City girl, are you? And traveling alone? Don't know what the world's coming to. Why, in my day—"

"I'm definitely *not* a city girl. My hometown is even smaller than Sunset Valley. And I think you showuld dress your best when you travel. You never know what interesting people you might meet, especially when you're on your own."

"Maybe so, but you be careful in that café. Don't pay any attention to those cowboys in there. They don't have anything to occupy their time, what with it being mud season and all, so they can get a little antsy. And they don't always like strangers."

"I'll keep my head down."

"You do that."

While his concern was appreciated, I wasn't worried. I had grown up in my dad's saloon and had probably seen more brawls before I was twelve than the clerk had in his whole life.

When I entered, everyone stopped talking. The smell of burnt coffee assaulted me, and the familiar look of the place brought tears to my eyes. It was so much like Mae's Café on Main Street that loneliness and a homesick feeling overwhelmed me.

Peering through the cigarette haze, I spotted an empty stool at the far end of a counter that stretched the entire length of the room. I headed for it like it was an oasis in the desert. I seated myself, and signaled for the man behind the counter.

"What can I do for you?" he asked.

"A cold lemonade, please."

"Why don't you go sit at a table and I'll bring it over to you?"

"I'd rather have it right here."

"Well . . . the thing is . . . ladies don't usually sit at the counter."

"Then there's no problem. I'm not a lady, I'm a newspaperman." A little shiver went down my spine.

This is it. I'll either get thrown out with my tail between my legs or not.

He stared at me for a minute and then laughed. "Well then, I guess you're fine." He poured my drink and landed it in front of me. "Where you from?"

"Jericho Flats." He looked at me with a blank face. "It's a little northeast of here."

"Oh. No wonder it didn't sound familiar."

I took a long swig of the lemonade. It was ice cold and just what I wanted.

"Just passing through?" he asked, wiping down the area around my glass.

"Nope. I'm going to be a reporter for *The Sunset Valley Daily Star.*"

"You don't say. Guess we'll be seeing a lot of you around here."

"Guess so."

"Hey, boys," he called to the men seated at the counter. "This gal's going to work for the paper." Turning to me, he asked, "What'd you say your name was?"

"I didn't, but it's Alex. Alex Lawson."

"Name's Alex Lawson, boys. Make her feel welcome."

There was lots of grumbling and growling about a woman reporter, especially one sitting at their counter. A few ranchers shook their heads, finished their coffees, and left, but my host had decided my fate and that was that. Obviously, his word stood as law in this room. He was a big guy and in good shape, so I was sure no one challenged his decisions.

I raised my nearly empty glass to them. *Gee, guess I really was thirsty.* "Gentlemen."

"You're welcome here anytime, Alex. I'm Pete. I own this place."

We shook hands and I knew I had made my first friend—and contact—in Sunset Valley.

Pete wiped down the counter again and looked at me.

"You know, for a young lady, you're real comfortable sitting here on a stool. How's that happen?"

"Back home, my dad owned the only saloon in town and I practically grew up there."

"That explains it then. Ready for another?" he asked, pointing to my empty glass.

"Sure."

While I drank my lemonade, I took a full inventory of the room. It had the same tin ceiling as the hotel. The wooden counter was scarred from years of use, the edge worn down to raw wood from hundreds of belt buckles rubbing against it. My fingers traced the scratches, nicks, notches, and initials carved there and I wondered what ancient stories they held. Ceiling lights bounced off the brass cash register, which sat in the middle of a back shelf stocked with enough sweets and desserts to provide a dentist with a lifetime's work of filling cavities. Mottled mirrors behind the colorful syrup bottles swallowed the light and distorted my reflection. The black and white tile floor was worn, but clean. Booths lined the opposite wall, stuffed heads of every beast that roamed Montana, or thereabouts, mounted over them: buffalo, moose, deer, elk, and even some prize bulls. Just like home.

I noticed the men passing a flask under the counter and surreptitiously tipping it into their coffee cups. Now I knew why Pete had suggested I sit at a table. These days you couldn't be too careful where strangers were concerned.

"Another, Alex?" Pete asked, as I swallowed a big swig from my glass.

"I think I've had my fill for the day. I want to get settled and see about a place for dinner. Any suggestions?" I had decided to treat myself to a good dinner to celebrate my first night in Sunset Valley, even though I was working on a tight budget.

"Well, this place isn't bad, of course, but if you're looking for a good steak, and want to treat yourself, the Range Riders across the street would be my choice."

"Well, then, the Range Riders it is," I said. "Maybe I'll stop in later."

"Enjoy your dinner, Alex. And welcome to Sunset Valley."

I gulped down the rest of my lemonade and brushed down my skirt. As I left, I could feel the men's eyes following me, a feeling I knew well from my dad's saloon. At five-foot-ten, I was used to stares. I gave the men a little salute and strutted out, some of my old self-confidence creeping back.

I breathed a sigh of relief as I picked up my valise from the desk clerk. I hadn't been thrown out of the café, I thought I had made a friend, and I knew where to find my next meal. I was off for my first night in the city. And tomorrow, off to my first real job.

CHAPTER 2

The next morning, I walked into the Met Café at eight o'clock. The smell of freshly perked coffee hit me, as well as the greasy smell of the grill. I didn't see Pete, but maybe he was busy with bookkeeping, the bane of every small business.

My breakfast of bacon, eggs, home fries, toast, and coffee tasted better than I expected. The cook had worked his magic on the eggs to make them tasty. And the bacon. Just right, crispy without being burned. Checking the clock, I saw it was only eight forty-five. I lingered over my second cup of coffee as long as I could, but I still had plenty of time to spare before my eleven o'clock appointment with Mr. Gordon, editor of the paper.

I was glad the café served a decent breakfast. I had no idea when I'd get a chance to eat again if Mr. Gordon assigned me to a story right away. And food was always a top priority for me.

I paid my bill and went back to my room to brush my teeth and freshen my lipstick. I checked my purse, for the hundredth time, to make sure I had my notebook, pencils, and ruby red lipstick—my secret weapon. It seemed easier for a pretty woman reporter to get men chatting than it was for a hard-nosed man, at least in my limited experience.

Since I still had two hours to kill before meeting Mr. Gordon, I wandered around the town and browsed in some of the stores. I was too nervous to sit in my room or the hotel lobby. At quarter to eleven, I stopped in front of *The Sunset Valley Daily Star* building and looked up at the masthead of a setting sun engraved above the door. Excitement pulsed through me. This was it. A shot at becoming an ace reporter for a major newspaper. Not exactly the *San Francisco Chronicle* or the *Denver Post*, but still, a definite step up from the college newspaper. Besides, it was the only one that had offered me a job. I took off my coat, straightened the seams on my stockings, tugged my suit jacket down, and headed inside.

The minute I opened the door, I smelled the ink from the presses in the basement, more pungent than the whiff from a fresh newspaper. Although silent right now, I knew in a few hours the floor would vibrate and hum with their energy, printing tomorrow morning's paper. I waited while the woman at the front desk, both receptionist and switchboard operator, answered calls, and I wondered if the phone ever stopped ringing. Finally, she pulled the last plug.

"Can I help you?" she asked.

"I have an appointment with Mr. Gordon."

"Are you Alex Lawson?"

"Yes."

She covered her mouth and snickered.

"Well, he'll be surprised. Go right in. His office is against the back wall. He's expecting you—or at least he's expecting an Alex Lawson."

I felt my face getting hot.

I should be used to this by now; everyone assumes Alex is a man. Not that it matters. He's already hired me.

I walked across the cavernous room filled with mostly empty desks and covered typewriters. A couple of people were working, but for the most part it looked like a newspaper graveyard, desolate and gloomy. Mr. Gordon's door was closed, but I could see him through the glass insert. He sat behind a cloud of cigar smoke, head down, proofreading some copy, red pencil in hand. I knocked and he signaled for me to come in, never lifting his eyes from the galley pages.

"What?" he asked in a gravelly voice that likely came from years of smoking and drinking hard whiskey.

"Alex Lawson, Mr. Gordon," I said.

His head jerked up and the glasses perched on his forehead slid down to his nose.

"You're Alex Lawson?"

"I am. You probably thought I was a man. Am I right?"

"Umm, no, no," he stammered. "Well, maybe. Is Alex your full name? Or is it a nickname?"

"My full name is Alexandria Victoria Lawson, but that's a mouthful. I've always been known as just Alex, but I think I'll make a note to myself to sign my letters with my full name from now on."

"Humph." He moved papers around on his desk, then pulled a file out from the bottom of a pile, rubbing one hand up and down his face.

"Sit. Sit. Funny, your professors never mentioned you were a woman. Just referred to you as Alex. But I guess that's not important. What's important is whether or not you can write. I liked the clippings you sent, and your professors' recommendations were first-class. Of course, the *Star* is a world removed from a college newspaper. But . . . well, with so many men lost in the war, beggars can't be choosers, as the saying goes."

"Yes, sir. And I know I have a lot to learn."

I wriggled around in my seat, my hands twisting themselves into a knot.

Oh, dear God. He's not going to fire me, is he? Before I even get started? I won't be able to show my face back in Jericho Flats. How will I pay back the money Mom and Dad loaned me for this trip?

Mr. Gordon sat, hands steepled under his nose, staring at me. I took this opportunity to size him up. Early fifties. Thinning dark brown hair turning gray at the temples. Rolled-up shirtsleeves that exposed thick muscular forearms covered with dark hair. A stained tie hung loose from his open collar.

I felt the sweat trickle down between my breasts. I knew he was reconsidering his decision to hire me, but I needed this job to prove myself before I could get what I really wanted: a job writing for a major metropolitan paper.

After what seemed like an eternity, he asked, "What made you decide to come here? I hope you don't think you're going to find a husband in Sunset Valley. There aren't very many young men left after the war."

"That's not why I'm here." I felt my temper rising and face heating up.

How dare he think I came here to husband-hunt. Why does everyone assume every young woman wants to get married and have children? I'm a career woman and I came here to begin that journey, not to be claimed by a man and chained to a sink and cradle for the rest of my life.

"Then why don't you tell me why you are here?"

"Ever since I could read a newspaper, I've wanted to be a journalist. When I hear or read something, I become curious. I want to know all the facts of a story. What happened. Why it happened. Who the people are behind the news. Then I want to tell everyone what I've learned. Telling them the important news that affects their lives. Maybe even have a column of my own one day."

"Getting a little ahead of yourself, aren't you, Alex? That'd be a long way down the road. But what about getting married? Having kids? That's what most young women want."

I tamped down my rising temper and tried to sound as rational as possible.

"Afraid that's not for me. A career as a journalist is all that's important to me. I can't see myself as a housewife and mother."

The minutes ticked by as he sat staring at me. Finally, he stood, reached his hand across the desk, and said, "Welcome to the *Star*."

"Thank you. I can't wait to get started."

He walked around his desk, opened his office door, and yelled, "Betty! Find a desk for Alex, here. She'll be starting with community news. Show her the ropes."

He turned and faced me. "Betty's our star reporter and one of the best. You'll learn a lot from her."

Community news? Not a beat that will get me noticed. But I guess I have to start somewhere. I just have to make sure I don't get stuck there.

A blonde-haired woman got up from her desk and walked toward me, hand extended.

"Hi, Alex," she said, shaking my hand. "Betty Hughes. Welcome. You can have the desk next to mine. That way if you have any questions I'll be nearby. That okay?"

"Sounds perfect."

"Oh, and Lou," Betty said, "I heard what you told Alex. Maybe it's time to ask for a raise."

Mr. Gordon grunted and walked back into his office. Betty shook her head and laughed. She threaded her arm through mine and led me away.

"It'll be swell having another woman around here," she said.

I breathed a sigh of relief. I was officially a reporter, the first step toward something I had dreamed about all my life.

CHAPTER 3

"Feel settled in?" Betty asked once I had looked in all the drawers, found a place for my purse, and tested the keys on my typewriter.

"I guess so," I said. "I just wish the butterflies would stop flying around in my stomach and settle down."

She laughed. "They will as soon as you do. Now, today, you'll go along with me and start to get comfortable. You know, meet some people, learn the layout of the town, that kind of thing. I won't throw you into the lion's den on your own just yet. How about we go to the courthouse and City Hall and see if we can scare up some news."

"I'm ready."

I grabbed my purse and hat while Betty grabbed our coats. She tossed mine to me, eyeing me up and down. I shimmied into it and followed her out, the clickety-clack of our high heels the only sound in what should have been a room filled with shouts and typing.

Outside, I asked Betty, "Where are all the other reporters?"

"I'm afraid we're it," she said.

My mouth hung open and I stopped dead in my tracks.

"Come on. Don't look so surprised. The war took a lot of young men, you know."

"Sure, I know, but are you saying *all* the reporters were killed?"

"To be honest, there were never a lot of us. There're still a couple of older guys, like Lou, who are probably out talking to some ranchers. It might be months before you meet them, since Joe does the agricultural news, but his report is weekly, and Tom is in charge of advertising. Sometimes he goes right to typesetting and works with them on the ads. He's in and out before I get back to the office. So, for the most part, it's you and me."

"Wow. So that's why so many of the desks in the newsroom are empty. But you can't be responsible for the whole paper, can you?"

"No. Lou takes care of all the state and national news, and any from overseas. They all come through from the wire services. He figures out what to include, or rewrite, and where it should go. I only have to handle the local news, community calendar, and feature articles, the ones that Lou, or I, think will interest our readers."

"That still seems like an awful lot to do."

"It hasn't been easy. We had a few young guys from the local college, but they got drafted. Then a woman from another town came to work here, but found it was more than she wanted to do every day. I have a couple college students who write some stories—English majors only, of course; I don't need to add massive editing to my list. Simple stuff. Human interest. Nothing that could do any damage, you know. But they'll be leaving at the end of the semester."

"Sounds like you're a real one-woman show."

"Welcome to Sunset Valley. Everyone here does the job of at least three people. Hope you're ready for that."

"Don't worry about me. I'm used to juggling. When your dad owns the only saloon in town, you learn how to waitress, bartend, study, and cook, all at the same time. College was easy. I only had to waitress and study."

Betty laughed. "You'll fit right in then." She checked her watch and said, "Damn, I didn't realize it was twelve o'clock already. The courts will be on lunch recess, so I guess we should stop for lunch too."

"Lunch?" I asked, thinking about my very limited finances.

"Peanut butter sandwiches all right with you? I only live a couple of blocks away, and I go home for lunch."

"Oh, I couldn't impose like that," I said.

"I invited *you*, remember? C'mon, it'll be nice to have someone to talk to for a change."

"Okay, thanks."

We walked a few blocks to Betty's house. She told me about the owners of the different shops on Main Street, and who lived in each of the houses we passed in the residential section. Some life was starting to come back to the trees and bushes now that the deep winter freeze was over. Although it was only March, you could feel the warmth of spring in the sun. The wind had lost its bitter bite, and a few crocuses were daring to peek out from their underground hibernation dens.

"This is it." Betty stopped at the gate of a white wooden picket fence. She opened the latch and led the way up the cement path to a small white bungalow with a dark green door and shutters.

"Let's go have that gourmet lunch I promised," Betty said.

We hung our hats and coats on the wall pegs behind the door and I got a quick glimpse into Betty's bedroom to the left of the entrance. White ruffled curtains fluttered in the breeze from the open windows. A white chenille bedspread covered the full-size bed that dominated the room. A desk cluttered with books, notebooks, and loose papers left little room for the typewriter in the center.

I wonder if she's writing a book. Gee, I can't imagine doing that on top of writing for the paper.

The living room was to the right, with green fern design wallpaper, a dark green sofa, and a brown armchair. Overflowing bookcases flanked the brick fireplace.

"Gee, this is nice," I said. "I think I'm finding out some things about you."

"Like what?" Betty asked.

"Looks like you're writing something that's not for the paper. Maybe a book?"

"Okay. First lesson as a reporter." Betty turned to face me. "Never assume anything. You could be wrong, and if it goes into print, the paper could be sued. Especially if your assumption is about an influential person. Why not try to learn the ropes first before trying to find a big story? Besides, that's my job. Yours is to write the community news. Not make headlines. That's my job. Your time will come. Eventually."

I could feel heat radiating up my neck onto my face. Why couldn't I keep my mouth shut instead of trying to show her how observant I am?

"I'm sorry. I guess that was stupid of me. I don't know anything about you and guess I was just trying to find out a little something. I leapt to a conclusion based on what I saw."

"Yeah, well, don't be too hard on yourself, kid. Maybe next time, ask before assuming anything. Your job as a reporter means you have to rely on facts, not assumptions. I would think they would have taught you that in your journalism classes."

I knew she was right, but didn't appreciate being treated like a high school kid who had never reported on anything. After all, I had been the editor of my college paper. But now, I'd probably never find out whether or not I was right about the book.

"C'mon, let's get those sandwiches."

We walked down the hall to the kitchen. A bathroom lay at the end of the hallway, with a small bedroom to the left. I caught a glimpse of a single bed and night table, but Betty didn't offer to show me that room. I followed her into a spotless kitchen with a black and white checkerboard tile floor and white walls. Black and white plaid café curtains framed the back door window and the one over the sink that looked out onto the backyard. A square table with a red top and four chairs occupied the center of the room.

"Have a seat while I fix our sandwiches," Betty said. "Coffee? Tea?"

"I'll have whatever you're having. Is there anything I can do to help?"

"I think I can manage to slap some peanut butter on bread, but I appreciate the offer." She slammed the bread and a jar of peanut butter on the counter.

A definite chill had settled over the room and it wasn't from the weather. Betty filled the kettle with water, set it on the stove, and started to make our lunch. I couldn't tell if I had annoyed her by assuming I knew things about her, or if she regretted asking me to join her for lunch. Either way, if my future meant working with her, I had to clear the air somehow.

I twisted my college ring around my finger as my stomach played leapfrog with itself. I shuffled my feet and moved the condiments around on the tray that sat in the middle of the table.

"Alex," Betty said, turning away from the kitchen counter to face me, "stop beating yourself up. You made a perfectly valid assumption based on what you saw in there. I guess I'm just not used to having people ask me about my life, or even visit me here. This place has become a kind of sanctuary for me. A place I can be by myself away from work, away from competing with men in an attempt to be recognized as a good reporter. Come to think of it, you might be the only person I've ever invited here, aside from my family. Guess you reminded me a little of myself on my first day—a bit green, and nervous as hell. You'll be fine, I'm sure, once you get your feet under you."

"Really? Gee, that means a lot to me. I love this house. It's so homey and warm."

The kettle's whistle blew and Betty turned back to the stove to make our tea. I admired her independence and her drive to succeed. I knew I could learn a lot from her if I didn't make an enemy out of her first. I certainly seemed to hit a nerve when I asked if she was writing a book. Hopefully, she'll forgive and forget my prying. But isn't that what good reporters do? Maybe. Just not to colleagues.

While we ate, Betty said, "I'm curious. Since we're going to be working hand in hand, so to speak, tell me all about you."

"Not much to tell. I'm from Jericho Flats. My dad used to own a saloon called Cattlemen before Prohibition. Now it's a café. My mom's a schoolteacher. They both encouraged my writing, Dad more so than Mom. He thought I could be the next F. Scott Fitzgerald or Willa Cather. Mom thought I was chasing a pipe dream."

Betty laughed and said, "Don't all fathers think their little girls are destined to be someone special? But most parents think that includes getting married and having kids. Didn't he want that for you?"

"If he did, he never said so. He always said he wanted me to be happy. And now that I'm here, I can't wait to write something I can send them. I'm sure they'll be proud of me and show it to everyone in town."

"I can almost guarantee it will be posted on the mirror behind the counter, on full display. There is a mirror, isn't there?"

"Of course. I think that's an unwritten law for cafés and saloons."

"Any brothers or sisters?"

"Nope, just me. How about you?"

"Oh, I come from a whole mob. Nine of us. Five boys and four girls. It was fun growing up with them, but I was glad to get away when I got older."

"Get away from where?"

"Tiny town in North Dakota called Reeder. Population around two hundred fifty when I left. It's probably lower now, what with all the men lost in the war."

A faraway look came into Betty's eyes, and I didn't want to pry into why, so, for once, I kept quiet.

After we finished eating, Betty got up and took the plates to the sink.

I jumped up and said, "I'll wash these. You can relax for a minute."

"Thanks. I'll freshen up, and we'll be on our way."

While I washed and dried the dishes, I thought about how nice it would be to have a little home like this of my own. A sanctuary, like Betty said. Maybe someday.

"Ready?" Betty asked, breaking into my daydream.

"A minute to freshen up myself?" I asked.

"Sure. I'll wait for you outside."

I ducked into the bathroom, and on my way out, took a peek into the other bedroom, smaller than Betty's, with only one window facing the side yard. A plaid bedspread covered the single bed with a battered night table on one side.

Obviously, no one lives here. No personal effects at all in this room. Uh oh, there I go, making assumptions again. I've got to stop doing that, and being so nosy.

I grabbed my hat, coat, and purse before Betty started wondering what was keeping me. I hoped that someday I'd be as confident and independent as Betty. She was pretty terrific.

As we walked back into the center of town, she chatted away like we had known each other for years. Betty obviously wasn't annoyed with my prying anymore. Or at least she was hiding it well. I hoped we could become friends, not just work colleagues.

"Depending on how today goes," Betty said, "either later today or tomorrow you'll have to stop in at the town's churches. They usually have something going on that we need to report. In any event, you should meet all the pastors. Are you a churchgoing person?"

"Not really. When I was little, Mom made me go to Sunday school and services. But when I reached high school, it was pretty much left to me to decide what I wanted to do. And my bed seemed much more inviting than the fire and brimstone sermons at church."

"I know what you mean," Betty said. "But it's a good idea to stop in at the church offices and stay in touch. They'll all assume you attend services somewhere else, but are still interested in them."

"That's clever. I never would have thought of doing that."

"You're a reporter in a small town now, and that means convincing the people who live here that you're concerned about everything that happens. Whether it's who's getting married, who died, who's moving—although that rarely happens—when the church bake sale will take place . . . the list goes on and on."

"Gee, I never realized I'd have to cover all those things."

"How do you think they get in the paper?"

"At home, people just told Mr. Miller, the editor, about them, or dropped a note in his mailbox. Of course, the paper only came out once a week, so that makes a difference."

"Well, here, we have to ask about upcoming events, and they'd better be in there. That's probably what most people read. Gossip in print. If we're not on top of all that, believe me, people will stop buying the paper. Then you and I will be looking for new jobs."

"But how will I know about all those things?"

Betty looked at me and shook her head. "I thought you were a reporter. Didn't you ever have to do these types of stories in college? Make yourself known around town. Get out and meet people. Introduce yourself to everyone—store owners, schoolteachers, pastors, local organizations, you know. Think of Jericho Flats. Who was influential there? Those are the people you want to get to know, and have them get to know you."

I never realized I'd have to make myself known. Everyone in Jericho Flats knew who I was. Now I was the stranger in town. Somehow, I'd imagined working for the paper would give me instant acceptance and notoriety. Gee, I had a lot to learn.

"Okay, here we are. The Tyler County Court House. Let's see what's on today's docket."

I looked at the imposing three-story building. It had a cream-colored facade, and its three embedded columns on either side of the front door gave it a solid, stately look. Spanning across the top of the columns and raised from the rest of the building, the words "Tyler County Court House" were engraved into the masonry.

Betty stood at the top of the six steps leading to the front door. "Impressive, isn't it?"

"It sure is. It takes up the whole block. It would certainly intimidate me if I were brought here for trial."

"That's the general idea," she said.

I climbed the steps and Betty linked her arm through mine. "Remember, you're a reporter now. We're here to nose around and see if there's a juicy story or trial going on in one of the courtrooms. You can't look like you're afraid of this place, or anyone in it."

"I'll try my best."

"That's the spirit. I'll introduce you to any court officers and bailiffs we see today. It's important to get to know them so you can get into courtrooms without any fuss, and get the dirt on a trial. Maybe we'll even run into a judge or two, or one of the prosecutors."

I swallowed hard and felt those butterflies do more somersaults in my stomach.

"That would be swell," I said, hoping I sounded braver than I felt.

"Just remember to smile. You'll have those guys in the palm of your hand in no time. They can't resist a pretty young girl like you. Take it from one who's been there."

"You're still pretty and young." I'd have bet money she was only in her thirties, not much older than me.

"Not so much anymore. They're all used to me and my tricks, but you're new. You have a chance to catch them off guard. Don't worry—you'll develop your own strategies to get around them. Just remember to use them to get what you want."

I wasn't sure if I knew exactly what she was getting at, but figured I'd find out soon enough.

Betty strutted through the front door. She wasn't as tall as me, maybe around five foot seven or eight. Her blonde hair fell in perfect waves under her cloche hat, and when she pulled her coat off, I noticed her suit fit perfectly, just snug enough to show off her curves. Of course, her confidence protected her from any unwanted male advances better than a suit of armor.

She held her coat over her arm and told me to take mine off. "Gotta show them what you've got," she said. "Spark a little interest in the new gal in town."

I told myself it was all to get a story, although I wasn't sure my journalism professors would approve of her methods.

Once again, the click-clack of our heels on the marble floor were the only sounds in the great hall, until a woman's screams and two gunshots shattered the silence.

CHAPTER 4

"Come on!" Betty grabbed my arm and we ran up the marble stairs to the second-floor courtrooms.

One deputy lay on the hallway floor. It didn't look like he was breathing. Blood ran from a bullet hole in his chest. Another officer knelt next to him, clenching his stomach. An older woman stood further down the hall, plastered to the wall, her hand covering her mouth.

The prisoner—clearly the person who'd shot the deputy—waved a gun at us and fired again. The shot hit Betty and she toppled backwards down the staircase. I screamed and ran to her. Blood poured down her face from a gash on her forehead. More blood seeped through her suit jacket around a bullet hole near her left shoulder. But she was still conscious.

"Help! Help!" I yelled. "Someone get an ambulance!"

I looked back up the staircase to see if anyone was paying attention, but no one answered my calls. My heart pounded. My head swam.

I didn't know what to do. I'd moved here to write news stories, not take part in gunfights.

"Lay still, Betty. I'll find a phone and get an ambulance."

"I'll be fine. Go back and get the story."

"I can't leave you."

"Get the story," Betty said through gritted teeth.

I wadded up a clean handkerchief and pressed it against her wound. "Here. Can you keep pressure on this spot?" I asked. My whole body was trembling.

"Yes." Betty pushed her right hand over the makeshift bandage. "Now go. Get the story."

I crept up the stairs, but before I reached the top step, another shot rang out.

"There. That should hold you," a man said.

I peeked up from my crouched position and saw a tall wiry cowboy pointing a gun at the prisoner he'd just wounded. The cowboy had his boot on the criminal's wrist, his hand still holding the gun.

"Let go of the gun," the cowboy said, "or I'll finish you off right here. I won't wait for the judge to sentence you."

The prisoner loosened his grip.

"You," the cowboy said, looking at me, "come over here and pick up that gun."

I rushed over, grabbed the gun, and backed away. Even though I had been raised around guns and learned to shoot as soon as I could lift one, I had never seen a person shot before. I felt sick as I looked at the carnage of blood and bodies strewn around the courthouse floor.

"My friend's been shot," I said. "Is there a phone around here? I have to call for an ambulance."

His eyes still on the wounded prisoner, the cowboy said, "The judge was calling for help before I left the courtroom."

By now, other people had spilled out of the courtroom and their voices echoed off the walls. I watched people mill about and wondered if shootings were normal in this town. Certainly, no one seemed particularly upset.

Had I taken on more than I bargained for in moving here? Were we back in the Wild West, where arguments were settled with shootouts? Did I want to live in a town where violence was greeted with mute acceptance? My brain jumped from one thought to another and I couldn't make sense of anything.

I looked around and spotted the older woman whose screams had initially attracted our attention. I kept my eye on her as other court officers took control of the chaos in the hallway. She was still plastered against the wall, eyes wide with terror, her hand over her mouth, her face ashen.

I came to my senses and remembered that my job was to get the story. I pushed my way through the crowd to reach her.

"Did you see what happened?" I asked, turning her around to block her view of the bloody scene.

"What?" she mumbled, her eyes slowly focusing on me.

"Did you see what happened?" I asked as gently as possible, pulling my notebook from my purse. "Here, let's get you off your feet." I led her to a bench down the hall. "It must have been terrible."

"Oh, it was," she said, calming down a bit. "I was going to go into that room," she pointed to one of the courtroom doors, "but before I got there, the deputies came down the hall with the prisoner. Just before they reached the door, he started fighting with them, trying to get away, and then, somehow, he managed to get one of their guns."

As she described what had happened, I wrote down every word as fast as my shaking hand would allow.

"And then what happened?" I asked.

"Oh dear, oh dear, I'm so upset. I'm not quite sure."

"You're doing fine, Mrs. . . . ?"

"Mrs. Lynch. Edna Lynch. I come here every morning, you know. It gives me something to do, and sometimes I hear the most interesting cases."

"I'm sure you do," I said. "But to get back to what happened here."

"Oh, yes, of course. Now, where was I?"

"The man got the gun off one of the deputies."

"Yes, yes. Well, he pointed it at them, and that's when I screamed. He turned and looked at me. I don't think he even realized I was there before that. Well, that's when one of the deputies tried to jump him and the prisoner started shooting. I was terrified. In all the years I've been coming here, I've never seen anything like this before."

"Thank goodness for that," I said.

"You can certainly say that. I don't know what's come over this world lately. I blame it all on the war."

"I don't know about that, but I think he'll be spending the rest of his life in prison, or with the hangman. Any idea who the cowboy is, the one who shot the prisoner? Or the name of the deputies who got shot?"

"Of course. The young man is Henry Ferguson, the son of the man the prisoner killed. The whole family was here today for the sentencing. I'm not sure who the deputies are. I didn't pay much attention to them, I'm afraid."

"That's all right. I can get their names later."

She narrowed her eyes and stared at me. "Who are you, anyway?"

"My name's Alex Lawson, and I'm a reporter for the *Star*," I said, extending my hand.

"Oh, will I be in the paper?" she asked as she shook my hand.

"I imagine so. Your eyewitness account will probably make the front-page."

"Oh my, oh my. Won't my bridge partners be jealous," she said, her cheeks coloring a little.

"You've been great, Mrs. Lynch. Now I'd better see how my partner is doing. She got shot too. Thanks for your help."

"Anytime, dear, but I must say, I don't want to experience a situation like this again."

I smiled at her and left to look for Betty amid the ambulance drivers and stretchers lining the hallway. When I didn't see her right away, I looked around for Henry Ferguson, but it seemed most people had fled the courthouse.

I found some spectators downstairs discussing the shootings and quizzed them for more information. I got a few quotes from some of the family members and others who had come to see justice done. They gave me their impressions and thoughts about the prisoner, but, of course, those weren't facts, just conjecture.

I decided the best thing to do was follow Betty's instructions and get the story out. I ran all the way back to the paper. This was my first big scoop, and I wasn't about to let anyone else claim it.

CHAPTER 5

WOMAN'S SCREAM HALTS
PRISONER'S ESCAPE
by Alex Lawson

I could hardly believe it. My first day on the job, and already a front-page story, with a byline.

I read the article again. It was sheer luck that Edna Lynch happened to be standing right outside the courtroom and that I had been there to get her story. Of course, that wouldn't have happened if Betty hadn't been shot. It could just as easily have been me lying on the courthouse floor, a bullet in my shoulder. Days later, Betty told me that since Edna was at the courthouse every day, she often had information that was more accurate than the officers.

After talking to Mr. Gordon and rummaging through some past issues of the paper, I uncovered the whole story about the prisoner. Billy Webb had been found guilty of murdering his father-in-law,

Ben Ferguson, in Ismay, a town all the way over in the western part of the county. Since there were only about a hundred and seventy-five people living there, everyone knew everyone else. Most were probably related by birth or marriage. Half the Ferguson family sat in the courtroom ready to hear the judge's sentence for Webb. I guess Webb figured he had nothing to lose, so escape was the only option—that, or be hanged like the guy in Missoula last year. Of course, the judge could sentence him to life imprisonment, but I guess this chump figured a quick bullet would be better.

Turns out this Webb guy was a real no-good bum. He had drifted into Ismay from somewhere in Montana and managed to get work on the Lazy F, the Ferguson ranch. Rough-and-tumble as they come, he seemed exciting to the teenage Ferguson daughter. Before long, she got pregnant and married him. Webb figured being married to the boss's daughter put him on Easy Street, so his drinking went from Saturday night to every day.

Old Man Ferguson had no intention of supporting a bum and insisted he do his fair share of work on the ranch. But Webb didn't like that, and they constantly argued about it. According to Webb's testimony during the trial, which I was able to get from the court stenographer, the two men went out one day to check on the cattle. When his father-in-law started yelling at him for the hundredth time, calling him a shiftless, good-for-nothing bum, Webb got tired of all the harassment and decided he had had enough. So, he shot him. After that, he knew he couldn't go home, so he ran. It didn't take long for the sheriff to catch and arrest him. It became pretty obvious through the course of the trial, according to Edna, that he was guilty and "not the least little bit sorry."

What a story for my first day.

I gathered copies of the paper to send home, and to my journalism professors back at the University of Montana in Missoula. This had to be the most exciting day of my life.

"How does it feel to be on the front-page?" Mr. Gordon asked, leaning over my shoulder, his cigar smoke fogging up the page as I read the article again.

"Great—really swell, Mr. Gordon," I said.

"Guess for now you'll have to be my ace reporter. At least until Betty comes back. When she does, you're back to community news. The job you were hired for. You understand that, don't you?"

"Sure, of course." My stomach dropped like it was made of lead. I went from floating on a cloud to finding myself back at the bottom of a mud bog. I understood, but that didn't mean I was going to take it lying down. I made a decision right then and there to fight with everything I had to keep the status this story had earned me. Maybe by the time Betty got out of the hospital, Mr. Gordon would have decided I was indispensable as his lead reporter. I set my mind to making that happen. Nothing was going to distract me from this goal.

"But, things being what they are, I guess you can start calling me Lou the way everyone else does."

"Thanks, Lou. I know I can't expect to make the front-page every day, but it sure feels good today," I said, trying to regain some of the elation I had felt earlier that morning.

"That's fine, but we have a paper to get out tomorrow too, so you'd better get to work, little lady."

"Sure, Lou. Anything special you want me to cover today?"

"Get with Betty and—oh, you can't, can you? Now that she's laid up in the hospital, it'll be up to you to get the local news. Think you can handle it?"

"Sure, Lou." I kept my hands clasped around the newspaper so he wouldn't notice them trembling. He chomped his cigar and stared at me.

"Humph. Guess I don't have a choice. All right, get off cloud nine and get another front-page story."

Lou walked away, puffing on his cigar and filling up the room with its smell and smoke.

I grabbed my hat, coat, and purse, tucked the papers away in my desk, and headed for the door. I didn't want my story to get ruined. It would be the first entry in my scrapbook.

I stood on the front steps, wondering where to start.

Yesterday—gosh, was it only yesterday?—Betty had promised to introduce me to all the town officials. But she wasn't around and wouldn't be for a while. Since Lou hadn't assigned anything special for me to cover, I decided to head to City Hall. I'd just have to introduce myself.

City Hall was a big brick building, not as imposing as the county courthouse. Two stories high, with six steps leading to a single door entrance, it also housed the Sunset Valley Sheriff's Department, the usual globe lights on either side of the door. Compared to the Town Hall back home, this was big city personified, and a little intimidating. At least for me it was.

Inside, deputies hurried past each other, women carrying folders scurried around, men in suits went in and out of closed doors that stretched the length of the hallway. While the interior of the county courthouse had been designed to be intimidating, everything about City Hall revolved around the business of running a city. No fluff. Nothing fancy. Strictly utilitarian.

The clatter of leather shoes, boots, and high heels on the terrazzo tile floor would have been deafening if not for the wooden doors, wainscoting, and benches lining the walls. Each door had a glass insert in the top half, the name of the city office engraved on it: Records Department, District Attorney's Office, Board of Appeals, Fire and Rescue, Archives, and Public Health.

I poked my head into the district attorney's office. No one was there, so I went upstairs.

I walked toward the front of the building and climbed the wooden staircase to the second floor. The city court and the mayor's office were the only two doors with brass plaques.

I took a deep breath and walked into the mayor's office. A pleasant gray-haired lady looked up from her typing. "Hi," she said. "What can I do for you today?"

"I'm Alex Lawson, a new reporter for the *Star*. Betty Hughes was going to introduce me, but—"

"Oh, we all heard about what happened at the courthouse yesterday. That was terrible. Were you there? How's Betty doing?"

"I was there, and I have to say it was pretty frightening. I'm afraid I haven't heard any news on Betty's condition yet. She was shot in the shoulder and had a pretty big gash on her forehead, but the ambulance had already taken her away by the time I finished talking to the eyewitness, Mrs. Lynch."

"What a way to be introduced to Sunset Valley. Yet here you are, the next day, back at work. You're a real trooper."

"I'm afraid I don't feel like one."

The woman smiled and extended her hand. "I'm Dot Ames, Mayor Kerns's secretary."

"It's a pleasure to meet you, Miss Ames," I said.

"You don't have to be formal with me, Alex," Dot said. "Call me Dot. Everyone does. I expect I'll be seeing a lot of you around here."

"Is the mayor in?" I asked. "Do you think I could meet him?"

"He is. C'mon, I'll introduce you."

She strode over to the impressive raised-panel walnut door, gave a quick knock, opened it, and poked her head in.

"Got a minute, Mayor Kerns?" she asked.

"What is it, Dot?"

"I want to introduce you to the newest reporter on the *Star*. Alex, this is Mayor Sam Kerns. Mayor, Alex Lawson."

He stood and shook my hand. "Nice to meet you, Alex."

"A pleasure, Mayor Kerns."

"You're not from Sunset Valley, are you?" he asked.

"No, sir. I'm from Jericho Flats, Montana."

"Jericho Flats, huh? I think I've passed through there once or twice. Nice little town."

"Yes, sir. I've always liked it."

"Dot, could you show Alex around?" He looked at me, then grabbed the newspaper that was on his desk. "Wait a minute," he said. "Are you the Alex Lawson who wrote this story?"

"Yes, sir."

"Well, well," he said. "Just in town and already a front-page story. I'll have to keep my eye on you. The next thing I know you'll be looking to take over my job."

"Oh, no, sir. This is the job I want, not politics."

"Well, that's fine then. Welcome to Sunset Valley, Alex. Stop in anytime. I'm always available to the press."

"Thank you, Mayor Kerns," I said.

"Goodbye. Remember, my door is always open."

Dot and I left his office and walked down the hall.

"Always open," Dot said with a smirk. "Unless he doesn't want you to know what's going on. Then he's like a bank vault. But with your looks you might be able to crack it."

I followed Dot around the various offices and met almost all the city officials, but I wasn't coming away with any groundbreaking news. Somehow, I felt I was missing something. I was sure Betty would have found a story, but for the life of me, I couldn't.

I shivered at the thought of facing Lou with no news. After all, that was my assignment. His exact words were: "Get off cloud nine and get another Page One story." Would I still have a job if I came back-empty handed?

Then I had an idea.

"Hey, Dot, do you have any information you could give me on that guy Webb? I got some of his story from Edna Lynch, but I'm sure you'd know more about what happened yesterday than she did. She was so upset, I'm not sure how reliable her facts were."

"Well, I'm not sure how much I could add, but I'll tell you what I know." Dot told me what she knew about the Ferguson family, and her thoughts on Webb and his marriage to Margie, the Ferguson daughter. It wasn't really information I could use in the paper, since it was Dot's perceptions, not facts. But it did give me some insights into how the people of this town probably perceived Webb. It made me want to talk to the Fergusons themselves and get their side of the story. Maybe I could even talk to Webb himself. I didn't know how much it would add to the story since his trial testimony pretty much laid out his whole case.

My head was spinning. I was determined to follow up on this story and prove myself to Lou before I was sent back to covering bake sales.

CHAPTER 6

On our walk to the courthouse the day before, Betty told me I'd be covering the town churches and their upcoming events as part of my community news assignments. With that in mind, I left City Hall and headed to the Methodist Church. I couldn't imagine there would be anything earth-shattering going on, but I figured it was all part of the job.

The building didn't look much like a church to me. I could imagine the crenellated castle-like bell tower commanding the parishioners to services instead of welcoming them. The sun reflected off the arched stained-glass window that glistened like a gem and somewhat redeemed the bleakness. A bleakness I felt deep in my bones.

Community news reporter. What a switch. From editor of my college paper to cub reporter. Guess it was to be expected. I was low man on the totem pole, at a smaller paper than I'd expected to be working at—notwithstanding the fact that it was the only paper that had offered me a job. Next time, I'll do more research before accepting a position.

About an hour later, after spending some pleasant time with the Methodist minister and his secretary and answering all their questions, I left the church office and headed for the Presbyterian Church. I looked up and down the street. The church was only a block away.

Another tall crenellated bell tower to the left caught my eye. Didn't the people here believe in steeples? A huge sand and fieldstone structure, the Presbyterian church's magnificent three-panel stained-glass windows sparkled in the sunlight like multicolored jewels.

I found the pastor's office behind the church. After introductions and politely refusing coffee, the secretary gave me a complete schedule of all upcoming church events, with a promise to call if any additional events popped up. The rector and his secretary were pleasant, and full of questions. Neither pastor had asked whether or not I'd be attending services on Sunday, or which church I attended. I'd been dreading that question.

Now I was back on Main Street, the courthouse right in front of me. I thought about popping in to see if anything interesting was going on, but knew that was probably not the best idea I'd ever had. Lou had made it clear that I was hired to do community news, so if I couldn't come up with a front-page scoop, I'd at least get that assignment done before I got fired and had to drag myself back home.

But, if I got in and out of the Catholic church quickly, maybe I'd still have time to stop at the courthouse. Anything would be better than writing about the next bake sale. I should have listened to my professor and applied for a job in Denver, or maybe even San Francisco. But no-o-o. I thought I'd be better off getting my feet wet at a smaller newspaper. I just didn't think it would be this small.

Let's face it, Alex, old gal—you were too scared to move that far away. Like you're ever going to find a Pulitzer worthy story here. Or one that will grab the attention of every big paper and wire service in the country. Now I'm stuck here in this backwater town, not much better than Jericho Flats. And I can't afford to even think about moving again so soon. I'll do more research on both the town and the paper before I jump into my next job.

I hurried to my last stop. The Catholic Church featured another square bell tower and more stained-glass windows. The only thing that distinguished it from the Protestant churches was the three crosses, noticeably absent from the others: one over the doorway, one atop the bell tower, and one on the roofline.

I found the office, left with the usual list of events, and practically ran down the street to the courthouse.

I sprinted up the marble staircase to the second floor and stuck my head in each courtroom. But . . . no trials, no activity at all.

I had resigned myself to writing up the church social calendars when someone tapped me on the shoulder.

"Excuse me, but aren't you Alex Lawson?" a woman said.

I was surprised that someone knew me until I turned around and saw it was Edna Lynch, my eyewitness from yesterday's story.

"Hello, Mrs. Lynch. How are you?"

"I'm fine, dear. I thought it was you, and I would never bother you if I thought you were in the middle of a big story, but you seemed a little lost, so I figured I could."

"That's fine. I wanted to check and see if any trials were scheduled for today, but everything's quiet."

"Yes. Guess the courts decided to take the day off to recuperate from yesterday. I just got here a little while ago myself. I've been so busy, what with everyone asking about my role in capturing that murderer. Seems I've become something of a celebrity."

"Oh, I'm sorry. I didn't mean to cause trouble for you."

"Oh, no, dear. Quite the opposite. I'm loving every minute of it. I feel ten, maybe twenty, years younger. Why, it took me an hour just to walk here. Everyone I passed on the street wanted to talk about the article. It's been one of the most exciting days I've ever had."

"You do look better today—not scared to death, like yesterday. Not that I could blame you." Her cheeks had a real glow to them, and her smile just didn't quit. Even her gray hair seemed curlier. "I'm glad you're enjoying all the fuss. But since nothing's going on here, I better head back to the office."

"Alex, dear—may I call you Alex?"

"Of course."

"Well, I was wondering. Since you're new in town, I was wondering where you're staying. I mean, a pretty young thing like you shouldn't be living just anywhere, if you know what I mean."

"I do, Mrs. Lynch—"

"Call me Edna. Everyone does."

"Edna, then. Right now, I'm staying at the Sunset Hotel, but I thought I'd go over to the community college and check the bulletin boards to see if anyone's looking for a roommate, or if there are any rooms to rent."

"Here's an idea for you. I have a couple of extra bedrooms in my house that I rent out. There's a young woman, about your age, in one of them. She teaches at the high school. But the other room is empty. It comes with breakfast and dinner, so you'd have to get your own lunch. If you're interested, I'd be happy to show it to you."

"That's swell. When can I see it?"

"Could you come by tonight around seven o'clock? We usually eat at six, so that would be perfect."

"I could. All I need is your address."

Edna wrote down her address and gave me directions on how to get there.

Maybe today wasn't a total loss. I had to find someplace to live other than the hotel; my finances couldn't take much more of the room charge and eating out. Maybe things were beginning to look up in Sunset Valley. At least I hoped so.

Now all I had to worry about was keeping my job.

CHAPTER 7

I walked back to the *Star* thinking about how to report the church events. Maybe Lou would give me a full page. I could design a banner for the heading and a template, one that could be changed or added to quickly. I'm sure the guys in typesetting would appreciate that. I walked through the newsroom door confident I could convince Lou that my new community page idea would boost sales and ensure that I kept my position.

"Where the devil have you been?" Lou shouted in my face as soon as I hit the newsroom floor.

"At the churches, Lou," I said. "Yesterday, Betty told me to go around, introduce myself, and get their schedules for the next few weeks. I even stopped by the courthouse, but it was deathly quiet today. No trials. No activity at all."

"Did you happen to think you should go to the hospital to check on the condition of Webb, or the deputy, or Betty?"

Lou's shouts bounced around the empty room and his face got redder with each question.

"And you call yourself a reporter. I never . . . in all my years . . ."

Lou charged into his office, sat behind his desk, looked at me standing in the middle of the newsroom, then immediately got up and lunged toward me.

"What are you still doing here? Do I have to do everything around here? Why aren't you headed to the hospital? Where's your nose for news? Good grief. Get going. And if you don't come back with a front page story, don't bother coming back. Just jump on the next bus headed to Jericho Flats and stay there until you figure out what a real reporter's job is all about."

He pounded back to his desk and grabbed one of the phones. They were ringing all over the place. The courthouse story had excited the community and everyone wanted to add what they knew about Webb, the Fergusons, or the shooting, even if they weren't there. The switchboard operator, Pat, couldn't answer the lines fast enough.

I stood there, frozen in place. *What hospital? And where? I'm in over my head now, for sure.* I felt tears threatening, but I couldn't let that happen. It would lower Lou's opinion of me even more.

Lou looked up from his desk and saw me. I thought for a minute he was going to leap over it to get to me. "You . . . you!" he sputtered, spit flying, eyes bulging.

That woke me up and evaporated the tears. I dashed for the door and ran down the steps to the street. I didn't know where I was going, so I ran to the café, burst in, and startled the afternoon coffee drinking, checkers playing crowd.

"Pete, how can I get to the hospital?"

"You hurt, Alex?" Pete asked.

"No, no, but I need to get there, and quick, before I'm fired."

"Got it, kid. Hey, fellas," he called out, "anyone have their truck with them today?"

"I do," one of them said.

"Give Alex a lift to the hospital, would you?"

"Sure, Pete," the man said, unfolding his long, lean body from the booth where he was playing checkers with another man. "Make sure this old geezer doesn't move any of my men while I'm gone. I got a dime riding on this game. Now where's Alex?" he asked, looking past me.

"I'm Alex," I said. "Could we hurry, please?"

"Pete, you didn't tell me I'd be escorting a lovely lady. I thought it was some old drunk sick from too much bathtub gin."

"Yeah, well, it's just me," I said, folding my arms across my chest, "and I work for the *Star*. Are you going to give me a lift or not?"

"Sure thing, little lady. I'm Adam, by the way." He took my arm and led me to the door. "See ya later, Pete," he called over his shoulder.

He stopped in front of an old, beat-up blue pickup; at least the parts that weren't dented or rusted away seemed to be blue. It was hard to tell with all the mud splashed onto its sides. The truck looked older than him, and I figured he was about thirty or so.

He tugged open the passenger door which squealed at being disturbed. All kinds of litter—empty bottles, paper bags, old receipts, newspapers, and a slew of unidentifiable items—covered the seat.

"Sorry. Don't usually have passengers in here," Adam said, scooping up the garbage and throwing it into the truck bed.

"But it'll blow away back there," I said.

"That's okay. The bottles'll stay. I'll take them back to Jake's for the deposit one of these days. Get in."

I realized this was the first time I ever tried to climb into a pickup while wearing a skirt. When I drove Dad's truck, I always had my dungarees on. *Oh well, first time for everything.* I hitched my skirt up so I could get one leg on the floorboard, then grabbed the door and yanked myself up the rest of the way. Once settled, I realized good ol' Adam had been standing there, ogling my legs the whole time.

"Are you getting in, or should I drive myself?" I asked, sure my face was scarlet. It certainly felt hot.

"Just wanted to make sure you got in okay," Adam said. "Wouldn't want Pete to yell at me for not taking care of you."

I didn't know if I was more angry or embarrassed. I did know I wanted to smack that silly smirk right off his face.

Adam jumped in on the driver's side and we headed for the hospital.

"You're new in town, aren't you?" Adam asked.

"Yep. Just arrived two days ago," I said.

"Where from?"

"Jericho Flats. It's northeast of here."

"Uh huh."

While we drove, I tried to sneak a look at him. Not bad. Taller than me. Wiry frame like most of the cowboys and ranchers back home. Brownish hair peeking out from under his Stetson. The usual dusty dungarees, jacket, and plaid shirt. Seemed like that was the official uniform of Montana. Cute smile. One dimple I'd noticed when he was talking to Pete. Blue, blue eyes.

"What are you going to the hospital for?" he asked.

I almost bounced out of my seat. His deep voice had broken into my thoughts so unexpectedly.

"Sorry," he said. "Did I scare you? You jumped like a frightened rabbit."

"No, no, I was lost in my own thoughts, that's all."

"Well, sorry. So, what are you going to the hospital for, if you don't mind my asking."

"No, I don't mind. I need to check on the condition of the people who got shot at the courthouse yesterday, and then write up the story for the paper."

"Sounds important. Lou must think a lot of you. You seem pretty young to be taking on such a big story."

"I am not. I had a front-page story in today's paper."

Terrific. That sounded like something a ten-year-old would say.

He gave a little chuckle and said, "Didn't read it. Don't often read the paper. Usually too busy on the ranch, but I had to come to town today for a few supplies. Lucky for you, I guess. I'm not sure who else has a truck they bring to town. Most of them just ride in on their horses."

"Well, thanks. I appreciate the ride."

"Happy to oblige a pretty lady. Here we are—Holy Rosary."

"A Catholic hospital?"

"Guess so. But I'm sure it's the same as any other. Just has sisters for nurses."

The hospital covered an entire city block and stood three stories high—a lot bigger than I imagined it would be for such a small town. But I guess being the county seat made a difference. The front entrance had a Spanish look to it, and trees encircled the entire building.

I reached over to shake his hand. "Thanks again. I don't think I ever would have found this on my own. It's really outside of town, isn't it?"

"Sure is. And looking at those high heels you have on, I'm sure you'd need the hospital's help if you'd tried to walk all this way."

"Oh, I'm used to them."

I probably would have taken them off and carried them as soon as the sidewalk ended.

"Want me to wait?" Adam asked. "It'll be night soon. I don't know if you'll be able to find your way back in the dark."

"That'd be swell. But I don't want to keep you. I mean, you probably have things to do back in town."

"Yep. Gotta finish my game of checkers with Bruce."

I could feel my face getting red again. I didn't know what to say. And he didn't help matters any, just sat there with a silly grin on his face and watched me squirm.

"Tell you what," he said. "We'll both go inside. While you find out what's going on, I'll go to the cafeteria and get a cup of coffee. You can come find me and let me know if you want me to wait or not."

"That's a swell plan," I said.

I hopped out of the truck and headed for the entrance, hurrying up the few steps to the front door. Adam, right behind me, grabbed the door handle before I could reach it.

"I was always told to hold the door open for a lady," he said.

"Thanks."

I headed inside, not knowing what to expect.

CHAPTER 8

Potted plants and comfortable chairs and sofas filled the lobby, along with the stench of hospital disinfectant. You'd think someone could invent a sanitizer that didn't stink.

Adam pointed to the cafeteria and headed there. Left on my own, I walked to the reception desk.

The receptionist smiled and said, "Can I help you? It's not our regular visiting hours, but maybe there's something else I can help you with."

"I'm looking for Betty Hughes. She's a reporter with the *Star* and I work with her."

"Betty! Of course. You must be Alex."

"I am. Alex Lawson. But how do you know my name?"

"Apparently, Betty's been driving the Sisters crazy, asking them to call you, but the lines to the newspaper were all jammed. They finally called down here and asked me to be on the lookout for you. It seems they can't get her settled until she's talked to you, or someone named Lou."

"Can I see her? Where is she?"

"Now calm yourself, dear. Everything's fine. I'll call upstairs and see if the Sisters will let you go up for just a minute."

I paced back and forth in front of the massive wooden desk, wringing my hands.

She must be hurt worse than I thought.

"Alex?"

The receptionist's voice brought me back to the present.

"The Sister said you can visit for a few minutes. Betty's on the second floor, the women's wards. Room 213."

"Thank you."

I flew down the hall to the staircase and took the steps two at a time. When I reached the second floor, I stopped at the nurses' desk to ask directions to Betty's room.

"You can't go in now," the nurse on duty, not one of the nuns, said. "It's not visiting hours. Come back later."

"But the receptionist downstairs said—"

"She should know better than to send you up here. I'll have to speak to her about following the rules."

Just then, a nun came out of one of the rooms.

"Sister," I called. "Sister, can't I see Betty Hughes for a minute? One of the Sisters said I could, and—"

"Are you Alex?" the nun asked.

"I am. Alex Lawson. I work for the *Star.*"

"Oh, yes, dear. Give me a minute."

I waited while she went into another room, then reappeared a minute later. The nurse on duty never took her eyes off me. She glared at me like I was the person who shot Betty.

The nun took my arm. "I'm Sister Marcus. I'll take you to Betty's room. You can only stay a minute, though. She needs her rest."

"How is she?"

"She's doing well, just a little agitated right now."

As we got closer to Betty's room, I could hear her yelling. I couldn't make out the words, but she was angry, to put it mildly.

Sister Marcus opened the door a crack and said, "Alex is here, Betty. But you'll have to calm down or I'll send her away."

"I'M PERFECTLY CALM."

"Oh dear, that will never do," Sister Marcus said.

"All right, all right, I'm *calm*," Betty said, in a milder tone.

"You can go in, Alex, but only for a few minutes," the nun said.

"Thank you, Sister. I'll be quick."

Sister Marcus opened the door all the way and another nun, who had been sitting in the room, came out. As they walked down the hall together, I went in and found Betty swaddled in plaster casts. One went from her neck, down her chest and left arm, and disappeared under her hospital gown. The other covered her right leg, which she broke when she fell down the stairs. The broken leg now suspended above her body by a system of wires and pulleys. A bandage masked the left side of her face diagonally from her hairline, across her eye, and down to her jaw.

"My God!" I said. "You look like you've been fighting overseas."

"Charming, isn't it?" Betty asked. "Talk about being in the wrong place at the wrong time. And it is *so* frustrating. I can't get to a phone, and they don't seem capable of dialing one for me. I've asked them a million times to call Lou or you or anyone at the paper."

"Seems all the phone lines are jammed. Everyone in town either wants to contribute to the story or ask questions about it."

"Well, why couldn't they say so instead of just telling me I have to stay calm?"

"I don't know. But other than that, are you okay? Of course you're not. What am I saying?"

"Alex, stop babbling," Betty said. "I'll be fine—just a broken collarbone and a broken leg. And a bunch of stitches over my eye. But you didn't come here to find out about my condition. Think like a reporter. Get your pad out and start writing before they kick you out of here."

"Right, right, of course." I fumbled in my purse for my notebook and pencil. "Okay, shoot."

Betty winced at the word but told me what she knew about the officer and Webb—enough for another front-page story. I managed to write down all the important points before Sister Marcus poked her head back into the room.

"Alex, it's time."

"Just one more minute, Sister, please?" I asked. "Quick, Betty, anything else?"

"I think one of the officers is dead, but I'm not sure. Nobody wants to give me the whole story."

"Alex," Sister Marcus said, "that's enough." She grabbed my arm and pulled me out of the room.

"I'll see you tomorrow," I yelled through the closed door, where Sister Marcus now stood guard, arms crossed. Her eyes glared a challenge: *Say one more word and discover how formidable I can be.*

"Sorry, Sister, but I've got to get the story or I'll lose my job. And I just started yesterday."

Her eyes softened a little, so I thought I'd push my luck.

"You wouldn't happen to know how the officer or the prisoner are doing, would you?"

"Miss Lawson," she said, her voice as cold as the ice on the Yellowstone River, "don't try my patience."

"No, of course not. I only thought—"

"Well, you can stop thinking. Come back tomorrow during regular visiting hours. As far as any other patients we have here, that's not information we pass out to anyone but family members. Leave, Miss Lawson. Now."

"Yes, Sister. Thank you for letting me see Betty. I really do appreciate that."

"I shouldn't have broken the rules, but she was creating such a ruckus, it seemed the only way to calm her down."

"I'm staying at the Sunset Hotel, in case you need to get in touch with me for anything."

"Thank you. Now, you must leave."

"Yes, Sister. See you tomorrow."

I flew down the stairs, already composing the headline and story in my head. I headed for the front door and was reaching for the handle when I heard, "Don't you need your driver?"

Geez—Adam! I had forgotten all about him.

"Adam," I said turning around. He was leaning against the doorjamb of the cafeteria, coffee cup in hand, smirk firmly in place.

Does he ever stop smirking?

"Or did you plan on taking my truck and leaving me here?" he asked.

"No. It's just that I have to get back to the paper and write up this story. I was thinking about that and forgot all about you."

"Seems I didn't make much of an impression if you could forget me so quickly."

"No, no, it's not that. It's just that Betty's all wrapped up like a mummy and—"

"Betty?" he asked.

"Yeah. Betty Hughes. She's a mess. You know her?"

"Sure. Betty's a great gal. I didn't know that's who you went to see. All right, Alex, let me land this cup where it belongs and I'll drive you back. I might even be able to add a little something to whatever Betty's told you."

"Really? What?" I followed him as he walked over to the counter where the dirty dishes were stacked. He stopped and said a few words to a really good-looking guy standing there.

Oh, come on, Adam. I have a deadline. One more minute, then I'll drag him out.

"We'll see you then," Adam called to the man behind the counter as he walked away. "Ready?" he asked, taking my arm.

"I've been ready the whole time you were socializing." I scowled at him and jerked my arm away.

"Maybe you'd rather walk back to town," he said, "since I seem to be such an annoying escort."

"Maybe I would," I said.

Wait a minute. I don't even know which way to walk.

I knew I'd better get my temper under control before he left me here. I could wander around in the dark for hours before I'd find my way back to town.

Dad always said my temper would get me in trouble.

"I'm sorry, Adam. I'm just excited about this story. I'd much rather ride with you than walk."

"That may be the first sensible thing you've said today. Come on, let's get you back so you can write another front-page story."

When we got to the truck I tugged up my skirt and jumped in. I hoped he enjoyed the view today. From now on, I'd be wearing trousers. No more free leg shows for the men in Sunset Valley.

49

On our way back, Adam asked about Betty and told me Jimmy, the handsome cafeteria worker, was a guy he grew up with. They had been talking, and Jimmy told him what he knew about the officer and the prisoner.

"What did he say?" I asked.

"It's kind of complicated. Jimmy overheard some of the doctors talking, and he spoke to the ambulance driver, so it's a little of this and a little of that."

"That's fine, Adam. I can fill in the blanks. I'll make sure I credit Jimmy for his information."

"Oh no, you can't do that." He shook his head violently.

"Why not?"

"He only told me because we've been friends since we were kids. He'll lose his job if the hospital finds out he told a reporter about a patient's condition."

"But he didn't tell a reporter. He told you."

"He told me in confidence." Adam gripped the steering wheel so tight I could see his knuckles turn white. "I never should have mentioned it. Forget I said anything."

"I can't, Adam. It's my job. I have to tell the whole story, and if you know something about it, you have to tell me."

"I don't have to tell you anything, Alex. And I don't like your attitude. I don't know why you think you can demand I do something that will hurt my friend. He's been through enough already overseas. I don't give a damn if the paper ever gets printed, but I do give a damn about Jimmy."

I folded my arms across my chest and stared out the window. I couldn't understand why he was being so stubborn. It was probably something everyone would know by tomorrow anyway, so why couldn't I get the scoop first?

He pulled up in front of the newspaper building.

"We're here. I think you can get out on your own, can't you?"

"I certainly can."

I pushed the door open and slid out of the truck. "Thanks for the ride."

He looked at me and touched the brim of his hat.

I slammed the door and went inside to write what I now knew, still fuming over Adam's attitude.

CHAPTER 9

"What did you find out?" Lou yelled as soon as I opened the newsroom door. "Took your sweet time about it. I've got a deadline, you know."

"I know, Lou. I'll get it typed up as fast as I can."

"No time. Call down to rewrite and dictate the story to Phil. He'll take it from there."

Lou hovered over my desk, excited as an expectant father, chomping on his cigar. I wished he would find something else to do. He was making me nervous.

I took out my notebook and looked over my notes for a second before I picked up the phone and asked Pat to connect me to rewrite. Lou grabbed the phone once Phil got on the line and screamed some instructions to him. Then he shoved the phone back to me.

"Okay, Phil, ready?"

"Go."

Here goes nothing.

I started to dictate. I'd never written a story this way before. I hoped it would work.

"Courthouse Massacre. On Monday, March 8, convicted murderer, Billy Webb, was brought in for sentencing."

I kept composing in my head, trying to stay two sentences ahead of what I was dictating. It was a frantic way to write a story, and I had to combine what Dot told me with the information Betty gave me. I prayed I was managing to get all the details right. Hopefully, Phil would be able to rewrite it into a coherent piece.

As it turned out, Webb assumed the judge would order the death sentence. On the way into the courtroom, he spun around and grabbed the deputy's gun, killing one deputy instantly and wounding the second one. The shot he fired at me and Betty broke her collarbone and flung her backwards down the stairs, breaking her leg and splitting her forehead open. It took fourteen stitches to close the gap.

"At present, the condition of one officer and the prisoner is unknown." I paused. "Okay, Phil, that's all I've got for now."

"Great job, Alex," Phil said. "I'll get this on page one."

"That's some story, Alex," Lou said. "How's Betty doing? Just like her, trying to get the story even when wounded. She's a real newspaperman. This calls for a drink, provided you don't mind a little bootleg bourbon. Do you?"

"Not at all. In fact, I wish there was a speakeasy in this town where a girl could get a good drink every once in a while."

Lou raised his eyebrows and studied me for minute, then shook his head. "You're full of surprises, Alex. You know Pete, down at the café, don't you?'

"Sure."

"I'll give him a call. Next time you're in there, remind him that I vouched for you."

"Thanks, Lou." I didn't know what to say. Access to any speakeasy was a coveted privilege, but for a newcomer, it was more than I could have hoped for.

He led the way to his office, opened the file drawer in his desk, and lifted out a bottle of bourbon and two glasses. He poured a healthy shot in each glass and handed one to me.

"To a job well done." He raised his glass. "While I don't want people shooting up my town every day, stories like this sell papers. I should have asked you to do this first thing this morning, but ... I guess this whole incident with Betty has thrown me off kilter. Tomorrow I want you to find out about the other people who were hurt, and Webb's condition. And talk to his wife and in-laws. Find out what they think about him and everything that happened. Can you do that?"

"Sure, Lou. I'd also like to see Betty again."

"Sure, sure. I'll stop by tomorrow, too. See how she's getting along."

"Lou, I have one problem."

"What's that?"

"How am I supposed to get around in this town?"

"No car, huh? How did you think you were going to get around?"

"I didn't know. Guess I thought I'd figure something out once I got here. I kind of thought there'd be a newspaper car anyone could use. Even if I did have my own car, I don't know if I could afford the gas and maintenance."

"Hmm. Well, there's always a horse. You can ride, can't you?"

"Of course I can ride. Is there anyone in Montana who can't? But where would I get a horse?"

"Check the Saddlery Shop on Main Street. Or you could get a bike."

"That might be easier. But I'm a little short on cash right now. Can I get an advance?"

"Tell you what, Alex. If you can find a good used bike, cheap, of course, I'll pay for it."

"You will? Gee, that's swell, Lou. I'll look for one first thing in the morning."

I wondered if Pete could help me find one. I'd stop in and ask on my way home. Home! Oh no! I had forgotten all about Edna and the room she was going to show me.

I finished my drink, and as I left Lou's office, I looked at the clock above the newsroom doors. It was six-fifty.

Where did the day go?

Back at my desk, I asked Pat to phone Edna Lynch. A few minutes later, I heard, "Hello, hello, is anyone there?"

"Hi, Edna. It's Alex Lawson."

"Hello, Alex. I thought you were coming over tonight."

"I was, but . . ."

I explained everything that had happened. She was very sweet about it and said I could see the room the following night. I thanked her and finally left to try to find a place still open for a much-delayed supper.

Outside, at last, I felt like I was walking on air. I had just written my second front-page story in as many days. I was euphoric. The stars glistened brighter than I had ever seen them before. The full moon in the indigo sky lit the street in a ghostly otherworldly glow. Night creatures scurried around, but tonight they didn't bother me like they usually did. Tonight, they were part of my celebration.

I closed my eyes. The river's ice was beginning to thunder as it cracked and thawed. The world was never as alive for me as it was that night. I wished I could feel this way every night, but I was afraid my heart would explode if it was this full all the time.

"Still here, Alex?"

Lou's gravelly voice snapped me back from my musings.

"I remember feeling the way you do right now," he said. "Breaking a big story can do that to you. What I wouldn't give to be back in the trenches. Now all I do is stamp out fires all day. Oh well. Go home, Alex. You've got a lot to do tomorrow."

"I do, don't I? First on the list—get a bike so I can get those interviews done."

We said good night and headed in different directions.

It was late to get supper. I knew most places closed their kitchens by seven, but I decided to stop at the Met Café, just in case. When I got there, I saw the kitchen was dark.

Damn. And I'm hungry. Maybe Pete knows a place that's still open.

As I stepped into the cafe, Pete yelled over to me, "Alex, saved you a seat down here."

I walked to the end of the counter near the kitchen. A napkin covered a plate that sat in front of an empty stool. Pete placed a lemonade next to the plate and pulled off the napkin to reveal a ham sandwich and some potato salad.

"Have a seat," he said. "Hope you like ham."

"You did this for me?" I asked.

"Sure did. I figured you'd be working late, what with the story Adam told me, so I asked my cook to make up a sandwich for you before he left. Hope that's okay."

"Pete, you're a lifesaver." I plopped down on the stool and took a gigantic bite of the sandwich. "Heaven, absolute heaven," I said, swallowing the first mouthful.

"Seems you had another busy day," Pete said.

"Adam told you all about it?" I asked between bites. "And about me?"

"Just said it was a big story and you had to write it up for tomorrow's paper. That's all. Why? Something happen between you two?"

"No, nothing. Did he tell you about Betty? You know Betty, don't you?"

"Oh sure. She's a great gal. She's the only other woman I let sit at the counter. Come to think of it, now there's two of you, we're almost completely democratic here."

"Just like Montana should be. After all, if we can be the first state to send a woman to the US Congress, we should, at least, let all women have a seat at the lunch counter."

"I'll have to think about that," Pete said. "Excuse me for a minute, Alex. I'd better see what those gents want before they start a ruckus."

Pete went over to the men sitting by the window to fill their empty coffee cups and cater to the usual assortment of questions and complaints. I went back to eating my sandwich with gusto. The sweet, tender ham and the peppery potato salad made my mouth water with every bite. As I ate, I relived the day, oblivious to the others in the room.

"Get your story done?"

The voice startled me. I didn't know if I wanted to face Adam again so soon.

"Yep. All tucked in for the night."

"Glad to hear it." He leaned on the counter next to me and took a sip of his coffee.

I didn't know what to say. It embarrassed me to remember how I'd spoken to him earlier. After all, he didn't owe me anything. I had been unreasonable and had acted like a brat.

I knew I should apologize. Instead, I said, "Did you win your game of checkers?"

"Nope. Cost me a dime too. That old geezer probably cheated while I was away. But I guess it was worth it. I got to meet the new pretty little lady in town."

I kept eating, determined not to look at him. I hoped he wouldn't notice the flush that I knew covered my face.

"I, uh, I have to come back to town tomorrow to pick up some things that weren't ready today," he said. "I could take you back to the hospital if you want. I'll introduce you to Jimmy. Maybe he'll be able to tell you something new about those other guys from the courthouse."

"I thought you said he'd lose his job if he did," I said, turning to him. "All of a sudden, talking to him is permitted?"

"Well, maybe by tomorrow everyone at the hospital will know about them, so it won't matter who told you."

"I doubt that. Besides, first thing tomorrow I'm going to buy a bike so I can get myself around."

"Where are you going to find a bike?"

I hesitated for a moment because I didn't have an answer for him. "I'll ask Pete. He knows everything about this town."

"Yeah, well, you're right about that. Pete's usually the fella to go to for information. But I seem to remember an old bike in the barn, from before I got my driver's license. I could probably dig it out for you. Clean it up a little."

"Really?" A grin spread across my face.

Adam looked at me with that same silly smirk he'd had in the truck.

"Wait a minute," I said. "What's this going to cost me?"

"I'll make it affordable."

Now it was my turn to squirm. "What's affordable?"

"How about an apology for acting like a spoiled little girl, and dinner with me tomorrow night?"

An apology? How dare he!

I took another bite of my sandwich so I had time to calm down. I *had* acted like a spoiled child, and when I considered my dwindling financial resources, a free dinner was tempting. Plus, a free bike.

"It's a deal," I said, extending my hand to shake on it.

"First, the apology," Adam said.

"I'm sorry I acted like a dictator," I said through gritted teeth.

We shook hands and Adam started to laugh. I looked up at him, then laughed too.

"I'll bring the bike around first thing in the morning," he said. He touched the brim of his hat and walked away.

I didn't know if I was furious with him for making me feel like a ten-year-old idiot or thrilled by his attention. But there was definitely something about him that intrigued me.

Sunset Valley was getting interesting.

CHAPTER 10

The next morning, I woke early and hurried downstairs for a quick breakfast before heading off for my busy day.

"Miss Lawson," the desk clerk called.

I halted my beeline for the café and went over to the registration desk.

"Good morning," I said.

"A gentleman left this note for you and asked me to tell you your transportation is tied to the standpipe out front."

"Thank you," I said, ripping open the envelope.

Morning Alex,
Your bike is out front.
I'll pick you up at 6:00 for dinner.

Adam

The bike! Yesterday had been such a crazy day, I had forgotten all about it. I was glad Adam hadn't.

Now that I thought about it, I was sure it would be a boy's bike. I had forgotten my vow to wear trousers and had put on a skirt this morning. Now I had to run upstairs and change. I hoped this wasn't an omen of how my day would go.

Dinner at 6:00? What if I wasn't done by then? He hadn't left a phone number or anything. And I had to go to Edna's tonight to see about the room. My day was already getting fouled up. I wondered how he could be so arrogant. He had decided on a time and expected me to be sitting in the lobby, waiting for him. Like I had nothing better to do.

Typical man. They all think they'll lead and we'll follow. Well, not this filly. I was brought up to stand on my own two feet and not have people dictate to me. I'm not about to change now, even if I did have to bend those principles a little this week.

I ran back upstairs, struggled with my room key, finally got the door open. threw my purse onto the bed, and unzipped my skirt. I pulled my beige trousers out of the closet.

If I happened to be done with my story by six o'clock, fine. If not, he'd be the one waiting for me. I wasn't about to jeopardize my job for a free dinner. Especially one with an egotistical man who dictated a schedule for me and expected me to meekly comply.

I looked at my reflection in the mirror. "Damn."

I'd have to turn the pants up or do something with them so they wouldn't catch in the bike's chain, and I couldn't wear my dressy T-strap high heels. If I left my tan blouse on, I'd look like a bland bowl of oatmeal. This was definitely not the way to start my day.

Rummaging through my limited wardrobe, I cursed the fact that my trunk of clothes hadn't arrived yet. *I should write an editorial on how shipping companies' promises can't be trusted.* I finally settled on navy blue trousers, a white blouse, spectator Mary Janes, and a checked blazer. It was one of those unexpectedly warm spring days, so I thought my heavy blazer would do. I hoped I looked professional enough.

By the time I got to the café I realized I had wasted a half-hour changing clothes. I had wanted to get a really early start, but even with the unexpected delay, I still had time for a full breakfast, and just like yesterday, it was perfect.

While I ate, I got out my notebook and wrote down what I needed to do that day:

- Get address and directions to Webb's house.
- Get directions to hospital and find out about visiting hours *Something I should have done yesterday.*
- Visit Betty at the hospital.
- Write Community News column.
- Call Edna to change appointment to see the room sometime today (7:00 won't work with Adam's command performance dinner at 6:00).
- Write story about Webb's wife and in-laws.
- Leave note for Adam at desk in case I'm not back by six p.m.

I looked over my list and wondered how I would ever get everything done. Somehow, I had to. Lou was relying on me, especially now that Betty was laid up.

Talk about a baptism by fire.

As I finished my second cup of coffee, Edna walked past the window. I jumped up and ran out to catch her, yelling "I'll be right back" to the waitress.

"Edna," I called as soon as I hit the sidewalk.

She stopped and turned around. I ran to her and said, "Hi, Edna. I'm glad I saw you."

"Morning, Alex," she said. "How are you today?"

"I'm fine, but a little discombobulated. Do you think I could see the room this morning? You see, I've got to go to the ranch where Webb and his wife's family live, and the hospital, and write the community news column, and the lead story, and—"

"Well, let me think," Edna said. "I'm on my way to the market, but I guess that would be all right."

"Gee, that's swell. I have to go back and pay for my breakfast. Should I wait for you here, in front of the hotel?"

"Yes, dear. That's a good idea. I shouldn't be long. Just want to pick up a few things for dinner. I hope I don't have to tell my story about the shooting at the courthouse again. It seems people just don't tire of listening to my part in stopping that murderer's escape."

"It was exciting, and I'm sure everyone's grateful you were there." I hoped the store was still fairly empty at this hour. Otherwise, I might be waiting here for a long time. "Meet you back here in a little while."

"All right, dear. I'll try to be quick."

I didn't know how I was going to fit this stop in with everything else I had to do, but a new place to live was essential.

I ran back to the café to pay my bill, collect my things, and leave a note for Adam with the hotel desk clerk. Then I went outside to look at my bike, which Adam had tied to the standpipe. It was going to be tricky, getting on and off the shiny black bike with the high bar that boys' bikes have, even with trousers on. But I'd manage. It was that or walking. The good-sized basket attached to the front would come in handy for my purse.

A few minutes later, I saw Edna hurrying up the block, huffing and puffing a little as she carried her groceries.

"All set, Alex?"

"Sure. You were quick."

"Well, it sounds like you have a lot to do today, so I didn't want to keep you."

"Thanks, Edna." I slung my purse across my chest. "You can put your parcel in the basket. No need to carry it."

"Thank you, dear. Where did you get this bike? It looks almost new."

I told her about Adam as we walked to her house.

"You mean the Phillips boy?" Edna asked.

"To be honest, I don't know his last name. Isn't that terrible? He drove me around, gave me this bike, I agreed to have dinner with him tonight, and I don't even know his last name."

Edna laughed. "Seems things are moving so quickly these days, I wouldn't worry about it. I can't tell you how many young folks in town ran off and got married lickety-split because the young man got drafted. Of course, I think they should have waited until he came home, but . . . war changes a man, you know. My son was never the same after he came home. I'm glad to see you didn't fall into that trap."

"No, ma'am. Not that I had any opportunity to. As soon as I graduated from college, I got busy trying to get my career started. I didn't have time to think about marriage."

"It's just as well. Now you know you don't have to rely on a man to survive. And you're young. You still have plenty of time to get married and start a family."

"I don't intend to get married at all. I want to become an ace reporter in a big city someday. Maybe even New York City."

"Really? Why would you want to go so far away? Sunset Valley is a lovely place to live. Big cities are so crowded and busy."

"That's exactly why. They're filled with a thousand stories, and I want to write about all of them."

Edna looked at me like I said I wanted to fly to the moon.

"Here we are," she said. "This is my home."

I looked at the two-story white clapboard house with a large porch that spanned the front. It was quite a bit bigger than the surrounding one-story houses.

"It's big," I said.

"Yes, my late husband added the second floor when our family outgrew the two tiny first-floor bedrooms. I guess we could have found a way to accommodate everyone, but we could afford it, and he liked to build things, so . . . Come in, come in. You can leave your bike on the porch."

The location at the end of Pleasant Street meant I would be within walking distance of most places I needed to go. The first floor had a cheery yellow living room to the right of the front door. Needlepoint pillows brightened the dark brown sofa and easy chairs. The mahogany coffee table had copies of yesterday's newspaper. Knickknacks filled the built-in bookcases on either side of the fireplace, and a large console radio stood against the back wall of the room.

"It's very cozy," I said. As I looked around, I could see that white doilies covered the well-worn arms of the furniture. White lace curtains hung at the windows and plants covered the sills. "What lovely flowers."

"I do love African violets, and I'm fortunate that they grow so well on that windowsill," Edna said.

We left the living room and Edna pointed out her bedroom to the left of the front entrance. The kitchen, at the rear of the house, had a door to the backyard. The second bedroom served as a sewing room. The layout of this floor was identical to Betty's house. We went upstairs to look at what would become my room. White curtains hung at the two windows that faced the back and side yards. There was a single bed with a white chenille spread, a small plaid upholstered chair, and a chest of drawers. Everything I needed.

"This was my daughter's room, but she's married now and living in Colorado. I miss her and my three grandchildren. Maureen Healy, the other boarder, is in my son's old room. He's gone, too. Moved to California soon after he came home from the war. I got tired of rattling around this big empty house by myself, so I decided to fill it up with boarders. There's a bathroom between your room and Maureen's, so you'll have to share. I'll clean, of course, but I expect you to keep the room tidy."

"Of course, Edna. How much rent are you asking?"

"I thought sixteen dollars a month would be fair. That includes two meals a day. And you can use the living room and kitchen whenever you want. Maureen and I usually listen to the radio in the evenings and have a cup of tea."

I thought about my present expenses. Breakfast cost me fifty cents this morning and supper at the café was around a dollar, judging from the menu I looked at. My hotel charged two dollars a night.

This is a steal.

"I'll take it."

"I'm so happy. I'm sure you'll get along fine with Maureen. Won't this be nice? All of us gals together." Edna grinned at me like I had just handed her an award. "When would you like to bring your things?"

"I'd like to do that today, if I can."

"Today's fine with me. Let me get you a key so you can get in if I'm not home, although I rarely lock the door."

We went downstairs and Edna rummaged around in a kitchen drawer.

"Here it is. Feel free to come and go as you please, within reason, of course. I'm not your mother, you know, although I probably remind you more of your grandmother."

I started to protest, but she waved me off.

"Never mind. I just want you to know that you don't have to report your activities to me. I do have a few rules: No men upstairs, no drinking, and no smoking. And I would like to know if you're not going to be home for dinner. I hate to waste food. All in all, just being considerate and respectful of my feelings will go a long way."

"Of course."

I hope this isn't a decision I'll regret. I know I can't stay at the hotel forever. May as well give it a shot.

"Speaking of food, as I said, Adam is taking me to dinner tonight, so I won't be here. I only hope I can get everything done by six."

"Well, if your plans change, you can call me. And there's always peanut butter if you don't mind having a sandwich."

"Oh, sure, that's no problem. I ate that a lot when I worked at my dad's saloon."

"Really? You'll have to tell me all about that."

"Some other time, Edna. Right now, I've got to pay for my room, check out, and get to work."

I asked her for directions to the hospital. I wanted to go there right after stopping at the hotel. Pocketing the key to my new home, I thanked her for showing me the room, hopped on my bike, and pedaled down the street.

After I paid my bill at the hotel, the desk clerk agreed to hold my valise for the day. That problem solved, I took off to check in with Lou before I went to see Betty.

With a more permanent place to stay, I felt better about the prospects of staying in Sunset Valley than I had since I'd gotten off the bus.

Next time I move, I'll arrange for a room or an apartment ahead of time. Live and learn. Live and learn.

CHAPTER 11

Once again, the disinfectant stench assaulted me as soon as I entered the hospital. Today, a few people sat around the lobby. Some flipped through dog-eared magazines, others looked at random pages of the *Star* that were scattered across the waiting room, while a few sat staring at nothing, sniffling and wiping a handkerchief across watery eyes.

I'll just gather up all these stray pages of the paper and put them back in order.

I started to do that, but stopped dead in my tracks when I saw my story on the front-page. It had been such a crazy morning, I hadn't had time to read it when I stopped at the office earlier. I tucked that page under my arm. As much as it hurt my pride, I knew none of these people really wanted to read the paper anyway. It was simply a place to focus their eyes for a few minutes and maybe distract them from thinking about why they were sitting there.

I walked to the reception desk to get my visitor's pass. A different woman sat there today. At least, I thought she wasn't the same person I'd seen the night before; it was so hard to tell. Lately, it seemed every receptionist I came across was in their sixties with short gray hair. The war had taken a lot of young people—mostly men, but some women who had also gone overseas as nurses or ambulance drivers with the Red Cross. Small towns like Sunset Valley looked more like ghost towns inhabited by specters of what used to be.

"May I help you?" the receptionist asked.

"I'm here to see Betty Hughes," I said.

She reached for a file box filled with index cards and pulled out the ones behind the "H" tab.

"Here we are. Betty Hughes, room 213. Here's your visitor pass, although I'm afraid it's not visiting hours yet."

"What time do they start?" I asked.

"Ten o'clock."

That was almost an hour away, so I decided to get a coffee while I waited. Maybe I'd see Jimmy, Adam's good-looking friend. Maybe he'd talk to me if I smiled nicely.

I cursed the fact that I had to wear trousers to ride my bike. Men always appreciated my shapely legs. My college roommate had said they were my best asset.

I walked into the cafeteria and looked around, but didn't see him. I poured myself a cup of coffee from the industrial-sized urn and gave the cashier a dime. I noticed a number of people sitting at tables, sipping coffee, waiting for visiting hours to begin. Nurses sat at other tables talking and joking. It was nice to hear something other than sighs and sniffles.

My mind wandered for a minute over the news I could include in the next letter to my parents, along with my second front-page article, of course.

I finally had a chance to read my story. I hoped Phil had done a good job. Of course, I was sure that he had. He'd probably been doing it longer than I'd been alive.

I walked to a table, reading as I went. I was so engrossed in the paper that I walked right into Jimmy, busy clearing the tables.

"Oh, excuse me," I said.

"That's okay," he said. "I'm used to people not seeing me. I can't blame them, or you. Everyone's worried about the patients they came to see. I'm like part of the furnishings."

"Well, you're not. You're a person and deserve to be treated with respect. I apologize. I was too absorbed in this story. Say, aren't you Jimmy?" I asked, batting my eyelashes as I placed my coffee cup on an empty table.

"Yep. How'd you know my name?"

"I was here last night with your friend, Adam. He didn't introduce us, but he mentioned you on the drive back to town."

"Oh, Adam. Yeah, he gets all the pretty girls," Jimmy said.

I noticed the hard muscles in his arm as he reached down to put my coffee cup into his bus box.

"Hey, wait a minute. I'm not finished with that."

"Oh, sorry. I thought someone had walked off and left it there."

"That's okay. I just put it there so I could finish reading this story." *Perfect opportunity to ask him about the other victims.*

"Some news, huh? About the 'Courtroom Massacre'?" I said, pointing to the headline.

"Yep. Not often we get a hothead like that in Sunset. Most crimes are small-time. A guy feels bad he did it, confesses, and takes his punishment. They don't even go to trial. But this guy, Webb, he's different. You can tell he's not from around here."

"I guess it caused a lot of excitement, huh?"

"Oh, yeah. There was that reporter lady who got hurt, and the deputy. I think his name's Cody. He got shot. And another deputy got killed. The only thing that bum Webb got was a bullet wound to the thigh, and a black eye."

"How's the deputy doing? Hear any scuttlebutt?"

"I don't know. The ambulance guys said he was in pretty bad shape. He got shot in the stomach. That's never good. And I should know. That's where I got shot over in Europe. Ripped my insides apart pretty good, so the doctors decided to send me home to sit out the rest of the war. I still wish they hadn't. I wanted to go back to the Front and get a few of those Huns. You know—pay them back for what they did to me. But before I could try to do that, the whole thing was over."

"I'm awfully sorry to hear you got shot. I'm glad they sent you home before you got killed."

We stared into each other's eyes for a moment. I was mesmerized by his, deep brown with flecks of gold. Jimmy started to say something, but stopped when a loud bell clanged in the lobby.

"That's the bell for visiting hours," he said.

"I'd better get going then. I'm glad we had a chance to talk, Jimmy. Take care of yourself."

As I hurried out of the cafeteria I heard him call out, "What's your name?"

I decided it was better not to answer him. He seemed like a swell guy, and I felt like a heel, pumping him for information. When he found out I was a reporter, he'd be furious. Anyway, I didn't have time for a beau. I had my career to think about.

"Hi, Betty," I said as I walked in to her room. "How are you feeling today?"

"Achy."

Last night, I had been too shocked by her injuries to notice anything about her room, but today I saw that it was pretty big.

"Gee, what is this? The Presidential Suite?"

There was a large window opposite her bed. Sheer white curtains fluttered in the slight breeze that came through the partially opened sash. A small wardrobe next to the doorway held her personal belongings. Metal night tables flanked either side of her bed, one with a huge vase of flowers.

"Those flowers are beautiful," I said.

"Aren't they? They came this morning from the paper. Lou's so thoughtful."

"Wow. I didn't think Lou was that tenderhearted. Guess he's a real softie under that crusty demeanor."

"Every once in a while, he can surprise you. Actually, I didn't expect to see you today," Betty said. "Figured you'd be running around, following up on your big lead story."

Using her one free hand, she tried to fold the newspaper she'd been reading, gave up, and heaved it onto her tray table, muttering under her breath the whole time.

"I'm going to, but I wanted to stop by and see you first."

"How sweet," she said, her voice dripping with sarcasm. "Lou came by last night. He said you're doing a swell job. Jumped right into the fire, didn't you?"

"I guess so. It's exciting. I never thought I'd be writing lead stories on my first two days at the paper."

"Enjoy it while you can. Just remember, it won't last. I'll be out of here soon and you'll be back covering bake sales and community dinners. But very few, if any, shootouts in the courthouse, or any other sensational front page stories."

"I know." I fiddled with my purse, refusing to look at Betty. Here I was gloating about writing big stories while she was pinned to her hospital bed. Still, she didn't have to be mean about it. It wasn't my fault she'd gotten shot.

I decided to try to patch things up a little.

"I'm sorry, Betty. This should be your story, not mine."

"Oh, it's not your fault. It could have just as easily been you who got shot." She looked away, lost in thought. "Guess I'm feeling sorry for myself."

I didn't know what to say to her. She was right, of course. It could have been me lying there.

"Umm, Betty? Can I ask you something?"

"Sure. What do you need?" She positioned herself straighter in her bed and looked at me with her unbandaged eye. She scratched at the bandage and said, "The doctor's going to take *this* off today, at least. He said it was only there to prevent infection. I don't know how anything could get infected in here. I think they soak the room in disinfectant while I sleep."

"I think they do that to the whole hospital," I said. "It stinks in here."

Betty started to laugh and so did I. In no time we were back to the easy camaraderie we had started to form yesterday.

"So, back to business," I said. "Did you find out anything more about the deputy who got shot?"

Betty told me everything the nurses had told her. She was good at getting information from them. I was sure they'd never tell me anything. Judging by the way they glared at me when I walked past their desk, they didn't even seem to like me. I repeated the news Jimmy had told me about the deputy and Webb.

"Apparently Cody—that's the officer—will recover," Betty said, "but it'll take time. He was in surgery for quite a while last night. His wife stopped by to say hello. You might want to talk to her about what his recovery looks like, how she's getting along, things like that."

"Good idea," I said, jotting down everything Betty told me. "I'm going out to Webb's house today. I want to talk to his wife and find out about his condition, and any other background story she has."

"Great. Talk to the whole Ferguson family. It won't be easy. Remember, they've just buried their husband and father. You'll have to use kid gloves. Don't go barreling in hell-bent for leather."

"Right. Any idea when you'll be able to go home?"

"Hopefully soon. The doctor might have some news for me today when he comes to take this bandage off. I need to get out of here as soon as I can."

"Don't rush it. You don't want to do any more damage than has already been done."

"I'm just not used to being laid up."

We talked a little about other news, and I told her about renting a room in Edna's house.

"You sure you're ready for that?" Betty asked.

"What do you mean?"

"Edna's the town busybody. She'll want to know everything about you—where you go, with whom, and what story you're working on. The list goes on and on." Betty rolled her one visible eye.

"Don't worry. I've learned how to avoid answering questions I don't want to answer."

"I hope so, or your front-page stories will be around town before they get printed."

Now I regretted telling Edna my plans for the day. I wouldn't make that mistake again.

"Gosh, look at the time. I'd better get going. Do you know if the Webbs live on the Lazy F Ranch? Or, for that matter, where the Lazy F Ranch is?"

Betty did, of course, and gave me directions, as well as the names of all the Ferguson family members who lived and worked there.

"Thanks," I said. "I'll try to stop in later and let you know what happened."

"Just get the story out. Don't worry about me. I'm not going anywhere for a while. Tell me something before you leave, though. Just out of curiosity, how are you getting around without a car? I assume you don't have one yet—or do you?"

"I don't, but I now have a bike."

"Where did you get a bike? I know there isn't a bike shop in town, and I doubt you brought one on the bus with you."

I told her about Adam and what went on last night.

"Wait a minute," she said. "Adam Phillips, the rancher? He drove you here last night? And gave you a bike? And he's taking you to dinner?"

"Yes, yes, yes, and yes," I said, counting off my answers on my fingers. "I think that answers all your questions."

"I don't believe it. You're in town one day and you snag the most elusive, eligible, taciturn bachelor in Sunset Valley."

"Now *you* wait a minute. I didn't *snag* him, as you say, and I don't want him. I only agreed to go to dinner with him to get the bike. Plus, my finances could use a break. Of course, that was before I knew I'd be able to eat at Edna's tonight. Now I can't cancel, since it was part of the deal."

Betty started a chuckle that soon turned into a full belly-grabbing laugh.

"Oh, this is rich," she said. "You have no idea how many Sunset Valley girls have tried to catch him. And you don't even want him. I wish I could be a fly on the wall at this dinner. This will be a hoot and a half."

"I'm glad you find it so amusing. I'm the one who has to eat with him. What am I supposed to talk to him about? All we did last night was bicker."

"You're on your own, Alex, but I want a full report tomorrow. Oh, why do I have to be stuck in this hospital bed? This could be the story of the century: 'Adam Phillips Lets New Girl in Town Break Through His Armor.'" She started laughing again. "I'm sorry, Alex. It's just that I've never heard Adam say more than ten words to anyone. I don't know what you've got, but it's obviously his cup of tea."

"Too bad I drink coffee." I tucked my notebook in my purse and waved goodbye.

I could still hear Betty laughing as I ran down the stairs and headed for my bike.

About seven miles to the ranch, according to Betty. That's a lot of pedaling, and I haven't been on a bike in years.

Guess I'll be sore tomorrow.

CHAPTER 12

I figured it would take about an hour to get to the Ferguson ranch. That is, if I didn't hit some steep bluffs along the way. I pedaled southeast on Route 59 toward Volborg. Betty said the ranch was just past where two rivers, the Tongue and the Pumpkin, split. It was a beautiful day, and the sun radiated some warmth, a harbinger of spring.

Sandstone bluffs looked like sculptures against the clear blue skies of the eastern Montana plains. White cotton ball clouds drifted around the sky but never obscured the sun. Stands of cottonwood trees ran along the banks of the Tongue River, an occasional stray one standing alone, proud and majestic. Herds of mustangs and cattle grazed the sagebrush-covered prairies, and pronghorn antelope feasted on the hardy wheatgrass. The plants and animals urging spring to hurry and break winter's grasp. The ice on the river continued to thaw and head downstream, ready to feed the grasslands and open watering spots for the herds.

This was what I'd miss the most if I moved to Denver or San Francisco or New York. Everything was ready to burst out of its winter hibernation and display its beauty. In no time, these plains would be covered with wildflowers and new life. I'd have to remember to come back when the new foals and calves were born.

It seemed like no time at all before I reached the gate at the Lazy F Ranch. I got down from my bike, unlatched the gate's chain, and carefully replaced it after I wheeled my bike inside. Not knowing how far away the ranch house was, I decided to ride instead of walk. But after about a minute, I changed my mind. The dirt road was pitted with ditches and ruts. The warmth of the spring sun, which I'd enjoyed on Route 59, had turned this road into a mud pond. As the days got hotter, this mud would harden, but for now it was more like a bog than a road. I slogged through it, wondering if my spectator Mary Jane pumps would ever look the same again.

Are these interviews really worth this trek?

Then I spotted the house. It was a typical old wooden frame farmhouse. At one time it had been white, but so much paint had chipped off that now it looked gray, or brown in places. A large porch ran across the front of the house. The steps up to the porch had long ago given up any pretense of color.

As I got closer, a couple of dogs wandered over from the backyard. They didn't look mean or vicious so I said. "Hi." They left me alone, and soon lost interest in me entirely.

I leaned my bike against the base of the porch, climbed three steps, opened the screen door, and knocked on the closed front door.

"Hello," I called. "Is anyone home? I'm a reporter from the *Star.* I'd like to ask you a few questions."

The door flew open and the cowboy I remembered from the courthouse—the one who shot Webb—glared at me, a shotgun aimed at my chest.

"What the hell is wrong with you?" he asked, advancing toward me, his eyes burning right through me. "Don't you people have any respect at all for this family? First my father and now my sister's husband, and all you can think about is getting more juicy gossip for your rag of a paper!"

By now, I had backed all the way up to the porch railing. He loomed over me. If I could have bolted, I would have, but he blocked my way to the steps. My only exit.

"I told the last reporter who came here not to come back, didn't I? And to tell everyone else at that rag the same thing. Did you think I was joking? My family has been hounded enough. We have nothing to say to you or anyone else. Is that clear?" He raised the shotgun to his shoulder. "Now leave."

He spat out his words with more vehemence than I had ever experienced before. My insides knotted into a ball. I didn't know if he planned on killing me or just beating me to a bloody pulp. I thought about Webb at the courthouse and took his threat seriously.

He held the gun so tightly his knuckles were white, his eyes bulged, and his face was crimson. *Maybe he'll have a heart attack before he can kill me.*

"Hey! What do you think you're doing? Is this the thanks I get for taking the gun away from Webb?" I managed to blurt out, although I don't know how I had enough breath to utter a word.

"Huh?" His grip on the shotgun eased and he calmed down a little. Clearly, he didn't remember me, but I used his confusion to shove the barrel away from my chest.

"I've never been here before, so get that out of my face."

I couldn't believe all this was happening. My heart pounded and my breakfast was making a beeline from my stomach to my throat.

"I only started working for the paper two days ago. You must have spoken to . . ."

Betty! She must be the one who came here, before the incident at the courthouse. And she never said a word. She sent me off with an angelic look and a reminder to treat these people gently. Maybe she wanted me to get shot.

"Who?" he said.

"What?"

"Who do you think we spoke to if it wasn't you?"

"I don't know, but that doesn't matter, does it? I'm sorry for what your family is going through, but I don't know anything about being told not to come here."

Of course, by now, the dogs realized I wasn't welcome and barked and growled at me from the bottom of the porch steps.

"Shut up!" the man said.

I wasn't sure if he meant me or the dogs.

"I apologize for bothering you, Mr. Ferguson. It is Mr. Ferguson, isn't it?"

He didn't answer, so I kept talking.

"I'll leave now, and I'll make sure everyone at the *Star* knows not to come here again. All right?"

I waited for an answer, my whole body trembling.

"Henry, what's all the yelling about out here?"

A tall, lean, gray-haired woman came out onto the porch.

"Nothing, Ma. Go back inside. I'll handle this."

"Don't you start ordering me around. You may be the head of the family now, but I'm still your ma. Why, you have this poor girl scared to death. She's white as a sheet. Don't pay him no never mind, miss. Come sit over here on this bench with me and calm yourself." She took my arm and led me away from my tormentor, giving him a scathing stare.

"Now, what's this all about?" she asked after we sat down. "You're shaking like a newborn calf. Henry, make yourself useful and get the girl a glass of water instead of trying to terrify her."

"But Ma, she's from the newspaper. All she wants to do—"

"Is her job," she said. "Now go. Water, Henry."

"Thank you, Mrs. Ferguson," I said. "He's pretty scary."

"Oh, pay no attention to him. All bluster, that's all. He's been angry since the draft board told him that cattle ranchers would do more good for the country by staying home and raising beef than going off to get shot at by those Huns. Now, why did you come here?"

"I'm Alex Lawson, and my editor at the *Star* wanted me to talk to some members of the family. Get an idea of how you feel about Billy Webb, how he's doing, how his wife is holding up—you know, all the things people want to know."

"Sounds like a lot of gossip to me," she said.

"That's why I got mad, Ma," Henry said, handing me a glass of water.

"Thanks," I said to him.

I turned back to Mrs. Ferguson and said, "That's the whole reason I'm here. The people in town will say whatever they think, or can imagine, about your family unless I write a story that gives them the truth. This way, you have a chance to tell your side of things. How you feel. What your daughter is going through. Anything else you want to say. The town gossips can't make up stories if I write what the family says. Or if they do, no one will believe them. It's always amazed me, but it seems that once the story's in print, people believe that's the only truth. This is your chance to tell your side."

I held my breath while I waited to see what Mrs. Ferguson would decide to do.

She sat there, still as a rock, and looked out over the fields. I'd never seen anyone stay as motionless as she did for as long a time. I don't think she even blinked. Finally, she turned and looked at, and through, me with dark, troubled brown eyes.

"All right. I'll have my daughter Margie talk to you. But—and this is a guarantee—if you write anything that isn't the truth as she tells it, I'll come after you with a vengeance the likes of which you've never seen before. This is my family, and I'll protect them to my dying breath. Is that understood?"

"Yes, ma'am." Her eyes bore through mine and terrified me more than her son and his shotgun.

"We are not going to be ashamed or embarrassed to walk through town. Nor will we allow anyone to pity us. What's done is done. You can write what we say. No more, no less. No opinions."

"Fair enough."

"I'll send Margie out."

Mrs. Ferguson stood and walked into the house.

Henry was still on the porch, but he wasn't glaring at me anymore. Guess his mother's blessing on my interview held a lot of weight with him. I felt my stomach start to unknot and reached for the notebook and pencil in my purse. My palms were so sweaty that I couldn't hold onto either item. I wiped my hands dry with my handkerchief, then ran it over my forehead, also covered in sweat.

I think I've aged ten years. This story better be worth it.

Margie came out a few minutes later. She was a skinny little teenager with mousy brown hair and dull hazel eyes. Her shapeless cotton shift only added to her forlorn air. She plopped down next to me and looked at me, her eyes wide in abject terror, like a deer who spots a hunter at her morning watering hole. To her, I was the hanging judge and she was the accused. I thought I'd ask her some easy questions to get her to relax. Questions about school.

"Oh, I don't go no more," Margie said. "Once I got married, I had household chores to do and didn't have no more time for schooling or books."

"Think you'll go back now?" I asked.

She shrugged. "Don't think so, being a widow and a ma and all, it don't seem right. And I think I've learnt all I need to know anyhow."

A widow?

"Did Billy die?" I asked.

"Not yet," she said, "but it don't matter if he dies in the hospital or they hang him. Either way, I'll be a widow, and it don't seem right to be a widow lady and in high school."

I didn't know how to answer that, so I thought over the other topics I really wanted her to talk about. What was Billy like at home? How did he treat her? Her family? Was he sorry for what he had done? What was his physical condition right now? Would he live? Did the family plan to ask the judge for mercy?

I didn't have to worry about turning my thoughts into questions or even being gentle with her. Once she started talking, Margie was like a dam breaking. Everything spilled out. She told me how she felt about Billy when he first came to the ranch. What wonderful fun times they had together. But her family didn't trust him or like him. She felt they never gave him a chance to be a real part of the family. She went on and on, telling me how Billy was treated and how that contributed to his anger toward her father.

"And then he started to change. He drank more. He was angry all the time. He scared me sometimes with all his yelling and throwing things around our cabin. But I know he never meant anything by it."

The faraway look on her face and the sparkle in her eyes told me that even after all that had happened, Margie still loved Billy. She told me how they had plans to buy a ranch of their own as soon as he could save some money. And how her father refused to help them, even though he could have. She told a sad tale of dreams thwarted and ambition killed.

I wondered how much of this was teenage fantasy about the life she'd always imagined would be hers, and how much was reality. But I wasn't here to judge. I was here to report the story as it was told to me.

Margie finally slowed down. Like an old Victrola that needs to be rewound, her words came out slower and slower until finally she stopped altogether.

"And now, I have little Billy to raise." She paused. Her mournful sigh made my heart ache. "I guess that's all," she said, and stood to go back inside.

"Thanks, Margie," I said. "I'll make sure your side of the story gets told."

She gave me a slight smile and dragged herself away.

As soon as the door closed, Henry said, "She's a fool."

I jumped at the sound of his voice. I had forgotten he was even there. He hadn't budged or made a peep the whole time Margie was talking to me.

"Why?" I asked. "Because she's in love?"

"Because she walks around in a dream world. Always has. We all know she's a little simpleminded, but we never cared. Everyone loves Margie, and we'd never let anyone hurt her. But when Billy came here, she thought her Prince Charming had arrived to take her away to some magical fairyland. She never saw him for what he was—a no-good drifter. A bum. But Pa would do anything to make her happy, so he offered Billy a job. When she said she was pregnant and wanted to marry him, we all objected. But she cried and begged, and Pa always gave her whatever she wanted."

He paused for a minute and looked out over the fields.

"So, Billy became part of our family. We all knew he was trouble, but Pa thought that maybe, just maybe, if he gave him enough work here on the ranch, he'd settle down and try to do right by Margie. I had my doubts, but Pa ran the ranch, not me. You know the rest of the story. Margie's right about one thing. None of us ever liked him, or wanted him in our family. And I don't think he ever really wanted to be Margie's husband, or a father.

"He figured he had a gold mine here, marrying the boss's daughter. Never did a whole day's lick of work, but expected to be paid more than men who have worked for us for years. And he was furious when Pa wouldn't stake him for a ranch of his own. Not that I think he really would've bought one. I bet as soon as Pa gave him the money, he would've run off with it and left Margie and the baby without a second thought."

Henry stopped to take a breath. It amazed me that Henry commented on Margie's story. I watched him fight to control his emotions. I could see the hatred he had for Billy. It made me think Billy had a real motive for shooting Mr. Ferguson. Not that it was right . . . but there are always two sides to a story.

"Maybe now, Margie will have a chance to meet someone decent," Henry said.

"I hope so. She's a sweet girl."

"Remember that when you write your story. I'll see if Ma wants to talk to you." In two steps, Henry was across the porch and in the house, slamming the door behind him.

I waited for a while, but Mrs. Ferguson never did come out to talk to me. I assumed she felt she had made herself clear already. And she had.

By now, the dogs had wandered away. I walked down the steps, grabbed my bike, and trudged back down the muddy road to Route 59.

On the ride back to town I wondered how I could write the story in a way that would please everyone. I couldn't wait to see Betty again. I wanted to wring her neck for not telling me she had already been out to the ranch, and been thrown off the property. She was infuriating. Colleague. Ha! More like my nemesis. Well, if it was a fight she wanted, I was ready to give it to her.

A truck horn honked and I realized I was pedaling furiously right down the middle of the road. I had to calm down before I got myself killed. Wouldn't that be ironic. Escape being shot only to be run over by a speeding truck. I bet Betty would get a kick out of that! No more competition for front-page stories. When I thought about how she let me walk into such an explosive situation without tipping me off first, it made my blood boil. Why would she do that? It wasn't like she could write the story from her hospital bed. Well, sorry, old gal. Like it or not, I'm here to stay.

CHAPTER 13

By the time I got back to the hospital, I was ravenous. As soon as I walked through the door, an amazing aroma assaulted me. Not the usual antiseptic odor, instead it was one of roasted meat. My stomach growled to let me know that eating was *the* priority at that moment. I looked up at the clock: 1:40. No wonder I was hungry. It wasn't visiting hours yet anyway, so Betty could wait. Right now, time for lunch.

I rushed into the cafeteria hoping they were still serving whatever smelled so wonderful. The blackboard announced today's special—roast beef with mashed potatoes, gravy, and green beans. My mouth watered and I hoped my wallet could pay for this feast. Fortunately, hospital cafeterias were not as expensive as restaurants, so the special was only fifty-five cents. That and a cup of coffee made a grand total of sixty-five cents, well within my budget.

I'll have to remember this place for lunch from now on.

I grabbed a tray and headed for the steam table section, bypassing all the luscious looking desserts. Neither my waistline nor my wallet needed to indulge in those.

Still lost in the aromas and salivating over the anticipated flavors of the roast beef dinner, I was surprised to hear someone say, "You're back."

Jimmy was behind the counter, dishing out food.

"Hi, Jimmy."

"You ran out so fast this morning, I never got to ask you your name."

"Oh, yeah, it's been a busy day so far."

Guess I may as well tell him the truth about who I am and what I do. He'll probably find out soon enough anyway, so I'd rather it come from me.

"I'm Alex Lawson. I'm a reporter at the *Star*."

"So, that's why you asked me all those questions about the guys who got shot."

"Guilty. Guess I forgot to mention that before. I'm sorry. I won't print anything you told me unless I hear it from someone else too. Okay?"

"Aw, don't worry about it. The scuttlebutt's all over the hospital. Everyone's talking about what happened. So, is that the only reason you came here earlier today?"

"No. I wanted to visit my friend, Betty Hughes, before I headed out to the Ferguson ranch."

"The lady who got shot?"

"That's the one. She's a reporter for the *Star* too. Any more news on the deputy?"

"I heard he's going to be okay. Probably laid up for a while, but okay."

"That's great. And Webb?"

"Aw, he got off easy. He'll live to see the hangman."

"That's a gruesome picture."

"It's all he deserves. Mr. Ferguson was a nice man, and Mrs. Ferguson is the sweetest lady I know."

Sweet? More like an angry polecat.

I didn't answer him. Instead I asked, "Can I still get the special?"

"Oh, sure. Sorry, that's what I should have been doing instead of chewing your ear off."

"I like talking to you," I said. I smiled one of my best smiles and watched Jimmy add an extra slice of roast beef to my plate.

"Here you go. Gotta make sure you don't starve to death," he said, winking at me. "Coffee's over there." He pointed to the giant urn on the next table.

"Thanks." I grabbed my tray, filled a cup with coffee, and stopped at the cashier to pay. She eyed my plate with one eyebrow raised, looked at me, then at Jimmy, but didn't say anything.

The cafeteria was pretty empty since it was late for lunch, so I sat at a table by the window and thought about my morning. I also thought about what I would say to Betty. I didn't understand how she could have put me in that situation. When I remembered how threatening Henry had been, I wanted to run upstairs immediately and let her have it. But my growling stomach had other ideas about what should come first.

"Mind if I join you for a few minutes?"

Jimmy stood next to my table, coffee cup in hand.

"Not at all."

"I only have a ten-minute break, but I thought you might like some company. I know I hate to eat alone."

"I'm getting used to it," I said. "I never thought I would, but it's not too bad. And I always seem to have a story going through my head—either one I have to write for the paper, or one I'd like to write for myself, like a novel or short story."

"That's my problem. I don't have enough to think about. This job doesn't take any brains. I just come in and do whatever they order me to do."

"What do you want to do?"

"Build things. You know, office buildings, houses, hospitals." He looked around the room as he said this. "This place, for instance. I see so much that could be done better. Ways to improve the layout to benefit everyone—staff, patients, visitors. But that's all a pipe dream. In ten years, I'll probably still be here, slinging hash and cleaning tables."

"Why? Why don't you go to college? Study architecture? Or, at least go somewhere where you can work in construction. See how things are built from the ground up."

"There's a little thing called money that's standing in my way. Plus, my gut's never going to go back to normal."

Damn. I forgot he got shot.

"Oh. Are you still in a lot of pain?"

"No, nothing like that. I just have to watch what I eat for the rest of my life. And the doc says I have to be careful about heavy lifting. So, construction's out for now."

"Sorry."

"Forget it. I shouldn't be crying the blues to you anyway. You've got enough troubles, with your friend being shot and all."

"Oh yeah, her."

Jimmy stared at me. "That didn't sound too friendly."

"Huh? Oh, it wasn't meant to be. It seems she let me go out to the Ferguson ranch when she had already been there, been thrown off the property, and told not to send anyone else back to talk to the family. I thought Henry was going to kill me, he was so mad."

"Are you sure it was your friend who went there?" He tilted his head and peered at me from the corner of his eye.

"Who else would it be? We're the only two reporters."

"I don't know about that, but I'd give her a chance to explain."

I thought about that while I finished my lunch. "Delicious. That was just what I needed," I said, wiping my mouth on the napkin.

"Glad you enjoyed it," Jimmy said. He sipped his coffee and watched me over the rim of his cup.

I took out my compact and lipstick to freshen up before heading upstairs to confront Betty.

"Uh, Alex," he said, "do you think you'd maybe like to go to the movies with me some night?"

I patted my lips with my napkin and looked across the table into Jimmy's blushing face. He fiddled with his coffee cup and I could hear his feet shuffling back and forth beneath the table.

"I think I'd like that very much, Jimmy," I said.

His face exploded in a huge grin and his brown eyes crinkled at the corners.

"Gee, that's swell," he said. He jumped up, knocking over his nearly full cup, spilling coffee all over everything. I pushed my chair back out of the way of the brown liquid mess that was running down the sides of the table.

This was definitely not the day to wear spectator shoes. Between the mud and the coffee, they're a disaster.

"I'm so sorry, Alex," Jimmy said. He ran to the counter, grabbed a rag, and flew back to the table. He threw the cloth over the spill, somewhat containing the damage.

"Did I get any on you?" he asked. "I'm such a goon."

He ran back for another cloth, since the first one was already soaked. He returned with a bus box and a good supply of rags. He tossed the clean ones on his seat, the saturated ones in the box, along with my dirty plate, and dropped a couple on the floor to mop up the spreading spill.

"I'm really sorry, Alex." His face was bright red again. "It's okay if you want to cancel going to the movies with me. I know I'm a jerk—not a big success, like you."

"Success? I'm barely keeping my head above water. And you're not a jerk. You spilled some coffee, that's all. It was an accident. Of course I still want to go to the movies with you."

While I spoke, I grabbed one of the rags and mopped up the rest of the coffee.

Jimmy was on his knees, cleaning up under the table.

"Jimmy," I said, "wouldn't it be easier if you got a mop?"

"Huh? Oh yeah." Now even his ears were the color of ripe apples. "I just wanted to get most of it up before it spread and someone slipped on it. That's all I'd need. Have someone fall and break an arm or something. Gee, I'd be fired for sure."

"I think you got most of it now. Danger of that happening is over."

Jimmy was still on the floor and I wondered if he'd ever look at me again. I reached down and tugged on his arm. "Get up, Jimmy. It's fine now."

"I feel like such a jerk," he said, his chin almost buried in his chest.

"Well, you're not. Now, when are we going to the movies?"

"You still want to go? You're sure?"

"I'm sure," I said, smiling up at him.

His face lit up like a Christmas tree. "I'm off on Friday, if that's okay with you."

"Friday sounds perfect. I rented a room in Edna Lynch's house. Do you know her?"

"Oh sure, everyone knows Mrs. Lynch."

"Why don't you call there and leave a message about what time I should meet you, okay?"

"That's swell. I'll stop by the theater tonight on my way home and find out what time the movie's playing."

"Okay. Meanwhile, I guess I'd better get upstairs and see what Betty has to say for herself."

"Don't be too hard on her, Alex. Maybe she forgot or something."

I raised one eyebrow and smirked. "Okay, for your sake, I'll go easy on her."

He grinned, and I sauntered out, waving goodbye over my shoulder.

CHAPTER 14

I stopped at the reception desk to get my visitor pass, but was told I'd have to wait until two o'clock to go upstairs. I paced the room. The warm feelings that Jimmy's attention had kindled flickered out, replaced by the cold hard reality of Betty's betrayal.

By the time the bell rang to signal the start of visiting hours, I was ready to confront her. I flew up the stairs and burst into her room, full of piss and vinegar. But she was asleep.

How infuriating!

I walked over to the window and stared at the trees. The sight of lime-green buds on the branches relaxed me. Soon spring would arrive and they'd transform into bright leaves that would conceal the nests abandoned last fall. I could still make out some remnants of them, but the Montana winter had gnawed away at their beauty.

As I stood there, I heard geese honking. I looked to my right and saw their familiar V-shaped formation wending its way back from their winter migration. Everywhere I looked, signs of life popped up, heralding spring's approach and the end of winter. Even the grass was beginning to turn a shade greener, shedding its winter brown hue. A few hardy flowers tentatively poked through the patches of snow that refused to melt, shielded from the sun and wind by the hospital's walls.

"Alex?"

I turned around. Betty was awake and watching me.

"Hi," I said. For a minute I forgot about being mad at her. She looked so pitiful, encased in plaster, one leg suspended above the bed. At least the doctor had removed the giant bandage on her face. Now there were only a few small strips over her stitches. But she did have a beauty of a shiner.

"How did the interview with the Fergusons go?" she asked, pushing herself up on her pillows.

All my feelings of sympathy for her dissolved the minute she said that.

"How do you think it went?" I asked. I crossed my arms to control their trembling. I could feel the heat rising across my chest, neck, and face. "I guess I should feel lucky Mrs. Ferguson was there. Otherwise, Henry might have killed me. How could you let me go there when you knew he had already threatened you, or anyone else from the paper who came on the property again? How could you? I thought we were at least colleagues, if not friends."

Betty stared at me, her mouth open, a deep frown creasing her forehead.

"What are you talking about? You're making no sense. Calm down. Tell me what happened, and start from the beginning."

So, I did, then said, "I don't know what your motives were. All I know is that I feel betrayed. And I'm hurt, Betty. I thought we could be friends. It seems you only see me as competition. And if that's the way you want it, then hold onto your hat, because I'm not going anywhere but up."

Betty's eyes never left mine during my monologue. They followed me as I paced back and forth, and now they were locked on me as I stood, defiant, at the foot of her bed, my hands gripping the footboard's metal rail.

The silence grew until Betty shook her head as if she needed to shake out the images I had painted.

"Alex," she said, her voice little more than a whisper, "I'm sorry that happened to you. I probably would have scampered off like a scared rabbit at the first sight of Henry's face, or his gun. But . . ."

She stopped talking and turned her face toward the window.

"But what?"

"Never mind. With the way you feel right now, you probably won't believe me anyway."

"Let me make that decision, will you? I don't need you deciding what I should or shouldn't know, or do, ever again."

"I'm pretty sure you don't want to believe me, but if you think about it for a minute, you might. Right now, you're so angry, and rightfully so, that I doubt you can even consider an alternative."

"As I said, let me decide that."

Betty sighed and looked at me. "I wasn't the one who went to the Ferguson ranch."

I watched her as she sank back against her pillow, exhaustion overcoming the bravado she usually displayed.

"But Joe must have," she said in a whisper, her eyes closed. Betty slowly shook her head from side to side. Her face was so pale, the purple around her eye looked darker than a moonless night.

"Joe? Who's Joe? I thought you reported all the local news. What does he have to do with this?" I asked.

"I mentioned him to you on your first day. He reports on agriculture, farming trends, and livestock prices. But he's always wanted to have a front-page story."

She was silent for a minute, then said, "Joe must have gone to the ranch after Mr. Ferguson was killed to find out the family's plans. Whether they were going to keep it running, or sell, or what. He always reports on those kinds of things when they do happen, which isn't too often, so it's big news. But he never said a word about being run off the property. I never would have let you go out there if I'd known. I wouldn't have gone out there, either. Some of these cowboys shoot first and ask questions later. I can't believe Joe never said anything to me. Or to Lou. I know Lou would have told you not to go *near* the Lazy F if he knew."

Betty's face was bright red.

"You'd better calm down," I said, "or you'll have a heart attack on top of broken bones."

"I'm furious," she said. "I know Joe'd like to get off his beat, but to put someone else in danger is going too far. This is a lot more than competitive headline grabbing, or sending someone off on a wild goose chase to get them out of the way for a while. Damn him. He's gone too far this time."

I figured I'd better give Betty some time to calm down. "You want a coffee or something?" I asked.

"I'd like a bourbon and a chance to land a solid right on Joe's jaw."

"I don't think the Sisters would approve of either."

"You're probably right, but they'd both make me feel a lot better." A minute later, she looked at me, a half-smile on her face. "Can you imagine Sister Marcus's surprise if she came in and saw me sitting here, drinking bourbon?"

I started to giggle at the image of her walking in on us drinking whiskey, and bootleg whiskey at that. I guess Betty was picturing the same thing, because she began to laugh, and soon, we were both howling.

I knew I had to get back to the paper and write up my story, but first I had to set things right with Betty.

"Betty, I'm sorry. Once again, I made assumptions without getting all the facts. I made a big mistake. I came in here loaded for bear and made some pretty horrible accusations. I let my temper rule and run away with my mouth. Can you forgive me?"

Betty said nothing at first. She just stared at me. Maybe she was trying to figure out whether or not my apology was sincere.

Please say something. Anything.

"You did paint a pretty black picture of me," she said. "But I realize Henry terrified you, and so did Mrs. Ferguson. I can imagine the ride back was spent thinking of how much you would love to strangle me, right?"

"Pretty much."

"Can't say I blame you. That's how I feel about Joe right now."

She shifted her gaze from my face to the window. I could almost see her mind racing, trying to figure out what she should do. So, I waited while Betty tapped her fingers against her blanket.

"Okay, here's what I'd like you to do," she said. "But I'm not ordering you, you understand. This is just my opinion."

"So, are we okay? I'm forgiven?"

Betty let out a huge sigh. "Yes, Alex. But for a cub reporter, you seem to keep finding yourself in the middle of some sensational stories and situations. And you'd better get your temper under control. A good reporter has to rely on her wits, not be ruled by her emotions. And I've already talked to you about assuming you know what's going on before you get all the facts. It's a bad habit to fall into.

"Okay, enough of the lecture, here's what I want you to do. I want you to tell Lou everything that happened today, including Joe's part. Let Lou deal with Joe. Then write the best possible story you've ever written about the Ferguson tragedy."

"That was kind of my plan, but I'm glad we're on the same track. And it's something I can do without causing a tirade in the newsroom. Thanks, Betty."

I grabbed my purse and headed for the door.

"Oh, Alex," Betty called.

I stopped and looked back.

"Tell Lou if he plans to stop by tonight, to make sure he has a flask full of his finest bourbon with him."

"I can do that, too," I said, grinning from ear to ear.

CHAPTER 15

Back at the paper, I typed up the Ferguson piece and got it to Lou ahead of the day's deadline. I set my idea for a full-page community news section on the back burner until Betty was back. No sense upsetting the apple cart any more than it had already been thrown out of kilter. Maybe for now I'd pass off news of the bake sales and 4-H meetings to one of the college kids, like Betty used to do—at least until this whole Webb/Ferguson story died down. I wasn't sure I could cover the community events and the other local news and do a good job on both.

I covered my typewriter and looked at the clock: 6:20. Time to go home, kick off my shoes, and relax. It had been a hell of a day, and my legs were starting to ache from all the unaccustomed bike riding.

I poked my head into Lou's office. "Anything else before I leave, Lou?"

"Don't think so, Alex. I'm sorry about the Ferguson incident. I'll deal with Joe tomorrow, if I can find him. Half the time, he sneaks in and out of here after I've gone. Maybe I'll let Phil know I want to see him. He seems to be the only person around here who's in regular contact with Joe. But that's my problem, not yours. Enjoy yourself tonight. I heard you have a big date," Lou said, grinning.

"A date? Oh, gosh. With everything that's gone on today, I forgot all about it. And now I'm twenty minutes late, and look at me. I'm covered in mud and coffee. Oh, gee. This is swell. Just swell."

I pushed my hand through my windblown hair and realized I hadn't combed it all day.

"I'm a real mess." I searched through my purse, looking for a brush or comb or something to try to tame my unruly brown bob. Normally it was sleek and shiny, but today I had taken my hat off to enjoy the breeze in my hair, and now it was a tangled mess.

"Here, Alex." Lou handed me his comb. "Go make yourself pretty. I don't have enough hair left to worry about."

"Thanks, Lou."

I ran to the washroom. Halfway across the newsroom, I turned back and yelled, "Don't forget Betty's bourbon!"

Lou nodded and waved for me to get going.

In the washroom, I looked at my reflection and gasped. My hair was in tangles, my face was blotchy, and my shoes and trousers were splattered with varying shades of brown. I was in need of a major renovation, not a quick nose powder and lipstick refresher.

Swell. I yanked the comb through my hair and tried my best to make myself look presentable.

I didn't know why I was even bothering. I didn't care what Adam thought about me. I was only having dinner with him to pay him back for the bike. I kept yanking the knots out and finally figured it would have to do, ran the powder puff over my face, the lipstick over my lips, pinched my cheeks for some color, and left.

By the time I got to the hotel, it was 6:30. I looked around the lobby, but there was no sign of Adam.

"Miss Lawson," the desk clerk said, "Adam said he'd wait for you in the café."

"Thanks."

Great. Now everyone will see my filthy disheveled state.

I walked in, head held high, determined to act like I meant to look this way. I spotted Adam right away. He was standing by the window, talking to a couple of men I had never seen before. And, of course, to make matters worse, he looked amazing in a pristine white shirt, the crease on the sleeves sharp as a knife's edge, slacks instead of the usual cowboy denims, boots shined to a mirror gleam, and a bolo tie. A leather jacket, that looked soft as velvet, was draped across the back of a nearby chair.

One of the men spotted me and motioned to Adam by a nod of his head that I had arrived. A smile crept across the stranger's face as he eyed me from head to toe and back again.

Determined not to be intimidated, I strode over to them.

"Hi, Adam," I said. "Sorry I'm late. I had a couple of stories to write before I could get away."

He turned his head and looked at me. His blue eyes mocked me as he looked down at my mud and coffee stained shoes.

"You sure you told her you'd be taking her to dinner and not a cowboy jamboree?" one of his companions asked, sipping at his coffee that reeked of bootleg booze.

"Thought I did," Adam said with his usual smirk.

I could feel my face getting hot. "If you don't mind waiting, I'll go home and change. It's been a hectic day, and it's pretty hard to ride a bike fourteen miles and arrive here looking fresh as a daisy."

The men stifled a laugh and Adam said, "If you'd feel better getting changed, I can wait. But you look fine to me."

His buddies stood there with stupid grins on their faces, waiting to see what would happen next.

They're loving every minute of this.

"I rented a room at Edna Lynch's house. Do you know where that is?"

"Sure do."

"Fine. You can pick me up there in half an hour."

I spun around and stormed out of the café, humiliated and furious at his friends' quips and stares. I knew I shouldn't have cared, seeing as they were three sheets to the wind, but their superior attitude riled me.

When I hit the lobby, I realized I hadn't even said hello to Pete, who had watched me leave with an openmouthed stare. I'd have to apologize to him later. Couldn't have my local restaurateur mad at me.

I grabbed my valise from behind the registration desk and thanked the clerk for watching it for me. Now I had to figure out how to get the bike and my valise to Edna's. It took some maneuvering, but I finally arrived there with everything still in one piece. After parking the bike on the porch, I lugged myself and the bag upstairs to my room.

"Is that you, Alex?" Edna called from the kitchen. "Maureen and I are finishing up, but I can make a plate for you if you'd like."

"No, Edna, that's fine," I said. She stood at the bottom of the stairs, looking up at me. "I'm having dinner with Adam, like I told you this morning. I just need to freshen up and change my clothes. Adam will be here in a little while to pick me up."

"Oh, that's right. Guess I just forgot, what with all the phone calls about your newspaper story and me," she said, retreating to the kitchen.

I didn't need, or want, another conversation about that right then. I needed to try and make myself look like a lady, not a six-year-old who'd been playing in the mud.

I washed my face, cleaned my teeth, and brushed my hair until it shined, knot free.

Back in my room, I rummaged through my unpacked clothes for something that wasn't a mass of wrinkles. I didn't have time to iron anything. Then I spotted my burgundy rayon crepe cocktail dress. It would be perfect for dinner. I had bought it for my college graduation party and everyone said I looked stunning in it. It had a jewel neckline with a wrap-style skirt that fell in soft folds from the low-slung waist down to the handkerchief hem. The three-quarter length sleeves added some elegance. I had a pair of black strapped pumps and a black clutch that would be perfect with it. My single strand long "pearl" necklace would add a little oomph.

I finished my makeup and adjusted my burgundy and white striped headband to sit in the middle of my forehead. I gave myself a final look in the mirror just as the doorbell rang.

I heard Edna say hello, then Adam's reply, and my stomach fluttered a little. One final check to make sure my stocking seams were straight and I was ready.

The extra time I'd taken to choose everything was worth it when I saw Adam's jaw drop as I came down the stairs.

Too bad his snarky cowboy buddies can't see me now.

"Ready?" I asked.

"You look beautiful," he said, twirling his hat in his hands.

"Thank you. You look pretty swell too."

We stood for a minute, both with smiles on our faces, not sure what to say next.

"Have fun, you two," Edna said, breaking the spell.

"Thanks, Edna. I won't be too late."

"Oh, don't you worry about that. You just go and have a good time."

Adam tipped his hat to her, took my arm, and led me to a gleaming black sedan.

I stopped dead. "Is this yours? Where's your truck?"

"Of course it's mine. You don't think I stole someone's car, do you?"

"But your truck—"

"That's for work, not to take a lady to dinner."

He opened the door for me and waited until I was settled, then gently closed it. He folded his long lean body behind the steering wheel and we took off.

"Where are we going?" I asked.

"It's a surprise," he said.

We drove out of town, heading west toward the sunset. Adam asked about my day, and how the bike had worked out. I told him about my trip to the Lazy F and the muddy drive to the house, but nothing else.

"It's that time of year, mud season. You should see the mess my dogs make. I think they find the biggest mud puddle they can and roll around in it before they come in, just to drive me crazy."

"What kind of dogs are they?"

"The Heinz 57 variety."

"They're the best kind. I miss my dog, but I didn't think it was a good idea to bring him, since I didn't even have a place to stay. I don't think Edna would appreciate it if I smuggled him into my room."

"'Spect not."

We drove for a while before he spoke again.

"How's your friend? The one who got shot? Heard one of the officers got shot. Is that who you were so upset about? I know you saw Betty, too, but I doubt you'd be that worked up over someone you work with, especially since you've only known her for a few days."

I looked at him, amazed. "I've only been in town about three days. Do you think I already have an admirer?"

"Well, do you?"

"No. Well . . . no, I don't think so."

"What's that supposed to mean? Either you do or you don't."

"Either way, I don't know what difference it makes to you. Look, can we drop it? We've been getting along so well, I don't want to spoil the night."

Adam shook his head. "Sure. Forget I asked."

Neither of us spoke until we got to the restaurant.

CHAPTER 16

It was a steakhouse and what used to be a bar, before Prohibition. The parking area was pretty full, so I hoped that meant the place was busy with people eating, not just cowboys drinking hooch.

We walked in through the barroom door and the men, "coffee" mugs in hand, greeted Adam like a long-lost son or brother. If they didn't come over to shake his hand and say hello, they nodded to him. All the attention and visible affection people felt for him surprised me.

An older woman came out from the kitchen and Adam kissed her cheek.

"Mamie, this is Alex Lawson. She just moved to Sunset Valley."

"Welcome, Alex," she said. "I'm Mamie. I hope he's treating you all right."

"He is, or I wouldn't be with him."

Mamie laughed and said to Adam, "I like her. Now, let's get you settled at a table and I'll get you something to eat."

"Thanks, Mamie," Adam said.

We sat near an enormous fireplace where a fire roared and took the evening chill out of the air. The stone structure covered most of the restaurant's back wall, and a mounted buffalo head held the place of honor above the center of the mantel. A few books lay beneath the hunting trophy, along with pieces of local Crow Indian pottery. Sconces on the walls between the windows lit the room with a subtle glow. The overall effect gave the small twelve-table dining room a homey feel.

Adam hung his jacket on one of the upturned deer hooves that hung below the sconces and served as coat hangers. Wood paneling covered the walls and gingham swags hung from the windows. A corner cupboard filled with sparkling glasses and china sat at the other end of the room. In front of it storybooks, coloring books, and a box of crayons covered a kids' table. It was more like someone's home than a restaurant.

Six other couples sat eating dinner, and most of the men waved over to Adam. An old-fashioned swinging wooden saloon door separated us from the bar at the other end of the building. Although the bar was crowded, there wasn't a lot of noise. The men all talked quietly among themselves.

Obviously, Mamie doesn't tolerate ruffians.

"That's quite a fireplace," I said.

"Yep. All the stones came from right around here," Adam said. "One of the local guys dug them up and built it."

"It's amazing." I let a minute pass, then said, "You seem to be well known in here."

"My ranch isn't far, and my family's been providing Mamie with her beef for years. We're old friends."

An uneasy silence settled over the table.

Guess I ruined his friendly attitude when I tried to sound mysterious about a beau.

"Hey," I said, "I'm sorry I snapped at you earlier. I guess I don't like answering questions about myself. Especially about possible boyfriends. Okay?"

"Sure. I had no right to ask you anyway. We had a deal—a bike for a dinner. I shouldn't have expected anything more, like friendly conversation, or getting to know something about you."

"There you go again. You're acting like a spoiled little boy who's going to pout all night because he didn't get his way."

"Would you rather I take you home right now?"

I felt my stomach drop to my knees.

The way the firelight bounced off the gold flecks in his light brown hair and highlighted his cheekbones made my heart jump. His eyes looked like two bright circles of a summer sky. I could stare into them forever.

God, he is so good-looking.

"Well, do you?"

I forced myself back to reality.

"No, no, not at all. Sorry. You're being so nice and I'm . . . well . . . I'm not. Let's change the subject. Tell me about your ranch."

I'd hit on the right subject. His jaw muscles stopped twitching and his eyes melted. His whole face glowed and became so serene that he didn't look like the same person.

He told me his grandfather had called it Long River Ranch because the river that ran through it never seemed to end. At least that's what he thought when he first saw the property. It had a little more than 100,000 acres and some of the "finest cattle in Montana."

"When he first arrived there, he built a small log cabin for him and his wife. Of course, over the years, as they had kids, he expanded it. Then my father extended it even more. Made the kitchen bigger with an area big enough to fit a table and eight chairs, a room off the kitchen for our housekeeper, bigger porches, lots of new appliances to make life more comfortable."

"Jeepers, it sounds wonderful."

"Oh, you're in for it now, Alex," Mamie said, placing two platters in front of us. "Once he starts talking about that ranch, he never stops. I may as well set up two cots in the kitchen for you. That's how bad he is." She patted his shoulder and walked away.

"This looks delicious, and I'm starving," I said.

Although we hadn't ordered anything, it was exactly what I wanted. A huge rib-eye steak, baked potato, and peas and carrots that filled the entire platter. I cut into the steak. It was perfectly cooked, just rare enough, and positively melted in my mouth.

"I don't think I've ever tasted a better steak."

Adam beamed like he had just become the father of a newborn son. "Glad you like it." He speared a chunk and chewed. "Not bad, if I do say so myself." He cut another piece, then said, "Damn. I forgot to order something to drink. What would you like?"

"Just coffee, I guess."

Adam signaled to the waitress and ordered Mamie's special blend. When it arrived, I took a gulp and instantly regretted it. Heavily laced with bourbon, I choked on my mouthful.

"Sorry," Adam said, slapping my back and handing me a glass of water. "Guess I should have warned you about Mamie's blend. You okay?"

"I'm fine," I said between coughs. "I'll be sure to sip the coffee from now on, not take big gulps."

Adam gave me a sheepish grin and for the rest of the meal, he talked about the ranch. Fortunately, I grew up listening to ranchers talk about their properties and livestock, so I was able to ask some intelligent questions, which I could tell Adam appreciated.

I swallowed the last morsel of beef and sopped up the remaining juice with my bread. I sat, full and content.

Adam looked at me and smiled. "You look lovely, and happy."

"A wonderful dinner, good coffee, and a pleasant companion will do that to me."

"Was I pleasant?"

"More than I imagined you could be. I'm happy you made this deal with me, Adam. It's been a terrific evening."

"I'm glad. I think so, too."

We sat staring into each other's eyes and I wished I could freeze this moment.

Mamie walked over to our table. "Well," she said, "did you enjoy your dinner, Alex?"

"It may have been the most perfect dinner I've ever had," I said.

"Good, good. Now, how about another coffee?"

Adam looked at his watch and said, "I don't think so, Mamie. It's pretty late, and I still have to drive Alex home. Ready?" he asked.

"I am."

We walked out into a chilly night.

"Here, put my jacket on," Adam said. "It got cold out."

My stomach lurched as he wrapped it around my shoulders, and a feeling like an electric shock surged through me.

"Guess spring's not here yet," I said. The jacket felt like a velvet cloak and smelled of Adam's aftershave, citrusy and tangy and all man.

The ride back to Sunset was comfortable in a way I never expected. We talked about everyday things and Adam filled me in on some of the town's annual events.

When we arrived at Edna's house, Adam came around the car to open the door for me. He took my arm, and at the top of the porch steps, he said, "I'd like to see you again, Alex. Can I?"

"I'd like that too," I said. "And thank you for a wonderful evening."

He leaned over and gave me a chaste kiss on the cheek, just like the one he'd given Mamie. I shook my head and went inside.

CHAPTER 17

The next morning, I dressed and hurried downstairs to breakfast. Edna was at the stove cooking scrambled eggs. Another woman, who I assumed was Maureen, was making toast. The table was already set for three.

"Anything left for me to do?" I asked.

"Oh, good morning, Alex," Edna said. "Did you have a nice time last night?"

"Yes, I did. Much to my surprise." Turning to the other woman I reached out my hand and said, "Hi, I'm Alex Lawson."

As we shook hands, I looked into the most beautiful green eyes I had ever seen. "Wow, your eyes are gorgeous."

"Oh, thanks," she said, her face turning as red as raspberry jam. "It's nice to meet you. I'm Maureen Healy. Edna told me you work for the paper. That must be exciting."

"Oh yeah, the paper. The last few days have been exciting, although I don't think it will always be that way," I said.

"Alex, could you pour the coffee?" Edna asked.

I grabbed a pot holder from a hook on the side of the cabinet and reached for the percolator. While I filled the cups, I looked at Maureen. She was about the same age as me, maybe a couple of years older. Her hair was an amazing copper color, thick, wavy, and shiny. Simply parted in the middle and pulled back on both sides, it stayed out of her face, which I guess was necessary when you're leaning over students' desks all day. She wore a simple skirt, blouse, sweater, and flat shoes. *Very utilitarian.*

"I hope you like eggs and toast," Maureen said, bringing a plate loaded with toasted bread to the table.

"I do."

Maureen sat, hands in her lap like a perfectly behaved schoolgirl. *She seems to be much more of a homebody than me, but that doesn't mean we can't be friends. And we are around the same age. Maybe she just needs someone to help her loosen up a little. And I'm just the gal for the job.*

I landed the coffeepot back on the stove while Edna dished out the eggs. There was a butter dish and a jar of homemade jam on the table.

"This jam smells delicious," I said, scooping a teaspoon of raspberry preserves onto my toast. I tasted it, and it didn't disappoint.

"Um, delicious." It wasn't too sweet, just the right amount of tartness to thrill my taste buds. And the aroma was heavenly, like being in the midst of a berry bush.

"You do make the most wonderful preserves," Maureen said, scooping another dollop onto her toast. "I can't wait to start harvesting all the fruits and vegetables from your garden again so you and I can put them up for next winter. That was so much fun. Hard work, but fun."

Edna smiled at Maureen. I could see the two of them were remembering their hours over the stove, boiling, crushing, canning, and whatever else needed to be done. When I was little, I remember a neighbor putting up vegetables and making jams, but my mom never had time, or the inclination, for that. Between sewing new winter clothes for me and managing the saloon's accounts, her days were filled to overflowing.

Stomachs full, we lingered over our coffee. Edna asked me about my night, and I told them about Mamie and the restaurant. Neither of them had ever been there, so they wanted to hear every detail. After describing the entire evening, I helped Edna clear the table.

Maureen and I washed and dried the dishes while Edna wiped down the stove.

We finished cleaning up and Maureen and I left for work. Since we were headed in the same direction, I walked my bike alongside her instead of riding it.

"You're lucky to have a bike," Maureen said. "They don't sell them in town, and I never seem to get to Billings to look for one."

"Guess I am lucky—but just try telling my legs that. They're still aching from my fourteen-mile trek to the Ferguson ranch yesterday."

"Gee, that is a lot. And you had enough energy left to go out last night? I would've been curled up on the couch, or in my bed, with a hot water bottle."

"It was part of the deal I made. Dinner for a bike."

Maureen looked at me like I said I sold my soul to the devil or something.

"Well, I need a way to get around. I have stories to cover, and they're not always right in town, you know. And like my dad always says, you've got to look out for number one, because no one else will."

"Sure, sure. It's just that . . . I don't know. It seems wrong somehow."

"I can't afford to stand on the moral high ground when my job is on the line. I don't have a car, and I can't afford to buy one. Lou, my editor, told me to get a horse or a bike, but to get the story. Considering how my legs feel, a horse may have been the better option. But that dinner was amazing."

"The food or the company?"

"Both."

Maureen looked at me and sighed. I guess she now considered me an amoral lost cause to decent women everywhere, but I didn't care. I had had a wonderful time last night and didn't regret a minute of it.

When we got to Montana Avenue we turned right and headed for Main Street. I asked Maureen what she taught at the high school, and when she said English, an idea began to form in my head.

Maybe she could help out at the paper until Betty's back on her feet.

At South Center Avenue, she and I parted. She went south toward Tyler County High School, about a block away, and I headed to the office.

I walked into the building still thinking about how to approach Lou with my ideas about Maureen and the community page when I heard him shouting.

I leaned my bike against the wall near the switchboard and walked into the newsroom. Lou's door was closed, but I could see him through the glass panel.

He paced back and forth in front of a man who stood, hat in hand, looking defeated. Every few paces, Lou stopped and poked the man's chest, his cigar coming dangerously close to his victim's nose. Lou's face was red, and when he stopped to puff on his cigar, I thought he would suck it down his throat.

I could see the man trying to talk to Lou, but that seemed to be a losing battle.

That must be Joe. Gee, I hope Lou never gets that angry with me. Just watching him lacing into Joe terrifies me.

I went to my desk to see if Lou had left an assignment, maybe something special he wanted me to cover, but there was nothing there. I decided it would be a good idea to get out of the office before he spotted me. I didn't want to get involved in Joe's dressing down. I decided to head to the courthouse and see if there was any news about the officer or Webb. Maybe the judge had set a date for the execution, if that's what he had decided on as Webb's sentence. If the courthouse was quiet, I'd stop by the mayor's office. Dot might have something for me. I also wanted to go to the hospital and see Betty. I hoped she knew how to get in touch with the officer's wife. I wanted to ask her what the prognosis was for her husband.

And I might be able to sneak in a few minutes with Jimmy. I liked him a lot and wanted to make sure we were still on schedule for Friday night. Imagine. Two beaus. At home, no one paid the slightest bit of attention to me. I was either too tall or too independent for the Jericho Flats' high school boys. The college boys felt differently, of course, but none of them had really interested me very much.

I was glad I had decided to move here. Two beaus made life interesting, even if I didn't plan on marriage. A little fun never hurt anyone.

I stopped at the reception desk and told Pat where I was going in case Lou came looking for me. I also told her I'd stop back before I went to the hospital. Hopefully, Joe would be gone by then and Lou would have calmed down.

CHAPTER 18

As I suspected, the courthouse was quiet. I roamed around and stopped to introduce myself to the District Attorney and the Assistant DA. They were both busy working on upcoming trials, or said they were, and gave me a schedule of future court dates before coolly dismissing me. But they did make time to ask how Betty was doing. I filled them in on her condition and asked about the officer. They didn't know any more than I did, which wasn't a lot. There was also a State Police office in the courthouse, so I went through the same routine with them, and was dismissed with the same coolness the DA had shown.

I was a little surprised at how concerned everyone was about Betty. It seemed she was well known and well liked. I wondered if there was a special trick to getting in these people's good graces. I thought about baking a treat for them but nixed that idea after about a minute's reflection. I didn't need them thinking about me as a happy homemaker instead of a serious career woman. Guess I'd just have to polish my feminine charms to win them over. I certainly couldn't do it with my figure when I had to wear trousers and flat shoes every day, especially since some people still didn't approve of women wearing pants.

And riding a bike did nothing to enhance my looks; instead, it turned me into a windblown mess.

If I had a girl's bike, I could wear a skirt. This is definitely going to be a wardrobe challenge, at least until my trunk arrives.

I thought about my clothing problem on the way back to the paper. I wasn't sure if there was even a store in town where I could buy something other than dungarees or daytime dresses. Maybe Pat or Betty would know about a place close to town. I knew I couldn't pedal all the way into Billings, but there might be a bus.

I was thinking my way through this dilemma when a man charged out of the newspaper building and knocked me down.

Sprawled in the gutter, I looked up and said, "Hey, watch where you're going."

"Sorry, sorry. I wasn't looking. Are you hurt? Here, let me help you up."

"Wait a minute," I said, brushing off the seat of my pants, "you're Joe, aren't you?"

"How do you know my name?"

"I'm Alex Lawson. I'm the new reporter here."

"Oh, so you're the one who went out to the Fergusons' yesterday. You're the one who caused me to get reamed out this morning. You're the one who almost cost me my job."

The whole time he spoke, he kept walking closer and closer until I was backed off the sidewalk and into the gutter again, this time still on my feet.

"Hold on. You could have gotten me killed," I said, poking him in his chest. "You're the one who didn't tell anyone the ranch was off-limits. You're the one who went out there and got Henry infuriated with the paper. You're the one who caused this whole thing, not me."

I had reversed our steps so that now Joe's back was up against the wall.

"Don't try to blame me for your mistake and foolhardiness," I said. "I was in serious danger out there. With no quick escape vehicle, just my bike and two strong legs. Which could have been shot out from under me. I should punch you right in the nose for getting me in that situation."

Joe pushed his fedora back on his head and scratched his forehead. "Well, when you put it like that . . ."

"What other way can I put it? You know I'm right."

"I guess you have a point."

"Ha!"

"Okay, look, I'm sorry you had to deal with Henry, but he's usually all bark and no bite. I never thought he'd actually threaten anyone from the paper. Honest. Can we start over? I'm Joe Davis. Shake?"

He extended his hand and smiled at me. I thought about how pitiful he had looked in Lou's office, so I gave him one firm shake, but refused to smile.

"That's better," he said. "After all, we're on the same team, aren't we?"

"It sure didn't feel like that yesterday," I said.

"How about I buy you a cup of coffee and fill you in on the ranches, and ranchers, around here? You never know when you'll have to go see one of them one day, even if it's only to report on a birth, anniversary, or his prize bull winning a blue ribbon or getting the highest rating in the rodeo lineup."

I didn't answer right away. I had a lot I wanted to do that day.

"Come on," he said. "Consider it my peace offering."

"Oh, all right."

We walked back the way I had come and went into the Met Café. Pete wasn't in yet. The waitress greeted me like a long-lost friend. Overtipping can create instant friends.

"We'll sit at that table in the back, Mae," Joe said. "We'll both have coffee, and bring Alex here a piece of apple pie."

"I don't want any pie."

Joe rolled his eyes, shook his head, and nodded to Mae. "Bring it anyway."

We talked about the paper and Joe asked about where I came from and how I landed in Sunset Valley. He was a real gentleman and I felt bad that he had endured two people yelling at him that morning.

He told me he had worked for the paper for the past twenty-five years. He grew up on a ranch just outside Sunset Valley and loved ranching and everything that went with it. But his father died when he was only eleven and his mother couldn't keep the place going with just the two of them, so the bank took over and he came to work for the paper. Little by little, he worked his way up from the presses, to doing rewrites, to finally doing the agricultural reporting. Since he knew all about ranching, it was easy for him to talk to the ranchers in their own language. Now, no one thought twice when he drove up to their home, or rode out to meet them on the range.

"So, if there's anything you want to know about any of them, just ask," he said, and waited for questions.

"Do you know Adam Phillips?" I asked.

"Sure do. Knew his whole family before the accident. Now that was a tragedy."

"What happened?"

"Well," he said, tilting his chair back, ready to tell a long story, "Adam's parents and older brother went out to round up the cattle one spring, about ten, maybe fifteen, years ago. Going to bring them in from the winter grazing land. They had their usual gang of cowboys working, too. Somehow, something spooked the herd and they started to stampede. Adam's parents got caught in the middle and his brother tried to wade through the pack to get to them. Of course, the roundup crew did everything they could to get the herd under control, but by the time the dust settled, all three members of Adam's family had been trampled to death."

I had absently popped a piece of pie into my mouth while Joe talked.

"That's horrible," I said. I wasn't sure if my pie was going to stay down after that story. "What an awful way to die."

"Yup. Young Adam took it real hard. Quit high school and just stayed at the ranch. Nobody in town saw him for months. If it wasn't for Clint, his foreman, and Martha, his housekeeper, I think he would have died out there. They kept things running, made sure he ate, and finally brought him out of his shell. Adam wanted to slaughter all the cattle, but Clint talked him out of that. Kept reminding him that his granddaddy wouldn't want such foolishness."

Joe stared at me for a while, then asked, "You have a special reason to ask about that one particular rancher?"

"No, no special reason, just curious," I said.

"This have anything to do with that fancy dinner he treated you to last night?"

"How do you know about that?"

"This is a small town, Alex. And the ranchers all talk to one another."

"More like gossip with one another."

Joe laughed. "Some people might call it that. Well, I've got to get going. It was nice to meet you, Alex. If you ever need anything, just leave a note on my desk. I check there most nights before I go home."

"Thanks, Joe. I'm glad we had this talk, and thanks for the pie."

He tipped his hat and left me thinking about Adam. I couldn't imagine losing your whole family in one day, especially in the way they died. I shivered even though I wasn't cold.

"More coffee?" Mae asked.

"Huh? Oh, no, thanks," I said when she pointed to the coffeepot in her hand. "I've got to get back to work."

I left some change on the table and headed to the office. I couldn't stop thinking about Adam. I was glad I hadn't asked him about his family last night. That certainly would have put the kibosh on our evening.

CHAPTER 19

When I walked into the building, Pat said, "Be careful—he's in a mood today."

"Thanks for the warning."

I opened the newsroom door and saw Lou sitting at his desk furiously puffing away on his cigar. One look and I knew this wasn't the best time to talk to him about making changes to the paper, and adding Maureen to the staff. I tiptoed to my desk, but he spotted me.

"Alex," he bellowed through his closed door.

"Coming, Lou."

"Nice job on the Ferguson story," he said when I poked my head into his office. "Oh, and I spoke to Joe today."

"I know. He literally ran into me a little while ago."

"You okay? I don't need another reporter banged up."

"I'm fine. He only bruised my pride and my rear end."

Lou's face colored a little and he shuffled some papers on his desk. "Look, Alex, I've got to work on my 'Old Montana' column today. It's a weekly feature every Saturday and I haven't even thought about a topic yet. Plus, there's whatever else comes over the wire. I need you to see to the rest of the news. Can you handle that?"

"Sure, Lou."

The rest of the news?

It amazed me how easily I could lie to him. The pie was jumping all over my stomach.

I'm in over my head now, but maybe this is the time to tell him about my ideas. If he agrees, it would take something off my plate.

"Uh, Lou, I was thinking about expanding the community news section."

"Into what?"

"Well, into a full page. I could set up a template with a banner. Then I'd just have to plug in the events, or change the times and dates. Maybe surround it with the local ads that run on a regular basis. It would be easier for the typesetters too. They could keep the basic headings and I'd let them know what changes to make each week."

"Sounds interesting. Work something up and show it to me. If it looks good, I'll have Paul talk to you about how it'll work. You haven't met him yet, but he's our chief typesetter." Lou went back to sorting through the papers on his desk.

"Thanks, Lou." I stood there for a minute.

He looked up. "Something else?"

"I rented a room in Edna Lynch's house and there's another boarder there, Maureen Healy. She teaches English at the high school. I was thinking maybe she could write up the community news events. It would just be until Betty gets back. She'd be more reliable than the college kids who leave at the end of the semester, and I'm sure she could use the extra paycheck." I said all this in a rush, crossed fingers behind my back.

"That's not a bad idea."

"Really?"

"When can she start?"

"Oh, well, I haven't even asked her about it yet. I wanted to talk to you first."

"I like it. See if you can get her on board right away. I feel like I'm working with my right arm tied behind my back. I never realized how much Betty did around here, but I do now."

She's like a goddess around this town. I'll never fill her shoes. I'll have to make myself indispensable another way.

"Speaking of Betty," I said, "I'm headed to the hospital now. I want to see if I can interview the bailiff and his wife, get their side of the story."

"Good idea. Tell Betty I'll try to stop by later."

"You got it, Chief."

I floated out of the newsroom. I couldn't believe Lou agreed to both my ideas. As I pedaled to the hospital, I thought about what I had to do: design a template for the community news, and talk to Maureen. I didn't think the template would be a problem. I had created one for my college newspaper that worked well for reporting the sports events and results. As I cycled to the hospital, I rehearsed what I could say to Maureen to convince her to take the job.

A lone rabbit ran across the road in front of me and jolted me back to reality. Moose and deer roamed freely down the center of the road. The grasses and plants reached out from the side of the new roads and invaded the tiniest cracks in the asphalt to establish their ownership. All were unwilling to give up their land to the ever more popular motorcars, which were changing the town. And on this beautiful almost-spring day, I had to agree with nature's stubbornness. The entire world seemed lovely and peaceful to me.

Maybe I was also leaving my minuscule mark on this town. And when I became an ace reporter for one of the major newspapers in Denver, or San Francisco, or New York, people in Sunset Valley would remember that I was the one who had figured out a new way to report community news to its citizens.

I was reveling in my future notoriety when a truck barreled past me, reminding me I wasn't the only person on the road and that I should try to stay to the right of the traffic.

I'd better get off my high horse and do my job or I won't be remembered for anything except getting fired quicker than anyone else ever employed by the Star.

I decided to have lunch at the hospital cafeteria, since all that slice of pie did was whet my appetite, and maybe I'd see Jimmy again.

I opened the hospital door and saw state troopers rushing around the lobby and darting up and down the staircase. Everyone seemed to be either shouting or whispering in each other's faces.

"What's going on?" I asked the first trooper I could grab. "I'm a reporter with the *Star.*"

"He finally made it. He escaped."

CHAPTER 20

"Webb? He's gone? How? Why aren't you guys out looking for him instead of milling around in here? Or is he still somewhere in the hospital?"

"Hey, lady, I don't know. I just do what they tell me to do. And so far, nobody's told me to do anything except report to the hospital. So, here I am."

"Who's in charge?" I asked.

"Probably the sheriff. But since it was his Keystone Kops that let the guy escape, I doubt he'll be sheriff much longer."

"Where is he?"

"How should I know? Probably on the third floor where all the hotshots are deciding what to do."

I raced up the two flights of stairs to the men's wards. The hall was jammed with state troopers, the Sunset Valley Sheriff and some deputies, the Mayor, and a whole bunch of men in suits.

I spotted Assistant DA Lewis and squeezed my way through the throng to talk to him.

"Mr. Lewis," I said, "do you know what happened?" I got out my notebook and pencil and stood poised to write down every word.

"Who are you?"

"Alex Lawson, from the *Star*. I met you this morning. Remember?"

"Oh, sure, sure. We're still trying to put it all together, but it seems that Webb managed to climb out the window and get away."

"Wasn't there a guard watching him?"

"Apparently there was one on the door, not in the room, and no one thought about the window, since we're on the third floor. His handcuffs had been removed so he could eat lunch. When the nurse came to collect his tray, he was gone."

"Gee, what a mess. Why aren't all these cops out looking for him?"

"You got me. Seems they're trying to figure out exactly how to conduct the search, but if they don't get that done soon, Webb'll be in North Dakota or Wyoming before they even start."

"Thanks, Mr. Lewis. I owe you one for this."

"Forget it, kid." He turned away and pushed his way through to his boss.

There was no time to see Betty, or Jimmy, or eat lunch. I had to get back to the paper. Maybe Lou could put out a one page special edition this afternoon. People had to be warned to lock their doors. Webb was desperate now. He might do anything. And taking hostages in return for his freedom seemed like something he would do.

I ran out of the hospital and jumped on my bike.

"Alex."

When I heard my name, I stopped and looked around.

Jimmy ran over to me. "Did you hear what happened?" he asked.

"Yeah. I'm on my way back to the paper to tell Lou. Maybe he can get it on the radio or do an Extra so the town knows about it."

"That's a great idea. People in town need to know that Webb's out there. Be careful, Alex. This guy's dangerous."

"I will be. You too, okay?"

"I'll stop by Mrs. Lynch's after work. I'd sleep better if I knew you were okay."

"All right, but I've got to go."

"See you tonight," he yelled after me as I pedaled down the road.

CHAPTER 21

I ran through the newsroom into Lou's office. "Lou, Webb's escaped. You've got to get it on the radio, or something."

"What? Slow down, Alex. What are you talking about?"

So, I told him everything I knew.

"This guy's a regular Houdini," Lou said.

"Sure is, and he could be really dangerous now. He's got nothing to lose. All he has to look forward to is the hangman's noose. Can you get the radio station to broadcast a warning? He'll want to find some kind of transportation, and maybe clothes. He might even want to take hostages."

"I'll call Bob over at KRJF and ask him to broadcast a bulletin. Meanwhile, see if Pat can find out if the Fergusons have a phone. He might be headed there."

"Got it, Lou."

I ran back through the newsroom to the switchboard and asked Pat to try to reach the Ferguson ranch. She got through to the local operator, but they didn't have a listing for Ferguson or Lazy F. Now I could only hope the police would send someone out there. Or maybe I could do something on my own.

"Tell Lou I'll be right back," I said to Pat.

I grabbed my bike and raced over to the Met Café. I burst through the door and looked around, but Adam wasn't there.

"Alex," Pete said, "nice to see you. Thought maybe you'd deserted us."

"Hi, Pete. Nothing like that. In fact, I was here yesterday, but before your shift began. I hoped Adam, and his truck, were here."

"Not today, but I heard you two were out on the town the other night."

"That's not important right now. That guy Webb escaped from the hospital, and I hoped I could get out to the Ferguson ranch and warn them. I wouldn't be surprised if he's headed there."

"What?! Escaped! Those poor people have been through enough. They don't need him showing up."

Pete looked around the room, then finally yelled, "Hey fellas, listen up. Alex here just told me that no good bum Webb escaped from the hospital. She thinks he might be headed for the Lazy F. Anyone going that way? It sure would be neighborly if someone could let the Fergusons know to be on the lookout for him. Those women are probably all alone in the house."

The men started talking all at once, and in a few minutes, the café emptied out and a caravan of trucks and horses headed for the Ferguson ranch.

"Didn't mean to chase away all your customers, Pete," I said. "I only thought someone should go there to warn them."

"These ranchers are a close group. When one of them is in trouble, they all try to help out. And everyone liked Ben Ferguson I think they all wanted to shoot Webb instead of capturing him, but the sheriff got to him before they could. Anyway, they'll all be back later to brag about how they saved the day. This place'll be full tonight, thanks to you."

"This place, or your speakeasy? Lou said to tell you he'd vouch for me, and I'm sure you don't need my help filling up that place." Since the café had emptied out, I felt free to mention it to him.

Pete fiddled around, picking up the coffee cups the men had left on the counter.

"How'd that topic come up?"

"Lou and I were having a drink in his office and I mentioned how it would be nice if Prohibition didn't exist and we could get a drink whenever we wanted."

"And he mentioned my place."

"Yup. I kind of figured there had to be one somewhere around here. My dad runs one at home."

"Well, got to make ends meet somehow. Of course, at this time of year, the ranchers have some time on their hands. Mud season stops almost everything, so the boys come into town to catch up, play checkers, and talk about the new lady reporter."

"That I don't believe. But I'd like to stop in sometime, if that's okay with you."

"Anytime, Alex. You're always welcome."

"Thanks, Pete. Right now, I'd better get back to the paper or I'll be the former lady reporter."

Pete laughed, and I left to go write up what I knew so far.

"He's looking for you," Pat said when I walked in.

"Good or bad looking?"

"I can't tell anymore. Seems he's angry about something all the time lately."

I braced myself for the worst and marched straight to Lou's office. He was chomping so hard on his cigar, I thought he'd chew off the end before he finished smoking it.

"Where in tarnation did you disappear to?" he asked as I opened the door.

"I went to see if someone could ride out to the Lazy F and warn the Fergusons. They don't have a phone."

"Oh, well..."

"I knew it'd only take a minute, and I figured I'd be back before you finished talking to the radio station."

"Humph. Well, until this thing is over, I want to know where you are. I don't want you involved in this manhunt."

"But Lou—"

"No buts about it, Alex. This is a matter for the police to handle, not you. Now, go write up the story, then go back to the hospital and see about interviewing the deputy and his wife. Just like you planned to do. That Webb guy won't go back there if he has any brains at all."

"Whatever you say, Chief."

"And stop calling me Chief."

"Okay, Chief," I said, smiling.

Lou slammed his cigar into the ashtray, splitting it apart like a dried-up piece of firewood.

I figured I had caused him enough aggravation for one day, so I retreated to my typewriter and wrote what I knew about the morning's escapades. There wasn't very much to write yet, but it might take up one column on the first page, or a special edition if Lou decided to do that. I checked it over before landing it on his desk, then told him I was off to the hospital for the second time that day. He grunted, which I guessed meant okay.

At the hospital, I decided it was time for lunch. After all, there was no urgency to my interview, or to seeing Betty. I had already written the big news of the day, and since there weren't any deputies or troopers milling around the lobby, I knew I wouldn't get any additional information from them. I headed to the cafeteria, hoping I'd see Jimmy, but a lady stood behind the steam counter dishing out the food today.

I decided I'd better cut down on how much I was eating or I'd wind up bending the bicycle's frame. I opted for a ham sandwich instead of the hot meal, which was also better for my wallet.

I took my tray to what was becoming my usual table by the window and sat there thinking over the questions I should ask the deputy and his wife. It hit me then that I didn't even know his name.

How could I have written all these stories and not know his name?

Everything had happened so quickly, it had never occurred to me before today.

"Back again?"

Jimmy pulled out a chair opposite me and plopped into it. "And eating here again too? You must be a glutton for punishment."

"I happen to think the food is pretty good here. And a lot easier on my pocketbook than the café."

"Yeah, well, it's not too bad. I've had worse."

I took a bite and thought there was nothing at all wrong with my sandwich. The bread was fresh and the ham was tender. I decided people were too quick to judge hospital food.

"So," Jimmy said, "what brings you back? Wait—I know. You couldn't get through the rest of the day without seeing me again." His eyes had a mischievous twinkle to them.

"That's not it at all," I said.

"Oh." Jimmy's face fell and his smile faded.

"Well, maybe a little."

He looked at me and grinned.

"But I also had to come back to do what I planned to do this morning, which is interview the deputy and his wife, and say hi to Betty. Have you heard any more about Webb?"

"Nothing yet. But I assume they'll bring his corpse in sometime today."

I almost choked on my sandwich. "His corpse?"

"Sure. You don't think the sheriff and his posse are going to take a chance on him getting away, do you? They're embarrassed enough about how he's played them for fools so far. They're not likely going to give him an opportunity to do it again. And besides, he'll probably be sentenced to be hanged, so what difference does it make how he dies?"

"But they can't just execute him because he embarrassed them. They have to bring him in."

"And chance him pulling something on the way to the hangman in Missoula? Not likely."

I couldn't believe Jimmy could be so cavalier about Webb being shot. I knew he had probably shot soldiers overseas and seen guys from his unit killed, but that was war. This was different. Wasn't it? I thought about the attitude of the trooper I talked to earlier and realized Jimmy was probably right. The trooper had a job to do, and he'd do it as quickly and efficiently as necessary. If that meant killing Webb so he could go home on time, he would.

"It doesn't seem right," I said.

"Maybe not. But it's not like he's some nice guy who made one mistake. He's a bum, a murderer, vermin infesting the earth. And I say good riddance to him."

Was this the sweet gentle Jimmy I had met the day before? He had transformed into a heartless brute who didn't care about seeing justice carried out. Instead, he only saw "vermin" who should be exterminated by any means possible, wherever that might be—field, house, or execution chamber.

"Jimmy, I can't believe you can be so . . . so . . . venomous. It almost sounds like you hope they do shoot him on sight."

Jimmy looked at me with dead eyes. "I do. I'm sorry you don't agree with me, but I have no use for a man who abuses women. Especially someone as gentle and loving as Margie."

We were silent for a few minutes, then I asked, "You were in love with her, weren't you?"

Jimmy lit a cigarette and stared out the window.

"I guess I was. Before I got drafted. Then I decided I had no right to ask her to wait for me. You never know how you're going to come back from a war, if you come back at all. I could've been missing legs or arms, or who knows what else. And Margie was still in high school. A kid. She didn't need worrying about me. So, I didn't say anything to her. Then when I came back, she was already married and a mom. Nothing was going to change that."

"You could let her know how you feel now."

"No. It wouldn't work. I don't feel the same way about her anymore, and she's not the same person I left. The Margie you met is a shell of the girl I knew. And he did that to her. That's why I hope the cops eliminate him as soon as they have the chance."

"Jimmy," the woman behind the counter called over, "they need you in the kitchen."

"Guess my break's over." He stood and crushed out his cigarette. "I'd still like to stop by tonight to make sure you're okay. Can I?"

"Sure."

He gave me a weak smile and left. I didn't know what to think anymore. I wasn't sure I wanted to go to the movies with him, or even see him again. But he looked so pitiful when he asked to come by, I couldn't say no. I'd always heard war could change a man. How some men came home with such different personalities their families didn't believe it was the same person. Some men chose never to go home again, knowing how much they'd changed. They didn't want to subject their wives to the monster they had become. Had Jimmy changed that much too?

I wondered if I could ask Adam about him.

On second thought, I realized that wasn't the best idea I ever had. What if Adam *did* want to see me again? He wouldn't appreciate being quizzed about another man. Maybe Jimmy was just blowing off steam. Maybe, maybe, maybe. All I knew for sure was that this wasn't getting my interview done.

I finished my coffee, carried my tray to the counter, and headed to the reception desk for my visitor's pass to Betty's room.

CHAPTER 22

"How's the patient feeling today?" I asked as I walked into Betty's room.

"Itchy," she said. "Itchy and bored. I never realized casts could be this itchy."

"Well, that's better than achy. Any word on when you'll be able to go home?"

"Not yet. The doctor says it will probably be another few days, at least. Even then, I don't know how I'll manage on my own."

"Can someone from your family stay with you for a while?" I asked.

"Maybe one of my sisters, but I don't know. They all have families to take care of. They can't just pick up and come when I call."

I didn't know what to say. I thought about my parents and knew if I were in Betty's shoes, they'd both be on the next bus to Sunset Valley to wait on me hand and foot. Business and school be damned.

"Guess you heard about Webb's escape this morning?" I asked.

"Are you kidding? It's been the only thing anyone *can* talk about today. What's the scoop?"

I told Betty what I knew, which wasn't much. Then I told her I wanted to interview the deputy and his wife, but didn't even know his name.

"I guess in all the excitement, I never asked," I said.

"It's Cody Clark, and his wife's Millie."

"Thanks. I'll go upstairs to the men's floor and see if I can talk to him now. Anything I can get you before I leave, or bring with me later?"

"Yeah, a new leg and collarbone," Betty said.

"Wish I could, but I'm not in charge of miracles this week. Anything else?"

"Maybe something to read? The magazines in this place are ancient."

"Okay, I'll stop by the library. Maybe they'll have a recommendation." I'd started to leave when Betty stopped me.

"Hey, how'd things work out with Joe?"

I told her about the dressing-down Lou gave him, and our peace treaty.

"Glad it worked out that way," Betty said.

"Yeah." I waved goodbye and went upstairs to find Cody Clark.

I got his room number at the nurses' station, but I didn't even need to ask. There was a trooper standing guard at the door. I was glad to see they were keeping an eye on him.

"Hi," I said to the guard. "Okay if I go in? I'm Alex Lawson from the *Star*. I'd like to ask Officer Clark a few questions."

The guard stared at me like I was speaking a foreign language. I reached for the doorknob, but he grabbed my arm.

"I'll ask Cody if he wants to talk to you," he said.

I nodded and waited outside while he went into the room to check with Clark. About five minutes passed.

How long does it take to ask if I can see him?

I paced the hall and tapped my pencil against my notebook. Finally, the guard reappeared.

"Okay, you can go in."

I brushed past him. I had no intention of being polite after he left me to cool my heels for so long.

Clark was sitting up in bed with a blanket over his legs. He looked healthy, with rosy cheeks and neatly brushed hair. Not what I imagined someone who had been shot and operated on recently would look like, but I guess some people recover better than others.

"Officer Clark, I'm Alex Lawson from the *Star*," I said, extending my hand.

He gave me a firm handshake and asked me to have a seat. There was a small wooden chair in the room for visitors, so I pulled it over next to him.

I asked him how he was feeling, his prognosis, all the usual questions you ask people who are in the hospital. He told me the doctors had removed the slug from his stomach and repaired the damage. He would have to watch what he ate for a while, but the outlook was good.

Just like Jimmy.

I asked him about Webb and how well he knew him before the trial. Turns out he didn't know him at all. He knew the Fergusons from church, but that was it. He grew up in a different part of the county and only relocated to Sunset Valley when he got assigned to the County Courthouse.

We talked a little about his life before Sunset Valley, and his wife. He and Millie had three children, which was why she wasn't there right now. Children weren't allowed to visit patients, so she couldn't bring them. She could only visit when someone was available to watch the kids.

He told me that he didn't hold a grudge against Webb; given the same situation, he might try to get away too. Especially if he was facing the hangman.

I asked him if he thought his wife would be willing to talk to me, and he said he didn't see why not.

"Great. I'll stop by today to see her. Any message?"

"Tell her she doesn't have to come every day. They're taking good care of me here. I say that every time she visits, but she says she has to see for herself. Women."

"I'm sure she's worried about you."

"Yeah, guess so. Oh, and let her know the doc says I should be able to go home in three or four days. That should make her happy."

"That's great. I'll be sure to let her know. Thanks for seeing me, Officer Clark."

"Sure, Alex, come back anytime. Always nice to see a friendly face."

I left his room and faced the guard's glare again.

"It wouldn't hurt to smile," I said. "I'm not the enemy."

His icy stare was the only response I got.

I left the hospital with a definite bounce to my step. I could envision the story writing itself. On my way to the Clark home, I thought about Jimmy. His attitude had unnerved me, to say the least. I wondered if he was that judgmental about other things. No gray, all black and white. I didn't know how I felt about that. But maybe my judgment of him was unfair. I didn't even know him yet.

Once again, I'm jumping to conclusions before I know all the facts. Maybe tonight I'll get a better picture of him and then I can decide whether or not I want to see him again.

When I arrived at the Clark home, my mind was more settled and peaceful. As I knocked on the front door, I heard a baby crying.

This might not be the best time for an interview, but I need to get it done.

I waited a minute before I called out, "Mrs. Clark? It's Alex Lawson from the *Star*. I've just come from seeing your husband."

That got a quick response. The door flew open and a frazzled looking young woman stood there holding a baby in her arms.

"You saw Cody? How is he today?" she asked.

"He's fine. Can I come in for a minute?"

"Of course. Where are my manners? Please, come in. Can I get you a cup of tea or coffee?"

"No, I'm fine. Thanks anyway."

The baby stopped crying and was inspecting me instead. "He's adorable," I said.

Mrs. Clark grinned and pushed back the hair that had fallen across his forehead. "Thanks. I think he looks like Cody. They all do."

With that, as if on cue, two other little ones, a boy and a girl, appeared.

"This is Martin, and Mary Lou, and this little guy is Stephen" Millie said.

"Hello, everyone. I'm a reporter from the newspaper, and your mom and I are going to have a little chat. Is that okay?"

"Guess so," Martin said. "C'mon, Mary Lou, let's go back outside."

They headed for the door to the backyard.

"Mrs. Clark, you might want to keep them inside today. Webb escaped from the hospital this morning."

Millie's face drained of all color and she gasped.

"Martin, Mary Lou," she yelled, "come back here."

She thrust the baby at me and ran to the back door. "Children, come inside. You can't play outside today."

I heard the children troop back inside, moaning and whining about not being able to stay out in the sunshine, and promising not to drag mud all over the house.

"Go play checkers or jacks or something," Millie said. "Just try to play quietly. I'd like Stephen to take a nap."

"Aw, gee, Ma."

"Now go."

Millie came back to the living room looking even more distraught.

"Where were we?" she asked, patting her hair and sitting on the couch. "Oh, Stephen," she said, reaching for the baby. "I'm sorry, Miss . . ."

"Call me Alex."

"I'm sorry, Alex. I didn't mean to throw him at you. It's just that when you said Webb had—"

"It's fine, Millie. May I call you Millie?"

"Of course. What happened?"

I told her the story, and the theories about how Webb could have escaped. I reassured her that her husband was being guarded and there was probably no need for anyone in town to worry since the troopers, the sheriff, and his deputies were out looking for him. I didn't want her to be any more upset than she already was.

"I imagine he's headed for South Dakota or Wyoming," I said. "Getting across state lines would be the best bet for his freedom, at least for a while. But I figure it's a good idea to keep the children where you can see them."

"Yes, you're right. They'll stay in until he's caught. They'll be fine. Maybe I'll have them help me bake cookies. It'll distract them, and I can take some to Cody."

I told her what he'd said about visiting, which she brushed off with declarations about how she needed to bring him "some decent food" to eat at least once in the day.

I thought about saying how I enjoyed the food in the cafeteria, but maybe the patients didn't get the same meals. And maybe I should keep my mouth shut.

Millie told me how difficult it was when they first arrived in Sunset Valley, not knowing anyone and being pregnant, and how now she couldn't imagine living anywhere else. She was only eighteen when they married and a mom by the time she was nineteen. Now, five years later, she had this brood of three.

Gosh, only twenty-four and all these kids. No wonder she looks the way she does.

We finished our conversation and I thanked her for taking the time to talk to me.

"Thanks for coming, Alex. If we had a phone and I could talk to Cody, I'd feel so much better about not being able to visit him every day."

"I can call the hospital for you if you'd like and get a message to your husband that you're staying here until the situation is resolved," I said.

"That would be perfect, Alex. Thank you. That way he won't worry. I'm sure it will all be over by the end of the day."

One way or another.

I said goodbye and headed back to the paper to write this episode of the story. But would it be good enough?

I felt overwhelmed, and wondered if I had what it took to be an ace reporter, or if I even wanted to be one anymore. Two handsome men pursuing me had me doubting what I really wanted for the rest of my life, and whether I was capable of achieving it.

CHAPTER 23

Later, I dropped my finished piece on Lou's desk and waited while he read through it.

"Great, Alex. This puts a human face on Webb's barbarity. Nice touch, including the kids and cookies. That should tug on a few heart-strings. People eat up stories like this."

I could never figure out how Lou managed to talk and chomp on his cigar at the same time. But he did. The smoke in his office was forming into a dense fog, and my clothes were beginning to smell like an ashtray. I'd have to see if Edna had a clothesline in the yard. Maybe if I hung my clothes outside, they'd air out a little.

"Did you speak to that teacher friend of yours yet?" Lou asked.

"No, Lou. I haven't had time today, and she's been at work." *How did he think I could squeeze that in?* "I'll talk to her tonight."

"Okay, just get her in here soon. I feel like we're drowning under a barrage of stories. I'm sure we're missing some of the local stuff that people really want to read."

I wasn't sure what local stuff he thought was missing. Webb's trial and escape—or at least, his attempts—seemed to be all people were talking about.

"I'll have an answer for you tomorrow," I said. "That is, I will if I get home before she goes to bed." I hoped Maureen was a quick decision person.

Lou glanced at me over the rim of his glasses, then looked at the clock on the wall, which read 6:20. "Is that your subtle way of saying you'd like to call it a day?"

"Not very subtle, was it?"

"More like a sledgehammer to my head. But I guess I need that every once in a while. Sure, kid, go home."

"It's just that I'd like to be off the streets before it gets dark. At least until Webb's caught."

"You're right. Absolutely. Get out of here. It'll be dark before you know it."

When I walked into the kitchen, Maureen and Edna were still eating dinner.

"Oh, you're here," Edna said. "I was worried that you'd miss dinner."

"Never," I said. "I might be late some days, but never a complete miss. Fasting is not something I do well. I apologize for not calling to let you know I'd be late. I guess newspaper work is a little too unpredictable for a set dinner hour."

"Well, as I told you when you rented the room," Edna said, "maybe if you *think* you might be tied up, you could let me know. Then I'll set your plate aside. Of course, if you know you won't make it home at all, I'd appreciate a call. I guess either way, I'd like you to call."

"I'll try, Edna, though sometimes I get so involved in what I'm doing, I have no idea what time it is."

"Yes, well . . . try to make more of an effort."

I nodded and helped myself to the meatloaf, mashed potatoes, and green beans. Turns out Edna was a good cook. Everything was well seasoned and delicious. I loaded up on the potatoes, my favorite side dish, and hoped my bike riding would take care of all the extra calories.

Dinner was the most relaxation I'd had all day. Maureen told us stories about her pupils, which were mostly funny, and reminded me of some of the shenanigans of my high school days.

Then Edna looked at me and asked, "How was your day, Alex?"

I realized I never told them about Webb escaping.

What a dunce! The door's probably wide open.

"Be right back," I said.

I jumped up from the table and locked the back door, then did the same to the front door.

"Whatever are you doing?" Edna asked when I returned to the table.

"Billy Webb escaped from the hospital today," I said, taking another bite of my meatloaf.

Well, that created pandemonium at the table. I was bombarded with questions from both women.

"Hold on. I can't answer both your questions at the same time. Edna, didn't you have your radio on today?"

"No, Alex. I usually only listen to it in the evenings, with Maureen."

"Maureen, didn't the school warn the students and teachers about him?"

"Not a peep."

I thought about that for a minute.

"Gee, I hope everyone got home safe. For some reason, I keep thinking Webb would want a hostage to negotiate his freedom. But maybe he just took off, hoping he can outmaneuver the sheriff and the troopers."

"How did this happen?" Edna asked.

I told them the basic facts, adding, "The whole story'll be in the paper tomorrow, along with Officer Clark's story."

"How exciting," Maureen said. "I can't wait to read it." She finished her dinner, and looked at me. "Alex, what's it like writing for the paper? It must be interesting, huh?"

"It is. I'm loving every minute of it, even if I am a little overworked right now. Especially with Betty laid up. I don't know how long she'll be out of work. In fact, that's something I wanted to talk to you about."

"Me? About Betty?"

"No—sorry. I guess I threw those things together, didn't I? No, about work. How would you like to work part-time at the paper?"

I cleared the table while I waited for an answer. I wanted to give Maureen time to mull it over for a few minutes.

"Who wants tea, or coffee?" Edna asked. "No dessert today, I'm afraid."

"I'd love a cup of tea," I said, "and I don't need dessert. I think I've eaten more since I moved here than I ever have."

"You're so skinny, you could use some fattening up," Edna said.

"No, thanks, I don't need to be buying all new clothes because I can't button my skirts or trousers anymore."

Edna laughed and filled the kettle. "Maureen, tea?"

"Huh? Oh, yes, please, Edna. Thanks. Sorry . . . I was a million miles away."

I started to wash the dishes while Edna put the butter away and got milk out of the fridge. Maureen never stirred from the table.

"Maureen," I said, "can you grab a towel and start drying?"

"Oh, of course. Sorry, Alex, your offer has my head spinning."

"It's not really a big deal. You'd handle the community news. You know, church events, bake sales, marriage and birth announcements, that kind of thing. Oh, and any sports news from the school."

"Oh, I see." She looked crestfallen. "Is that all?"

"Do you want more? I thought with teaching and grading papers and planning lessons, you'd be too busy to do much more than that. I know that keeps my mother busy."

"Your mother's a schoolteacher?"

"She is, and she also keeps the accounts for my dad's business. She's a busy lady."

"I'll say," Maureen said. "I've been a teacher for a few years now, and I've pretty much got my curriculum down pat, so I don't have a lot of planning to do. As far as grading, I could give fewer assignments. My students would love that. When do you need my answer?"

"Lou wants it by tomorrow, but I could probably put him off for a day or two."

"Tea's ready," Edna said. "Should we go into the living room and turn on the radio while we have our tea?"

"Good idea, Edna. Coming, Maureen?"

"Be right there," she said.

Edna turned the radio on and as we waited for it to warm up, there was a knock at the front door.

"Whoever could that be?" Edna asked. "It's a little late for visitors."

"I completely forgot," I said. "Jimmy said he'd stop by tonight to make sure I got home safe."

"Well then, go answer the door," Edna said.

Sure enough, when I opened the door, Jimmy stood there, hat in hand. It was the first time I'd seen him in anything other than his kitchen whites. Not that his outfit was a surprise. Denim and plaid seemed to be *de rigueur* for all Sunset Valley men.

"Hi, Jimmy. Come on in. You know Edna, don't you? And this is Maureen Healy, another boarder."

"Evening, Mrs. Lynch, Miss Healy," he said.

"Why if it isn't Jimmy Byrnes," Edna said. "How do you two know each other?"

"Jimmy works at the hospital," I said. "I met him there. Would it be all right if we used the kitchen to talk for a few minutes?"

"Of course," Edna said. "Unless Jimmy'd like to join us and listen to the radio for a while."

"Oh, no, ma'am. I won't be keeping you. I just wanted to make sure Alex got home safe tonight. You know, with that killer out loose and all."

"Isn't it terrible?" Edna asked. "I hope they catch him soon. I won't be able to sleep a wink."

"C'mon, Jimmy. Kitchen," I said. Knowing Edna, she'd have his ear for an hour if I didn't get him into the kitchen quickly.

I grabbed his arm and we walked down the hall and sat at the table. Jimmy asked about the rest of my day and I told him about Officer Clark and his wife and kids. He told me he had stopped by the theaters.

"We could go to the Palace Theater and see *The Kid*. It's a comedy with Charlie Chaplin. Or an adventure story, *the Three Muskateers*. That one's at the Deluxe Theater."

"Let's see *The Kid*," I said. "I could use a comedy after all the shooting that's been going on around here lately."

We sat in the kitchen and talked about other movies we'd seen and liked, our families, and what was good and bad about Sunset Valley.

When he said he should get going, I walked him to the door and said good night.

Jimmy was so nice, not at all mean like he had sounded earlier. Maybe this was the real Jimmy, not the cold and unfeeling one I'd talked to in the cafeteria. Maybe I had misjudged him.

I walked into the living room just as the announcer interrupted the program to say that Billy Webb had been shot to death by a state trooper.

"Well, we can sleep easy tonight," Edna said.

CHAPTER 24

Before I knew it, it was Friday. Maureen had accepted the job at the paper, and Lou had approved my design for the community page template. Paul, the chief typesetter, and I worked out any last-minute glitches.

The new page would debut tomorrow. I couldn't wait to see how the final product looked, and to send a copy to Mom and Dad. In their letter, they told me how proud they were of me. They touted my successes to everyone, and now the whole town seemed to be vicariously living my experiences. Dad's café had become the center for reports on my stories. Guess during mud season, any reason to celebrate was welcome.

Maureen was doing a great job. She jumped into reporting with both feet. Every day after school she checked in with the hospital to see if there was any news of births or deaths. Fortunately, she was friends with the head nurse, so it was easy for her to get this information. She planned on going to all the churches once a week to get their upcoming events and the topic for the weekly sermon. Being a schoolteacher, she was able to get a lot of information about other events around town from the faculty and staff. And the coaches filled her in on the sporting news, both local and state. Lou and I agreed she would become an invaluable asset.

Now I could spend my day at the courthouses, county and city, as well as the mayor's office, the sheriff's department, and anywhere else things happened in town. For what I initially thought was a sleepy little place, there seemed to be no end of activity in Sunset Valley. Since it was March, everyone was gearing up for the annual St. Patrick's Day festivities, and the Chamber of Commerce was a great spot for information about those events.

I decided to make a visit to Tyler County Junior College. There weren't many college students yet, but I thought I might be able to write a feature story on the school. Since the paper was delivered free to high school seniors, I knew Maureen would make them read the article and maybe they, and their parents, would get excited about attending.

The college had started five years ago and held classes in the same building as Tyler County High School, where Maureen taught. Since the redbrick high school was three stories high and spread across an entire city block, there was plenty of room to house both schools. The college offered classes in math and the sciences, composition, and public speaking. They even had a newspaper, the *Falcon*, men's and women's glee club, and a student government. The Dean of Students was happy to spend time with me and go through all the future plans for the college.

I left his office right around lunchtime and ran into Maureen. She invited me to join her for lunch. My memory of school cafeteria food wasn't great, but the hospital's food was good, so I took a chance. Maureen suggested I stick to something simple, like a sandwich and coffee. It was that or a bowl of mystery meat stew. I opted for the tuna sandwich.

We took our trays to the faculty lounge, which was much quieter than the cafeteria. The noise in there was deafening. I had forgotten how rambunctious teenagers could be. No wonder Maureen enjoyed the adult atmosphere of the newsroom on the evenings she worked there. At least it was quiet when Lou wasn't screaming about something or other.

Maureen grabbed a small table for two in the lounge and we gobbled our lunch in the twenty minutes left of her break. Between bites, I asked her why she was living at Edna's.

"You seem to know a lot of people in town, so I assume you grew up here."

"No, I didn't. I grew up in Rosebud," she said. "It's a small town about fifteen miles from here. After college, I saw there was an opening for an English teacher at the high school, applied, and got the job. And I drove back and forth every day."

"Gee, that's a long drive on the best of days," I said.

"Yeah, it can be. But a friend of mine from college got a nursing job at the hospital and had an apartment with two other nurses, so on bad snowy days I could always camp out on their sofa. The following May, I looked around for an apartment, but no one wanted to rent to a single woman. Then one of the teachers told me about Edna wanting to rent rooms, and that was that. I've been living with her for two years now."

I wanted to ask her how she liked the arrangement. I had an idea that maybe the two of us could get an apartment together. A place where we wouldn't have to worry about Edna's rules or schedules. But just as she finished her story, the bell for classes rang.

"I'll take the trays back to the cafeteria so you can get to your classroom on time."

"Thanks," she said, racing out of the lounge.

I gathered our things and opened the door, but the hallway was filled with teenagers. Between the slamming lockers, shouting, pushing and shoving, it was bedlam. I decided to stay in the lounge until they were all safely in their classrooms.

On my walk back to the paper, I thought about my conversation with the college dean. He had told me about all the grants that were available to pay tuition for veterans and, sometimes, provide an additional living stipend. The US Federal Board for Vocational Education, established to help World War I veterans, sounded like something Jimmy might be able to use. I needed to talk to him about this. If he really wanted to be an architect, this could be a golden opportunity.

I wondered if there were other veterans who didn't know about this program. I didn't know if Lou had written about it, so I decided to ask him as soon as I got back in the office. If he hadn't, I would. Maybe I could even provide an update about new programs if there were any. I'd have to find out where the American Legion was located. They would have all the information I needed.

I walked into the newsroom, my head full of stories about the college, available funding, and of course, the final story about Billy Webb. I had stopped by the state troopers' office on my way back and had spoken to the captain about last night's shooting. Turns out, one of the troopers came across Webb on the banks of the Yellowstone River. Ordered to stop and get on the ground, Webb grabbed an oar from a nearby boat and charged at the trooper. When Webb raised it to clobber him, the trooper fired, killing Webb instantly.

In a way, he got off easy. I'm sure it's much more painful to be hanged than shot through the heart.

My plan to talk to Lou had to be delayed, since he wasn't in his office. I couldn't imagine where he could be. I'd never seen his office empty. I asked Pat if she knew where he was, but she just shrugged.

I decided to work on my other stories while I waited for him to return. Goodness knows there were plenty of them. First on the list was the finale of the Webb saga. I felt like I'd been writing this story forever. I probably should've gone to the Ferguson's ranch to get their reaction to the shooting, but it was too late now. Maybe I'd go tomorrow. But tomorrow's Saturday.

I wonder if I have the day off? I never asked about that when I was hired. Hmm. Something else to discuss with Lou.

"What are you working on?" Lou's dulcet tones and stinky cigar broke through my musings.

"Right now, I'm writing the final episode of Webb's life. Then I wanted to write about the US Federal Board for Vocational Education. Have you written about that already?"

"What?"

"The Federal Board for Vocational Education. It's important. I bet there are a lot of veterans who don't know anything about it."

"Don't think I ever got around to that," he said, rubbing his chin. "And right now, there are a few other things on my plate, you know."

146

"Well, I'm going to write about it. Okay?"

"Sure."

He walked into his office, grumbling something about one less thing for him to do.

If I played my cards right, maybe features like this could become my sneaky way to keep reporting on news other than bake sales once Betty got back.

A new game plan formed in my mind. I smiled as I slid a fresh sheet of paper into my typewriter.

CHAPTER 25

I told Jimmy I'd rather meet him at the theater than have Edna making judgments about my dating two men.

As I walked down the street, I saw Jimmy pacing in front of the Palace Theater. He looked very handsome in his gray flannel slacks and Western-style blue shirt. His boots shined and he held a dungaree jacket over his shoulder. I had chosen a white sailor top blouse and a navy-blue pleated skirt for our first date. Jimmy was taller than me, so I was able to wear my black T-strap heels. I also brought along my navy checked blazer in case the night got cool.

I stopped on the corner before he spotted me and smoothed my hair one last time.

"Hi, Jimmy," I said, walking up behind him.

He spun around, gave me a quick once over, and said, "Gee, you look swell." He gulped a little and tossed his cigarette on the ground.

"So do you," I said.

He stood fiddling with his jacket for a minute, then said, "Well, I guess we should go in, huh?"

Jimmy bought our tickets, two at twenty-five cents each. As soon as he opened the door, I was bowled over by the smell of popcorn. Even though I had just eaten dinner, my mouth watered. Jimmy asked if I'd like a box and I instantly said yes. While he left to get our snacks, I looked around.

The theater was beautiful. Velvet ropes marked off both the concession stand and the padded doors that led from the wide-open foyer to the orchestra section. Huge cloth tapestries depicting bucking broncs and bulls covered the walls. The rich red carpeting with tiny gold squares looked brand new, even though I was sure it wasn't. But since the Palace had only been built a few years ago, it didn't have a lot of wear and tear. Beyond the foyer was the main lounge, filled with sofas and easy chairs in small groupings with vases on the occasional tables. White on black silhouettes of dancers and crooners decorated the walls. It looked like a sitting room in a Hollywood home.

Our seats were in the orchestra section, more expensive than the loge. At least Jimmy wasn't going for a cheap date night. Wood panels covered the walls with floor-to-ceiling vertical lights every ten feet or so. I picked two seats in the center of the theater. I didn't like to be too close to the screen. Jimmy thought they were perfect.

We settled into the comfortable red velvet cushioned seats and munched on the popcorn for a few minutes before the show started. I wanted to save some for the movie, but Jimmy said he'd buy more if I ate it all.

I had just asked how he'd spent his day off when the lights dimmed, the curtains parted, and the screen lit up with Pathé News: a rodeo in California, society news, a glamour girl contest, and a healthy baby contest. Finally, a report on sporting events.

After the news came a Walt Disney cartoon, *Kansas City Girls Are Rolling Their Own Now*. Next, *Never Weaken*, a short comedy with Harold Lloyd, and finally, the movie we had come to see, *The Kid*.

The cartoon and the Harold Lloyd film had the audience roaring. The movie was good, a nice light comedy with a happily-ever-after ending. Just what I needed after the hard news week.

After about two hours of sitting in the dark, the house lights came on. It took a minute for my eyes to adjust, so we sat and finished the last few kernels of popcorn. When the usher came down the aisle with a broom and silent butler, we knew it was time to leave.

Outside, Jimmy said, "That popcorn made me thirsty. Would you like to stop for a drink, or some coffee?"

"I'd love a beer," I said, glancing out of the corner of my eye to see Jimmy's reaction.

"Great. Me too. And I know just the place. It's down the street."

"Swell."

I was anxious to see where he took me. In one way, I hoped it was Pete's place; in another, I didn't. I didn't know if Adam would be there or not, but I didn't want to run into him. Not while I was with Jimmy. Adam would probably think it wasn't honorable for him to ask me out if I was dating his friend. Although with all the gossips in this town, he probably already knew. Right now, I didn't know which man I preferred. In fact, I didn't want to have to make a choice. I wanted to date both of them. For now, at least.

We talked about the show while we walked to the speakeasy. Jimmy led me down the alley alongside the Met Café and knocked on a black door. A small window slid open and when the eyes behind it saw Jimmy, the door swung open. The doorman held the door for me, we walked in, and went down a flight of stairs. I could hear music and people laughing and having a good time.

"Where is this place?" I asked as we walked down a long corridor.

"It's an old tunnel that was built to connect the two hotels above us, the Sunset and the Montana. Once upon a time, they were owned by the same family and used the same kitchen, so a tunnel was a convenient way to get food from one place to another."

We turned a corner and I was amazed.

The tunnel opened up into a large room with a long bar, brass cash register, animal heads mounted all around, the smell of stale beer, and cowboys in dusty denims and muddy boots with their wives or girlfriends.

Jimmy went to the bar to order our beers, and I chose a table away from the noise of the other customers so we could talk. Not that it was noisy right then. Everyone had stopped talking when we walked in. They were just beginning to resume their conversations, now that they recognized Jimmy as a local. I couldn't remember if my dad's

151

speakeasy was as unwelcoming to strangers as this one, but it probably was. I waved over to Pete, the bartender and master of ceremonies, who smiled and waved back.

"Here we are, nice and cold," Jimmy said, sliding two glasses across the table, and sitting himself in a chair opposite me.

"Just what the doctor ordered," I said. "Thanks."

We both took a sip and leaned back, letting the cold bitter taste wash away some of the popcorn's saltiness.

"Oooh, that's good," I said.

"Sure is," Jimmy said. He set his beer down and looked at me. "So, tell me, Alex. what brought you to Sunset Valley?"

"I saw an ad that the paper was looking for a reporter. I applied and was hired. That's about it."

"Aw, come on. There has to be more to it than that. If you really want to be a reporter, why didn't you try getting a job in a *real* city?"

"I'm not sure," I said after a moment's hesitation. "Maybe I got cold feet thinking about living in a big city. I've thought about that a lot since I came here. In fact, I've been thinking a lot about whether I want a career or a family. I know I can't have both."

"Why not?"

"Oh, Jimmy, let's face it. That's just not how the world works. Sure, some women were doing that during the war, but when the men returned from overseas, they got their jobs back and the women went home to be wives and mothers. I don't think that's what I want, but when I look at someone like Betty, who's all alone, I don't think I want that life either. Right now, I can't decide what I want. And I'm a little afraid I'll make the wrong decision."

"You? Afraid? You don't seem to be the type of gal who's afraid of anything. What exactly are you afraid of?"

"Ruining my life. If I move to a city, I'm afraid I'll get swallowed up. At a big paper there'd be a lot of reporters. It'd take me forever to get noticed by the editor. I thought maybe I'd get a big scoop here, and establish my reputation. But now that I'm here, I doubt that will happen. I guess it all seems a little overwhelming. It didn't seem that way when I was home, or at college, but now that I'm on my own, it scares me. I don't want to spend my life all alone."

"Makes sense, I guess."

"Do you know that Betty told me I'm the only person she's ever invited to her house? I don't want to live like that. I mean, at first, I thought it was homey and wonderful, but now it seems like such a lonely life. But, I don't want to be chained to a life of laundry and cooking and screaming kids either."

"You make it sound so awful. It doesn't have to be that way. My mom loves her life. And didn't you tell me that your mom works? Yet she still took care of you and your dad, right?"

"Yeah, but that's different. She's a teacher. She had the same school schedule I did when I was growing up. And my granny lived with us and did the household chores, so Mom didn't have to try to juggle work and be a housewife at the same time. I don't know how anyone can do that. And as a reporter, I don't have regular hours. If I got a job in a city, I might be sent to cover stories out of town. How could I raise a family and do that?"

"I don't know, but you'll have to decide what you really want to do sooner or later, or your whole life will fly by and you won't have accomplished anything. You've got to take a chance and hope for the best."

I stared into my beer, tears brimming my eyes.

"How about another?" Jimmy asked, jumping up from our table.

"Sure." I smiled up at him. "I'm sorry. I didn't mean to pile all my worries and doubts on you."

"Hey, that's what friends are for." He grabbed my empty glass and headed to the bar.

By the time he came back, I had shaken off my black mood and was determined to keep the rest of the night light and upbeat.

"So, now that I've bored you with my problems, tell me, what keeps you here in your hometown?"

"That I can't answer. When the army sent me home, it was the only thing I could think of. You know, coming home, having my parents and brothers and sisters around, being back with whatever friends were still here. It was comfortable. And I knew the hospital was here so I could get the medical attention I needed."

"But you could leave now, couldn't you?"

"I could, but I don't know where I would go, or why. I don't see anyone out there begging me to come work for them."

"You could go to school. Become an architect, like you dream about."

"No money, remember?"

"Oh, I'm so stupid—I almost forgot! That's just it, Jimmy. I was over at the college today talking to the Dean and he told me about the American Legion and the US Federal Board for Vocational Education."

"What's that?" Jimmy leaned back and furrowed his forehead.

I told him about the paid tuition and the stipend. He frowned, rubbed his fingers up and down his glass.

"What do you think?" I asked.

"Is this real, or a joke?"

"It's real, Jimmy. I wouldn't make up something like that."

He looked off toward the bar, and I took a gulp of my beer.

"You can go see the Dean and ask him about it."

"Maybe. Maybe I'll see what the American Legion knows first."

"That's a great idea. Then you can start to send applications to colleges that have architecture classes."

"I don't have to do that," he said, finally looking back at me. "I already know where I want to go." He eased out his chair and stood next to me. "How about another beer?" he asked, finishing what was left in his glass and reaching for mine.

He already knows where he wants to go to school?

A minute later, he set two fresh beers down on our table.

"Well, don't keep me in suspense," I said. "What school did you pick?"

"The Cooper Union in New York City," he said, taking a big swig of his drink.

"New York?" I guess I yelled, because a few of the men turned and stared at us.

"You don't have to let the whole town know."

"Sorry. You took me by surprise. How long have you known you want to go there?"

"For years. The only thing stopping me is my train fare and some money to live on. But if this bill will pay a stipend, maybe I can swing it. And The Cooper Union is tuition free."

"Free?!" Once again, everyone turned to stare.

"Could you please stop yelling? Yes, free. But they only accept people who they feel have real talent. I sent for all their information before I got drafted."

Jimmy described their acceptance policy. After his application was approved, the school would send him three projects to work on, with deadlines. Once completed and returned, they'd be judged, and only the best designs would be admitted. I could feel his enthusiasm. He talked so fast that I had to keep asking him to slow down so I could understand what he was saying. His arms flailed around his head as he described some of his design ideas, building them in his mind as he talked. He was more animated than the cartoon we saw earlier that night.

Gee, if he gets accepted, I'll probably never see him again. And I like him. Maybe I should have kept my mouth shut.

"Alex, I could kiss you for telling me about this new bill."

"Well, why don't you?"

He slid his chair around the table and squeezed it next to mine. Then he grabbed my face and gave me a long, lingering kiss. A couple of jerks at the bar started whistling and Jimmy's face turned red as a radish. I could feel the heat racing across my face as well.

"Maybe we should leave," I said.

"I guess we should."

Jimmy finished his beer and stood. I took another swallow of mine just as Adam walked into the room.

CHAPTER 26

I think my heart stopped for a minute when I saw him. I know my face must have turned ashen, because Jimmy looked at me and said, "What's the matter, Alex? You look like you've just seen a ghost."

I forced my eyes away from Adam, who had stopped dead inside the entrance and stood staring at me.

"Nothing, Jimmy. Just thought of something I forgot to do today. I'm fine."

Jimmy hovered over me, real concern on his face. "You sure you're all right?"

"Fine. I'm fine."

I pushed my chair back and stood, wishing the floor would open and swallow me whole. But of course that didn't happen. Instead, we would have to walk right past Adam.

Jimmy turned around and spotted him.

"Hey, Adam's here." He strode over to shake Adam's hand.

"Jimmy, Alex," Adam said, touching the brim of his hat.

To say this was awkward would be putting it mildly.

Adam and Jimmy walked over to the bar, and I followed them. Adam caught Pete's eye and ordered a beer for himself, and "whatever these two folks are drinking." I could feel my face burning and my legs shaking. I wished I could disappear.

Adam handed me a beer with that familiar smirk on his lips. I would have loved to toss my drink right in his face, but knew that would cause a scene even more embarrassing than this one.

"So, where have you two been tonight? Just here, or someplace else?"

"You don't think we've spent the whole night swilling beer, do you?" I asked.

"Don't know. Maybe. It's been known to happen," Adam said, eyes twinkling, a smug look creeping across his face.

Ohhh, I really could smack him. He knows I'm uncomfortable, and he's reveling in it.

Jimmy told him about the movie, and although Adam paid attention, he kept throwing sideways glances at me.

"Did you enjoy it too, Alex?" Adam asked.

"It was great. Just what I needed after a week of Webb and his escapades."

"Yup. Too bad nothing else went on this week to take your mind off him," Adam said, and took a swig of his beer.

I could feel my face burning up. "It's awfully warm in here, isn't it?" I asked Jimmy, fanning my face with my clutch purse. "Could we leave, please? I have to get up early for work tomorrow."

"Sure, Alex. I do too. No rest for the weary, huh, Adam?"

"So they say," Adam said. He turned to me and asked, "You're not off on Saturdays?"

"Actually, I'm not sure. But with Betty laid up and all, I figure I better go in and see what's what."

"Very conscientious," Adam said.

I put my glass on the bar and said, "Good night, Adam. Nice to see you."

He tipped his hat again, and I marched down the hallway and up the stairs, Jimmy trailing behind me.

Once we were in the street, I started walking to Edna's house.

Jimmy grabbed my arm and pulled me to a stop. "Why do I get the impression that you don't like Adam? He's a great guy, and a good friend."

I tugged my arm away and kept walking.

Jimmy hurried to catch up with me. "What? Now you're mad at me, too?"

"I'm not mad at anyone. He just annoys me. He's always so smug, so . . . so superior."

"Superior? Adam? You've got to be kidding. That's definitely one thing he's not. He's the exact opposite. And he'd do anything for anybody. When I came back from overseas, I guess I wasn't right in the head or something, I don't know. I just know I was fighting with everyone. My parents. My brothers and sisters. My doctor. Anyone who talked to me."

"I thought you said you were comfortable with them when you came home."

"I thought I would be, and I am now, but I wasn't when I first came home. Anyway, Adam saw how I was acting and asked if I'd like to come out to his ranch for a while. Said he could use a hand to fix up a few things, and he knew I liked to build stuff. I didn't really believe him, but I wanted to get away from my family. My mom was driving me crazy, constantly checking up on me to see if I felt sick, or was hurting.

"Anyway, I wound up staying with Adam for a few months. I took my anger out on his barn. Must've hammered a thousand nails into the addition I built. I had to rely on his ranch hands to do the heavy lifting, but I designed it and did what I could to help. Between the construction and the target shooting we did together, I guess I pounded out all the demons that I'd brought home with me. I don't know what would've happened to me, or where I'd be today, if Adam hadn't done that."

I didn't know what to say, so I said nothing. I thought about telling Jimmy I had had dinner with Adam, but decided not to. After all, I didn't know if Adam would ask me out again, so why bring it up? And it was only part of the bike deal anyway. It's not like it was a real date. Like tonight with Jimmy.

We stopped in front of Edna's house and I said, "Maybe I'm wrong about Adam."

"You are." He pulled a cigarette from the pack in his shirt pocket and lit it. Smoke concealed his face.

I turned and started up the porch steps, but stopped.

"Jimmy, I had a really nice time tonight. I don't want to end it with us fighting."

Jimmy puffed on his cigarette and looked at me. "Neither do I, Alex. Let's forget about it. Okay?"

"Okay." I walked back down the steps and stood in front of him. "Can I give you a good night kiss?"

"You sure can."

He tossed his cigarette on the ground and opened his arms. I stepped right into them and gave him a kiss I hoped he'd remember for the rest of the night.

CHAPTER 27

"Oh, Alex," Edna said, "I was just going to bed. Your young man, Adam, was here. I left his message on your pillow."

"Adam was here? Looking for me?"

"Yes, dear. Are you all right? You look so pale."

"I'm fine. Thanks." I felt my stomach drop.

I took the stairs two at a time. There on my pillow lay a folded sheet of notebook paper, which he probably got from Maureen or Edna. Now they'd both want to know what it said.

My hands trembled as I unfolded the note.

Alex,
Thought you might like to see my ranch since I talked about it so much the other night. If you're interested, call me in the morning and I'll drive into town to pick you up.

Under his name was a phone number.

Now I didn't know what to do. I thought about my behavior at the bar earlier. For some reason, Adam seemed to bring out the worst side of me. I couldn't help trying to best him in verbal combat, but it always seemed to backfire. And after seeing me with Jimmy tonight, he probably regretted leaving the note.

I decided a good night's sleep would clear my head. I could figure out what to do in the morning. After all, I didn't even know for sure if I'd have to work the next day.

I changed into my pajamas and climbed into bed, a thousand scenarios racing through my mind. If I didn't stop thinking about Adam and Jimmy, I'd never get to sleep. I turned over and forced my mind to think of happier events—like my wistful dream of winning a Pulitzer.

The next morning, I woke feeling refreshed and ready to take on the world. Until I saw Adam's note on the night table. The simple truth was, I was terrified to call him. What if he hung up on me? What if he told his housekeeper to say he wasn't home? Or worse. What if he asked me how I thought I could date Jimmy and him at the same time?

I realized I really wanted to see Adam again. Every time I saw him, electric shocks jolted through me. Something I'd never felt before with any other man, certainly not with Jimmy. Jimmy was more the cuddly teddy bear type, warm, comfortable, and safe. Adam was fireworks, bucking broncs, and bull rides. Two opposites. Each wonderful in his own way.

"Alex," Maureen said, tapping on the door. "Are you up? Breakfast's ready."

"I'll be down in a minute, Maureen."

I heard her go downstairs so I ran into the bathroom and washed up. Back in my room I quickly dressed in dungarees, a blue chamois shirt, and boots. I folded a scarf into a headband, knotted it above my ear, and let the ends trail down. A little makeup and my shoulder bag, and I was set for the day—whatever it might bring.

After breakfast, I biked over to the paper. Neither Edna nor Maureen had asked about Adam's note. Instead, they both wanted to hear about the movie. Thank goodness.

When I got to the paper, I walked into an eerily quiet newsroom. Pat wasn't at the reception desk, and the only sound came from the birds outside the windows. Even the phones were silent. I checked my desk, but there were no assignments waiting for me. I heard a metallic noise and decided to go down to the basement where the presses were located to see if anyone was there.

"Hello," I called into the room as I descended the metal stairway. Giant cylinders filled the space. They towered two or three feet over my head and gradually tapered down to the smallest ones, about three feet in diameter. Conveyer belts snaked around them and eventually out the loading dock door. Paper rolls ten feet across stood against the wall like soldiers waiting to be called to duty, to be transformed into messengers of all the good and bad news of the day. But right now, they were as still as a graveyard.

"Can I help you?" The words crackled in the air like radio static.

I must've jumped a foot off the floor.

"I'm sorry, miss. Did I frighten you?"

I grabbed the ice-cold metal railing and looked around. A man stood next to the largest print cylinder, wiping his hands on an oily rag. His thinning white hair gleamed in the sunlight streaming down from the ceiling-level windows.

"A little, I guess." My hands clutched my chest and my heart thumped almost as loud as the presses when they were rolling.

"What are you doing down here?" he asked. "Paper's closed today."

"Oh. I'm Alex Lawson," I said, walking over to him. "I'm the new reporter here."

"Yup. Heard all about you. I'm Mac."

We shook hands and stood awkwardly looking at each other.

"I wasn't sure if I was supposed to come in today or not," I said. "So, I did, just in case."

Mac chuckled. "That's Lou for ya. He thinks everyone knows the paper's schedule. But, since you're not from around here, seems like he would've told you. We don't publish on Sunday, so everyone has today off. I'm kind of the watchman around here now. Used to be chief mechanic, so on Saturdays I come in and make sure all the machines are running like they should."

"Then I'm glad I came in today and got to meet you."

Mac nodded and turned to leave, but stopped and looked back at me. "Nice writing on that killer guy."

"Thanks."

And then he was gone, disappeared into the giant mechanisms that turned my words into front-page articles for everyone to read.

I went back up the metal staircase to the newsroom.

I decided to call Adam. What was the worst thing that could happen? At least if he humiliated me, I'd be able to lick my wounds in private here. A luxury I wouldn't have at Edna's.

I walked to my desk and dialed the number on the note. The phone rang three times, and I was about to hang up when Adam answered.

"Hello," he said.

"Adam, it's Alex. I got your note. I'd love to see your ranch."

Silence on the other end.

"Adam?"

"Right. Sorry. I kind of gave up on you when you didn't call first thing this morning."

I looked at the clock on the wall. "It's only eight o'clock. I told you last night I was going to work to see if Lou had an assignment for me."

"I didn't think you really meant that—I mean, since there's no paper on Sunday."

"Yeah, well, I just found that out."

At first, I didn't hear anything, then I heard a muffled laugh. My face burned. I was glad I was on the phone, not sitting across a table from him.

"Why didn't you say something last night?" I asked. "I could've called a lot earlier. This is all your fault, you know."

"Guess I figured you should find out for yourself," he said, still laughing.

"I don't think it's very funny to make a fool of me just because I don't know the paper's schedule."

Catching his breath, he said, "I'm sorry, Alex, but it is pretty funny." I could hear him take a deep breath. "Look, why don't I drive in and pick you up? It'll be a lot faster than you riding your bike out here, and there's still plenty left to the day."

I wasn't sure if I even wanted to go to his ranch anymore; but the thought of spending the day in Edna's living room was less appealing.

"Okay. I'm still at the paper, or do you want to meet me somewhere else?"

"That's fine. Stay put. I'll be there in about twenty minutes," Adam said, and the line went dead.

Guess I'll go outside and wait. I'll leave my bike here. I wonder if there's anything to read around here... Read! Oh no. I promised Betty I'd get her something to read!

I rummaged around, found a telephone directory, and looked up the Public Library: 10th Street and Main, only a couple of blocks away.

I hurried over there and yanked on the door. Locked! Of course. The posted hours said it opened at ten o'clock on Saturdays. *Now what?*

I looked around and remembered Jake's market was open early.

I ran there and grabbed a couple of magazines off the newsstand rack, paid for them, and ran back to sit on the steps and wait for Adam. I got there just as he drove up in his old dented truck.

"Hi," I said, jumping in. "Could we make a quick detour? I promised Betty I'd get her something to read. I won't stay long."

Adam stared at me like I was from another planet.

"Hello. Is that okay?"

He shook his head, sighed, and said, "Sure." Then he pulled away from the curb and headed to the hospital.

"I'll only be a minute," I said when we got there.

I jumped out and ran up the steps. Once inside, I asked the receptionist if one of the volunteers could take the magazines to Betty's room, then scooted back outside and got in the truck.

"That was quick," Adam said.

"I told you I was just going to drop them off."

Adam started the engine and headed for the road out of town. "Thought you might stop to say hello to Jimmy."

"No. Why would I do that?"

"You two seemed pretty chummy last night."

"Really? We went to see a movie, then stopped for a beer. No law against that, is there?"

"Not at all."

"Are you jealous?"

"No. Just don't want to date my buddy's gal."

I didn't say anything, but I didn't like his answer. After all, why couldn't I date both of them if I wanted to? I didn't know either of them very well yet, and they didn't know me. Why couldn't we all take some time to get to know one another before settling for just one?

"Glad to see you didn't get all dressed up," he said.

"I have a little more sense than to wear a cocktail dress when I'm going to be on the back of the horse."

His head spun and he looked at me. "A horse?"

"Well, how else do you figure I'll be able to see your ranch? Fly over it?"

"I didn't know if a city gal like you knew how to ride."

"I don't think there's a person in Montana who doesn't know how to ride. Besides, I'm not a city girl, as I've mentioned before. I grew up in Jericho Flats, which is smaller than this town. I knew how to ride a horse long before I knew how to ride a bike."

I could see a little smile creeping along the corners of Adam's lips. "Good to know."

"Maybe you have me confused with some other girl."

The little smile broke into a full blooded one. "I don't think so, but it's sure easy to get your dander up," he said, and started to laugh.

I stared out the window and, once again, wondered why I had called him today.

CHAPTER 28

We left the paved road and drove onto a dirt one, then passed under a log archway with "Long River Ranch" carved into the lintel. Scrub grass stretched as far as I could see on either side of the road, the occasional tumbleweed rolling across in front of us.

Ahead, the road curved to the right behind a row of cottonwood trees and opened up to reveal a magnificent two-story log ranch house with a porch that wrapped around the building. Forest green shutters framed each of the four windows on the second floor and the two large picture windows on the first floor. The front door was painted a matching green with a gleaming brass knocker. I climbed the three steps to a welcoming porch filled with willow chairs with brightly colored cushions and glass topped willow tables.

The front door opened and a woman with gray hair, pulled back into a bun, and a smile on her face greeted me.

"You must be Alex," she said. "I'm Martha." She took my hand in both of hers and looked me straight in the eye. "You're quite lovely."

I didn't know what to say to that remark, so I just said, "Hello."

"Now, Martha, don't go swelling her head any more than it already is," Adam said.

"Adam!" Martha said, "don't be rude. I raised you better than that. Come in, Alex. Can I get you some coffee, or tea, or lemonade?"

Before I could answer, Adam said, "We're going to take a ride out to see the cattle, but we'll be back for lunch." He turned to look at me. "Or would you rather have Martha pack a lunch for us and we could eat on the plains? Which one, Alex?"

"Gee, that'd be hard for me to decide, since I don't know how far we'll be riding."

Adam thought for a minute and looked at Martha, who stood tapping her foot, arms crossed, an annoyed look on her face.

"Adam Phillips, you know perfectly well you already asked me to pack a picnic for you and this young lady. Why are you putting her on the spot? You're being very ungentlemanly. Honestly, I don't know what's gotten into you lately."

Now it was Adam's turn to be embarrassed. His face turned bright red and he looked down at the floor. "Sorry, Martha. Guess I forgot."

"Forgot nothing," she said. "You're just being difficult. I'm sorry, Alex. He's not usually this way."

"Really?" I said. "Good to know. I thought he was."

Martha shot Adam a look that would have scared a badger. "Come in the kitchen with me, Alex, and I'll show you what I made for your lunch. That way if there's something you don't like, we can change it. And Adam, *you* can go saddle the horses."

With that, she spun on her heel and marched down the long hallway to the back of the house.

The first thing that hit me as I entered the kitchen was the aroma of freshly baked bread and something sweet, like cake. The kitchen was bigger than any I had ever seen. A huge window stretched across the back wall to the right of the back door and looked out onto the plains and a few outbuildings. A table with seating for eight sat in front of it, and the side wall held another massive window with a gorgeous view of some faraway bluffs. A wagon wheel chandelier hung over the table to light that side of the room. The other half was the working space. On the far wall were two stoves with ovens and a deep sink with two basins, a large paned window above them. A wooden chopping table sat in the center of the room, and a cupboard that covered the entire wall opposite the stoves finished the room. The massive space took my breath away with its size and beauty.

Martha pointed to a small hallway off to the left of the kitchen and said, "There's a washroom down there if you'd like to freshen up, Alex."

I thanked her and headed toward the washroom, which was bigger than the bathroom I shared with Maureen. It had a large clawfoot tub, a pedestal sink, and a toilet. A vase of birch branches, eucalyptus leaves, and dried marsh reeds sat on top of a small cabinet set against the wall.

When I came back into the kitchen, Martha was looking over a slew of packages wrapped in wax paper.

"I made roast beef sandwiches, and there's some cake here," she said. "And a thermos bottle of coffee and one of lemonade. Now, is there anything else you can think of? Of course, I would have more if you were eating here at the house, but Adam insisted I pack a picnic lunch."

"It all looks wonderful, Martha. Thank you."

"You're welcome. I don't know why he's being so ornery today. Got up on the wrong side of the bed, I guess."

I thought I knew exactly why, but I wasn't about to say anything to Martha. Maybe seeing me with Jimmy really did upset him.

While Martha talked, she packed our lunch in a saddlebag. "That should hold you until dinnertime. Make sure he doesn't wear you out, Alex. That man forgets himself when he gets out on the range. I want you both home before nightfall. I've already told Adam that, but you make sure he remembers."

"I will, Martha."

"Will what?" Adam asked, coming through the back door.

"Get you home before nightfall," I said.

"Martha, you worry too much," Adam said.

"It's fine for you. You could get yourself around here blindfolded. But Alex can't. I don't want her horse stepping into one of the prairie dog holes and going down just because it's too dark to see. And then there's the coyotes, and—"

"All right, all right. I'll make sure I get her back here in one piece."

Adam grabbed the saddlebag, gave Martha a kiss on the cheek, and said, "Ready?"

"Oh wait," Martha said. She hurried down the little hall and came back carrying a cowboy hat. "This might fit you. It'll keep the sun off your face, at any rate."

I plopped it on my head. "Perfect," I said. "My hat is coming eventually, along with the rest of my clothes. I had them shipped since I couldn't manage everything on the bus."

"The bus? Where are you—"

"Not now, Martha," Adam said. "Plenty of time for that over dinner."

Hmm, so I'm staying for dinner, am I? Seems like he had this whole day planned before I even agreed to come today. Pretty cocky.

Martha scowled at him, but he grabbed my arm and pulled me out the door.

"She'd have us there for hours if I didn't stop her," he said. "It's not often we have company."

The back porch was as inviting as the front one, and for a minute I thought how nice it would be to just sit in one of the rockers and talk to Martha. But Adam had a firm grip on my arm and led me down the steps and across the yard to the barn. A couple of dogs trotted next to us, so Adam let go of me to lean over and rub their heads. So did I.

"I miss my dog," I said.

"These guys are my buddies. This one's Pal, and the other one's Blackie. Don't know what I'd do without them."

They followed us into the barn where two horses stood, all saddled and waiting for us. Adam threw the saddlebag across the larger one. I noticed both horses had rifles in their cases.

"You think we'll need guns?" I asked.

"Never know what you'll come across. This is Midnight," Adam said handing me the reins to the smaller black horse. "He's very gentle. Good for a city gal like you."

I ignored that remark and mounted my horse.

"Well done," Adam said.

"I told you I've been riding since before I could walk, didn't I?"

"You did," he said, and shook his head.

We trotted out of the barn and Adam led the way past the bunkhouse and an outdoor grill with wooden picnic tables and benches scattered all around. I could hear pigs and chickens but couldn't see them. They must have been on the other side of the barn.

We rode past the smokehouse where a thin stream of smoke drifted out of the chimney, the smell of meat smoking making my mouth water. Once we got past it, and a few other outbuildings, there was nothing but wide-open space and a bright blue Montana sky.

CHAPTER 29

That morning, we rode for hours before we reached the "long river" the ranch was named after, which was actually the Powder River. The sun glistened off the icy surface. I could hear the roar of the ice beginning to crack under the sun's warmth. We rode upstream to see if there was any open water yet for the cattle. If not, Adam and his workers would keep hauling tankfuls every few days.

The beauty of the land was amazing. Stands of cottonwood trees clustered close to the riverbank and sandstone cliffs rose majestically from the grasslands. Pronghorn antelopes roamed in herds, nibbling at the new growth emerging from its winter hibernation. White fluffy clouds drifted across the sapphire blue sky, only interrupted by flocks of returning geese and soaring eagles searching the plains for food.

We passed a few old ruins, remnants of early settlers or maybe stagecoach stops, now just piles of stones outlining the perimeter of a building, or crumbling crude log structures eaten away by time and weather. We followed the rough paths formed by these pioneers and I thought about the courage they must have had to venture through this wilderness, not knowing what lay ahead for them. I didn't think I'd ever have that kind of grit.

Today, I was glad Adam was a quiet person. It allowed me time to think about the people who lived here or simply passed through on their way to their future homes.

Adam stopped his horse and pointed ahead.

"Looks like the cattle have found a break in the ice," he said.

I looked where he pointed and saw dozens of the beasts either at the river's edge, or heading there.

"Does that mean you can stop hauling water?" I asked.

Adam rubbed his chin and watched them. "Don't know. I'd like to go there and see how open it is. But first why don't we ride over to that clump of cottonwoods and have lunch. Hungry?"

"I am. That sounds like a great idea."

We rode to the cluster of trees, dismounted, and tied up the horses. Adam untied a rolled blanket from behind his saddle.

"You came prepared, didn't you?" I asked. "Then why the charade of asking me if I wanted lunch at the ranch house or out here?"

Adam busied himself looking for a spot without too many rocks to spread the blanket.

"Adam? Why the charade?"

"Guess I wanted to see if you'd be the adventurous type or if you'd prefer the comforts of a warm kitchen."

"Is this the way it's going to be? You always testing me? Why can't you just ask me what you want to know? I don't believe in playing games."

I jerked the blanket out of his hand and flung it on the ground. At this point, I didn't care how rocky the ground was beneath us. In fact, the rockier the better.

Adam retrieved the saddlebag with our lunch and brought it over to the blanket. He sat down and started to unload the wrapped packages.

"Are you going to sit or stand while you eat?" he asked.

I plopped down on the blanket.

"Ouch," I said, landing on a pointy rock, now sorry that I hadn't cleared the ground first.

"You picked the spot," Adam said, biting into his sandwich.

I reached under the blanket and plucked out the offending rock. "At least it wasn't a clump of sagebrush."

As I rubbed my wounded rump, Adam stifled a laugh, but when I looked at him, he burst out roaring, and, in a minute, I joined him. "Guess it could have been worse," I said. "It could have been a cow pie." "Yeah, but at least they're softer." We both started laughing again.

The sandwiches were delicious. The meat was so tender it practically melted on my tongue, and the sharp tang of mustard woke up my taste buds. Thanks to our thermos bottle, the coffee was piping hot and smelled heavenly. Martha had packed two sandwiches for each of us, but they were so overloaded with meat I had trouble finishing the first one. Highly unusual for me. I think somewhere in the back of my mind, I was saving space for a piece of her cake. My sweet tooth was screaming for it. But I had to wait until Adam finished his second sandwich.

"Aren't you going to finish your lunch?" he asked.

"That sandwich was huge," I said. "I couldn't eat two."

"Martha always says if you don't finish your meal, there's no dessert."

I was horrified. No dessert!

Adam looked at me and burst out laughing again.

"If you could only see your face," he said, gasping for air. "You look like a little girl who's just been told there's no Santa Claus."

I couldn't see it, but I could feel it getting hotter. Adam's back was against the tree trunk and he held his stomach, he was laughing so hard.

"Maybe I don't want dessert." I crossed my arms and looked away, pouting like a two-year-old.

Then his arms were around my waist and he pulled me toward him until my back pressed against his chest.

"I'm teasing. You can have whatever you want," he whispered in my ear.

I felt my body turn to jelly while my insides burned with a ferocious desire. At that moment, the only dessert I wanted was the touch of Adam's lips on mine. He kissed my neck and the next thing I knew we were lying next to each other, locked in an embrace with our lips joined together, our tongues exploring.

I was burning up. I felt like I would never be the same person I had been earlier that morning. I felt transformed. Catapulted to a new level of existence.

Gradually, we pulled away from each other.

"Ready for some cake?" Adam asked, a huskiness to his voice that wasn't there before.

"I can think of something I'd like more."

Adam smiled and twirled a lock of my hair through his fingers. "We still have work to do today. I want to check on the cattle and see how much of the ice has melted on the river. But you can have whatever you want once we're done."

I traced his lips with my fingertip. "Promise?"

"Promise."

"Well, then," I said, shoving him away, "of course I want cake."

I sat up and rummaged through the packages.

Adam tucked his arm behind his head and watched me.

"So that's my competition, huh? Cake?"

"Right now it is."

Adam shook his head and sat up.

"Where's my piece? Or did you manage to gobble them both already?"

I gave him a playful smack on his arm and handed him a thick slice of spice cake. He grabbed my hand and kissed the inside of my wrist.

"Thanks." He looked into my eyes, and cradled my hand in his.

Thank goodness I have a horse. My legs are too wobbly to walk.

Lunch finished, we shoved all the debris back into the saddlebag. Adam lay down and placed his hat over his face to block out the sun.

"Think I'll catch forty winks."

"Okay. I'm going exploring."

He lifted his hat and said, "Don't go too far. I don't want to spend the afternoon looking for you."

"Don't worry. I won't get lost. I just want a closer look at that old cabin we passed."

"I don't know why. It's ready to fall down, but okay. Just keep this stand of trees in sight."

"And you say Martha worries too much."

CHAPTER 30

I walked over to Midnight, untied him, and looked at Adam, already back under his hat, hands clasped on his stomach. I guided Midnight out of the copse and decided to trot down to the ice break to let him have a drink.

The opening wasn't very large yet and the cattle pushed at each other to reach the water. I gave Midnight his head to find an opening. He wisely stayed at the very edge of the herd, managing to drink from the narrowest slit of water between the riverbank and the ice. While he lapped up his fill, I daydreamed about Adam and me.

I didn't know what to think about how he made me feel. Since I was a little girl, all I ever wanted to do was be a reporter in a big city. Now this cowboy had my head turned upside down. I knew he'd never give up his ranch. But could I be happy here? Could I keep working for the *Star*? Could I have both Adam and a career?

Every time I was near him, an electric current ran through my body, igniting every nerve, twitching every muscle. I thought about the kiss I shared with Jimmy the previous night. It was warm and soft, like cuddling up under a fluffy comforter in front of a fire. Adam's kisses were explosions, setting me on fire.

I completely lost myself in my imaginings of a life with Adam. I could myself working with Martha in the kitchen, making Adam's favorite meals, while our kids ran around the yard, dogs and chickens everywhere. But that would mean no more reporting, no career, no Pulitzer Prize. I'd have to give up everything I ever dreamed about. Could I?

I shook my head to clear away the fantasies of what Adam's kisses could lead to.

Time to stop fantasizing and go see that cabin.

I tried to steer Midnight around, but saw we were surrounded by cattle. Unwilling to wait their turn, some of them had stomped their hooves through the thinning ice at the river's edge to open it up further. Midnight and I were an island in a sea of cattle that were becoming more and more anxious to get a drink. Their lowing cries became louder. I couldn't believe I hadn't heard them through my daydream.

I tried to back Midnight up but he refused to move, his head swinging wildly back and forth, his eyes rolling around, wide in panic. We were trapped. I rubbed his neck, trying desperately to keep him calm while working to squelch the fear racing through me.

Come on, Alex. Use your head. There's got to be a way out of this herd.

I yanked my foot out of the stirrup and pushed against the closest beast. It was like a fly trying to knock down a wall. I could feel Midnight becoming more agitated as the herd pushed against us and each other. My heart pumped faster as the cattle squeezed against my legs.

I didn't dare go forward across the river. I didn't know if the ice would hold us, or if Midnight would be willing to try such an escape. The stench of the cattle's dung nauseated me. I could feel my panic rising, which I knew would transmit to Midnight and make matters worse.

Maybe if I fired a shot in the air, the cattle would startle and shift. Or stampede.

Before I could do anything, a whip cracked. Adam was at the edge of the herd, sending them back away from the river, and me. Begrudgingly, they gave in and retreated as Adam plowed through them, cracking his whip at any stubborn ones. As soon as he got close enough, he grabbed the reins and pulled Midnight toward him and away from the herd.

"Get out of here!" he said, and tossed the reins back to me.

I pointed Midnight back to the copse of cottonwoods and galloped to them, Adam following.

As soon as I was safely away from the herd, I slowed down. Adam rode up next to me.

"What the hell were you thinking?" he roared. "Don't you know they could have crushed you and Midnight to death?"

My whole body was trembling from the incident, and now, from Adam's wrath. My usual cocky attitude evaporated and I burst into tears. Great heaving sobs wracked my body.

Adam jumped down from his horse, dragged me off Midnight, and drew me into his arms. He rubbed my back and kept saying, "Shhh, you're safe now . . . shhh."

Gradually my sobs changed to whimpers and hiccups. I clung to Adam like a drowning man grasping a piece of driftwood. Adam stroked my hair and kissed my forehead. I looked up at him and saw such tender concern in his eyes that my legs didn't feel like they could hold me up any longer.

"You'd better sit for a minute," he said, and lowered me to the ground. He sat next to me and wrapped his arm around my shoulders. "You gave me quite a scare, Alex."

"I scared myself," I said.

"Why did you think you could push your way through that pack and be able to get out whenever you pleased?"

"That's not how it happened."

I explained everything to him and he listened carefully. Obviously, he was evaluating whether or not he would need to keep hauling water. In a way, that made me mad. I could've been killed, but he was thinking more about the workings of his ranch.

But that wasn't fair. I was safe, thanks to him. He was right to look ahead to what needed to be done next.

We sat for a while, my head tucked under his chin.

"Feeling better?" he asked.

I looked at him. "Much. I'm sorry, Adam. I don't mean to be so much trouble."

"It's okay. I should have known better than to let a city gal take off on her own like that," he said, that familiar little smirk sneaking across his face.

"I am *not* a city girl," I said, smacking his chest. "You're so infuriating. And wipe that silly grin off your face."

Adam burst out laughing.

"A minute ago, I was your knight in shining armor. Now you look like you'd like to throw me in that river."

"And I would, if it wasn't covered in ice."

Adam pulled me closer and kissed me. All thoughts of throwing him anywhere other than into my bed disappeared.

"We should probably head home," he said, drawing away from me.

"I wish we didn't have to."

"So do I. But we do."

He stood, reached out for my hand, and pulled me up into his arms.

"We really have to get going or Martha will send out a search party," he whispered in my ear, kissing my neck the whole time.

"If you don't stop, I'll never leave this spot. I don't care who comes looking for us."

I grabbed his face with both hands and kissed him firmly on the lips. "Now, stop tempting me and get on your horse."

CHAPTER 31

On our way back to the ranch house, we passed the cabin I had originally planned to explore. I pointed it out to Adam and suggested we ride over to take a look at it.

"Why?" he asked.

"I'm curious, that's all."

He hesitated, then turned his horse off the path and headed toward the ruin.

It wasn't in the best shape, but better than I expected. There were gaps in the mud mixture originally sandwiched between the logs where sunlight danced through, lighting up the dust mites. The roof seemed intact and solid, although a good rain might prove me wrong. The greased paper that had originally covered the window openings hung in tatters, held together by cobwebs. The dirt floor was covered in dead vegetation, with a few pieces of bone or rocks scattered around. The stone fireplace would probably still work, but I wasn't sure what the chimney looked like. A table and stool had survived, along with a few pieces of chipped or broken plates and cups. But, most importantly, there was a bed along the far wall. The mattress had been chewed at. Stuffing hung out and covered the floor all around it, but the frame was solid.

Adam looked at me. "Seen enough?"

"I've seen enough to know that this could be a perfect little rendezvous spot."

"What are you playing at, Alex?"

"I'm not playing Adam. I mean it. The mattress is useless, but that could be replaced. Or we could just throw a bedroll on top of it."

"You're not serious, are you?"

"Why not?" I looked at him. His face had drained of all color.

Oh no. Could I have this all wrong? Doesn't he feel the same way I do? I'm such a fool.

The blood rushed to my face. I ran out of the cabin and jumped on Midnight, wishing I could disappear, but I didn't even know which direction led back to town.

Adam was beside me in a second, grabbing Midnight's bridle.

"Just point me in the right direction and I'll get out of your sight," I said.

"Alex, get down. Please."

I didn't want to, but he looked so pitiful standing there.

I stood in front of him and stared at the ground. I couldn't look at those eyes again. I was ashamed of myself. I was sure he thought I was no more than a floozy.

Adam grabbed me by the shoulders.

"Look at me," he said. "I don't want to say this to the top of your head."

I looked up, but through my tears, he was a wavy watery image.

"Alex—it's not that I don't want you. I've probably never wanted anyone this badly before. But not like this. Not in some animal infested shack. I want our first time together to be perfect. Something we'll always remember because it was beautiful, not because we fought off the mice and won. And I don't want to be sneaky, like what we're doing is wrong or dirty. It won't be wrong. It'll be something we both want more than anything else in the world." He took a deep breath, then said, "Unless it doesn't mean that much to you."

I couldn't stop myself. I burst out crying.

Adam pulled me close.

"Adam," I finally blurted out, "what you said was so beautiful. And it does mean as much to me. It's just that I don't want to wait."

He tilted my chin up from his chest.

"You know what they say, the best things in life are worth waiting for. So, can you be a good little girl and be patient for a while longer? Maybe you won't even like me very much when you get to know me better. I'm not always this charming, you know."

"I already know that, but I like you anyway."

"That sounds more like the brat I've come to know."

"What? Brat—"

But I never finished. My words were swallowed by Adam's lips.

One thing I did know. If he kept kissing me like this, my patience was going to be very short-lived.

For the rest of the slow ride back to Adam's house, we talked about his ranch and the plans he had for its future. He wanted to add sheep to his livestock line. He had the acreage to do that, and income from the wool could be set aside toward future building improvements and updates without diminishing the flock.

As he laid out the plans he had, I saw Adam was a realistic and practical businessman, not just someone who had inherited a well-run and profitable ranch. It made me wonder even more if he'd ever be willing to leave this place, even for a little while.

We led our horses into the barn just as the sun started its descent. I began to unsaddle Midnight, but Adam told me he'd have one of his men take care of both horses.

"We'd better get inside and get cleaned up for dinner before Martha has my head on a platter," Adam said. "I didn't realize it was so late."

"But, it was a great day," I said.

"Sure was," he said, and gave me a quick kiss before we headed into the house.

Adam spotted one of his ranch hands and called over to ask him if he could have someone see to the horses. The man, Bill, said he'd be happy to do it, so, that taken care of, we went to face Martha.

"It's about time you brought Alex back," she said as soon as we stepped into the kitchen. "The poor girl must be starving by now. And sick of listening to you talk about this ranch."

"I'm okay," I said. "Our lunch was enough to keep me full. And it was delicious."

"Glad you enjoyed it," Martha said. "Now you two get washed up. Dinner's all ready. The men have eaten, but Clint waited to eat with us."

"Good." Adam gave Martha a peck on the cheek. "You weren't really worried about me, were you?" he teased.

"Not about you," she said, stirring something in a pot on the stove. "About Alex. I told you I didn't want you keeping her out after dark."

"And we made it back," Adam said, "in plenty of time."

Martha shook her head and sighed. "Go wash up."

I could tell Martha was much more than a housekeeper. More like his mom. She obviously loved him like a son.

As I headed down the hallway to the washroom, I thought about the events of the day. I felt like something inside me had changed, although I didn't know what to make of it.

Could I change my dreams for new ones and still be happy?

When I saw my reflection in the mirror, I couldn't believe how dusty and grimy I looked. I scrubbed my filthy face and hands until they shined. *So much for makeup.* Even though I had kept Martha's hat on the whole day, the tip of my nose and my cheeks had picked up a little color from the sun. I left the hat on a hook behind the door and went back to the kitchen.

As I walked down the hallway, I heard Martha and a man whispering to each other. I thought I heard my name, so I coughed a little before entering the kitchen.

"All freshened up?" Martha asked.

"Yes, thanks. I left your hat on the hook behind the door. Thanks for the loan."

"You're more than welcome. Alex, this is Clint, our foreman."

"Pleased to meet you," he said, walking over to shake my hand.

"It's my pleasure. Adam's told me a lot about you." I looked up into his deep brown eyes. He was as tall as Adam, broad shouldered, with jet black hair, prominent cheekbones, and a tan that only enhanced his weather-beaten face. He looked to be in his fifties, maybe a shade younger than Martha.

"Now don't you go believing everything he says," Clint said.

"What shouldn't Alex believe?" Adam asked, walking into the room.

"Anything you say," Clint said.

"More like anything *you* say," Adam said.

"Both of you," Martha said, "stop it, and sit at the table before this dinner isn't worth eating."

"Yes, ma'am," they said in unison.

"Alex, you can sit on the far side," Martha said. "I need to be able to get up and down."

I went where I was directed, Adam sat next to me, and Clint sat opposite me.

"Adam, I forgot, you need to get the meat out of the oven for me," Martha said.

He jumped up and did as he was told.

"I'm sorry," I said. "I should have asked if I could help."

"Don't be silly," Martha said. "You're a guest. You can sit and chat with Clint. Adam here'll be all the help I need."

I looked across the table. Clint was evaluating me in the silent way that only someone who spends most of his time with cattle, away from other people, can do.

"This is a great ranch," I said.

"Yup," Clint said.

"We rode around quite a bit today." I fiddled with my napkin, trying to think of something I could say that would require more than a one word answer. "Adam sure knows how to handle his cows. Good thing, too, since I got myself stuck in the middle of the herd and thought they'd crush—"

A dish crashed onto the slate floor.

I looked up and saw that Martha's face had turned white as the ice on the river. Even Clint's face seemed pale.

"It's all right, Martha," Adam said. "Nothing happened."

"How could you let her get into a situation like that?" Martha asked, scowling at him.

"It was my own fault," I said. "I wasn't thinking."

"What happened?" Clint asked, a frown across his face.

I told him the whole story while Adam cleaned up the broken dish.

"It was my stupidity," I said. "I should've known better."

"You're just not used to being around cattle," Adam said, absorbed in getting all the bits of crockery off the floor. "They're pretty dumb animals. You were where they wanted to be, so they figured they'd push you out of the way."

"Well, I'm fine, so no harm done," I said. I looked at Martha. Some color was creeping back to her face and Clint looked better as well. "I'm sorry I upset everyone."

"No, no you didn't. I'm just a butterfingers today, that's all," Martha said. The atmosphere in the room was definitely more subdued.

Clint got up, went over to Martha, and rubbed her back. He whispered something to her and she nodded her head. Then I remembered what Joe had told me about Adam's family and the stampede.

Damn. I'm an idiot. Of course everyone's upset. How stupid can I be?

Clint brought a bowl of beans and one of roasted potatoes over to the table while Martha carried a water pitcher and a bottle of wine. Obviously, Prohibition wasn't enforced here. Adam finished carving the meat and placed a platter of sliced pork loin on the table.

"Dig in while it's hot," Martha said.

Everyone helped themselves as the food was passed around. Clint asked Adam about the condition of the river and they talked about whether or not the men could stop hauling water. After that, there was an awkward silence hanging over the room.

"Alex is a newspaperman," Adam said.

"That must be interesting," Martha said. "We don't usually get to see the paper unless someone goes into town and buys one."

"She wrote the story about that guy who killed Ben Ferguson," Adam said.

That got everyone's attention. Clint and Martha wanted to know all about it, and how the Ferguson family was doing.

I silently thanked Adam for finding a topic to lift the pall hanging over the room.

After dinner, I offered to help clean up, but Martha said she and Clint could manage everything.

"Adam, I think you should see about taking Alex home," she said. "I'm not throwing you out, Alex, but it's late already, since you two were so long getting back here today."

"She's right, Adam," I said. "I'd love to stay longer, but I do have to go to work tomorrow."

"On Sunday?" Martha asked.

"Got to write the stories for Monday's paper," I said. "It was wonderful meeting both of you. And thank you again, Martha, for two terrific meals."

"You're very welcome. Don't be a stranger now that you know where we are."

Adam grabbed his hat, gave Martha a peck on the cheek, and we left.

"I apologize for babbling about my battle with the cattle," I said, once we were on the road. "Joe told me about your family. If I had remembered, I never would've said a word."

Adam pulled the truck over to the side of the road and stopped. "Joe told you? Why?"

"I asked him about you. I was curious. I just wanted to know more about you after we had our dinner date."

Adam rested his forehead against the steering wheel.

"Why didn't you tell me you knew about my family?"

"I don't know. Guess I thought it was something you wouldn't want to talk about. I figured you'd bring it up at some point, so I decided to leave it at that."

"You're right. I don't like to talk about it. But I guess I'm glad you know."

"I'm sorry, Adam. For that, and for my big mouth."

"It wasn't your fault. Martha and Clint are very protective of me ever since the accident. They try really hard to never talk about anything that will remind me of it. You couldn't know that. Let's forget about it, okay?"

"I'd like that. It's been such a wonderful day, I don't want to spoil it."

"You're right. We won't spoil it by bringing back old memories. C'mere."

He pulled me over next to him and kissed me.

"That's better," he said. "That's what I've wanted to do for hours."

"Me too."

I snuggled in next to him and he pulled back onto the road and headed for town.

CHAPTER 32

"Finally decided to come home, I see," Edna said when I walked into the house.

"Yep, and I'm going to have a cup of tea. Anyone else interested?"

Maureen and Edna both said no. The radio was off and the two women sat reading. A strained atmosphere hung over the room that I couldn't identify. Or maybe it was my imagination.

The kettle whistled. I made my tea and carried it into the living room. *There's definitely something in the air. The iciness in this room could freeze a slab of beef.*

Flipping through a magazine while I sipped my tea, I almost jumped out of my chair when a book slammed shut, the noise shattering the quiet.

"You know, Alex," Edna said, "I told you you could come and go as you please."

"Yes, you did," I said.

Edna's face was blazing, her eyes boring into mine. *What is this all about?*

"I also asked you to let me know if you wouldn't be home for dinner. I don't need to waste food. If you think you can go gallivanting all over town with no regard for me or this household, then maybe you need to find another place to live." She twisted her hands together throughout her speech.

Her vehemence took me by surprise. Gone was the grandmotherly Edna, replaced by this harridan I hadn't met yet.

"Edna, I'm sorry. I completely forgot. Adam took me out to his ranch and gave me a tour. We didn't get back to his house until the sun was setting. Even if I had called then, it would have been too late."

"Well, it was very inconsiderate," Edna said in a huff. "Maureen and I waited forever, thinking you'd come home. By the time we decided to eat, everything was overdone. I think you owe Maureen an apology as well."

Edna had regained her composure and sat like a headmistress reprimanding a recalcitrant schoolgirl.

Who does she think she is? Maybe I should *look for another place to live.*

"My apologies, Maureen," I said. "I'm sure this has been a difficult evening for you."

"Well, I never," Edna said. "I'm going to bed. Maureen, please see that the lights are out before you go upstairs. At least I know I can rely on *you* to be a responsible adult."

With those parting words, Edna marched out of the room and slammed her bedroom door shut.

"That was unpleasant," I said.

"She's been in a snit all night," Maureen said. "I don't know if it's because you didn't call or the fact that she didn't know where you were, or with whom."

"That's none of her beeswax," I said.

"I know, but let's face it, she's the town gossip and doesn't like to be kept in the dark about who is stepping out with whom."

I didn't say anything.

"Maybe we should continue this conversation upstairs," Maureen said, "where there's less possibility of being overheard."

"I don't think there's much more to say. I can't be on a leash like she seems to want. We never had family dinners at home. Mom ate her main meal at school, and, being in the bar, and now café, business, Dad ate whenever he could grab a few minutes. I was pretty much left on my own. I'm not used to a strict routine. Maybe this arrangement isn't right for me. I'll look around for another place to live tomorrow."

"Don't be so hasty, Alex. There aren't too many decent places to live in this town. And think of the advantages here. We don't have to cook for ourselves, or keep the place clean, and we can walk to everything. It could be a lot worse."

"I suppose, but I feel like she's spying on me. Like she wants me to tell her everything I do, where I go, who I see, aside from wanting to know what stories I'm working on for the paper. I don't know if it's worth it."

"Sleep on it," Maureen said. "Maybe everything will blow over by the morning."

"Maybe."

My anger grew with each step as I went up to my room. Edna had managed to ruin one of the best days of my life. She was nothing but an old biddy. A nosy old biddy.

CHAPTER 33

On Sunday, Edna left for church right after breakfast and I spent the rest of the day at the paper, helping Lou with the national and state news and thinking about finding a new place to live. At dinner that night, Edna never mentioned anything about my moving out, and neither did I.

I woke the next morning, still not sure what I wanted to do about my living arrangements. At breakfast, Edna was civil, but there was still a chill in the air. When she asked if either of us had other plans for dinner, I knew who she really wanted to ask. She only included Maureen so it didn't look like she was targeting me.

The heaviness in the room began to stifle me, so I gulped down the rest of my cereal and coffee and took my dishes to the sink.

A quick wash of these and I can get out of here.

Maureen joined me, and in a few minutes we had washed, dried, and tucked away all the breakfast items.

"Are you walking to the paper this morning?" Maureen asked. "Or somewhere else?"

"The paper. I don't know what Lou wants me to work on today."

"Want some company?"

"Sure."

"I'll just scoot upstairs and get my things. Meet you on the porch in a few."

I had brought my purse downstairs earlier, so I grabbed my hat and coat from the hall closet and went outside to wait for Maureen. Edna had retreated to her bedroom as soon as she finished eating, so I was spared any further conversation with her.

Maureen came out a few minutes later, lugging her briefcase filled with graded papers and textbooks.

"Have you given any more thought to moving?" she asked.

"I have. I think I'll have to look for another place to live."

"I wish you didn't feel that way. It's been so nice having you to talk to, instead of just Edna."

"You saw what it was like at breakfast," I said. "She could barely look at me. And asking if 'either of you girls' had other plans for dinner was a direct hit at me."

"Yeah, she wasn't very subtle."

"I can't live in a place where I feel like I'm walking on eggshells."

Before I knew it, we were at Maureen's street.

"Hey," I said as she turned right, "if you hear of anyone looking for a roommate, or an empty apartment, let me know, okay?"

"I will, Alex. You didn't even have to ask."

I trudged along the street to the paper. On the way, I remembered I hadn't gotten anything for Betty to read. The magazines I brought on Saturday might have lasted a day, and that was two days ago.

I decided to stop at the library and pick up a couple of books. I made a quick stop at the office first, to let Lou know where I'd be, then headed out.

I walked past the courthouse to the Carnegie Library. The redbrick building with tall arched windows could be a home for Andrew Carnegie instead of a library his foundation built. Inside, the round walnut circulation desk and wainscoting made the place feel homey. The leather armchairs were exactly the type I could spend hours in, curled up with a good book.

At the circulation desk, I introduced myself and filled out the form for a library card. Fortunately, the librarian knew Betty and recommended some books she thought she'd enjoy. I checked out three and thanked her for her help.

Next, I was on to the county courthouse. A few of the courtrooms had trials scheduled, so I jotted down all the pertinent facts from the bailiffs. Nothing seemed extraordinary, although there was a case of cattle rustling that sounded interesting. I decided I'd follow up on that one in the afternoon.

The city court had the usual cases: late fines, traffic violations, past due taxes. I made notes on all of them. The past due taxes case was worth looking into. It seemed the rancher might lose his ranch. The judge called for lunch recess, and as if on cue, my stomach growled.

Perfect timing. I could pedal over to the hospital, eat lunch, visit with Betty, and deliver the books.

Clouds blotted out the sun and the bike ride became an endurance test between my bare hands and the cold metal handlebars. I should have known the spring-like weather wouldn't last. Why hadn't I worn my gloves?

At the hospital, I tucked my bike out of sight behind some bushes and headed to the cafeteria. I picked up a budget friendly sandwich and coffee and headed to my usual window table. While I ate, I looked through the books from the library. *The Curious Case of Benjamin Button* by F. Scott Fitzgerald and *The Forsyth Saga*, a historical romance, sounded interesting, but the third one, *Scaramouche*, didn't appeal to me at all. I hoped the librarian knew Betty's taste better than I did.

"Hey, don't you ever return phone calls?" Jimmy asked, looming over my table, an angry scowl on his face.

"What are you talking about?" I was totally confused.

"Phone calls. You know. Usually when someone leaves a message, the other person gets back to them."

"Huh? What message?"

Jimmy folded his arms across his chest. "You trying to tell me Mrs. Lynch didn't give you any of my messages? She told me she did."

"What? I swear, Jimmy, this is the first I'm hearing about it. I wouldn't ignore you. Can you sit for a minute?"

"That's about all I've got," he said, pulling out the chair opposite me. "I already took my break."

"Honest, Jimmy, Edna never told me you called."

"Why would she do that? I thought she liked me."

"I'm sure she does. I think it's me she doesn't like."

I told Jimmy about going to Adam's ranch, missing dinner, and the argument with Edna.

"Oh." He stood up and pushed his chair in. "If you're dating Adam, I guess you don't want to date me anymore."

"I'm not *dating* Adam. I went out to his ranch. That's all. It was a nice day and I enjoyed the horseback ride and being out in the fresh air. Don't make a big deal out of it."

"Jimmy," someone called from the kitchen.

"Look, I've got to go," he said. "Can I take you out tonight so we can talk?"

"If it's about Adam, there's nothing to talk about."

"It's not. Can I?"

"Well, okay."

"Great. I'll pick you up around seven, okay?"

"Okay."

He hurried off to the kitchen where a woman stood, arms folded, foot tapping.

I'm so confused. When I'm with Adam, I don't want to be anywhere else, or with anyone else. But when I see Jimmy, with his puppy dog eyes, I melt.

How can I choose between the two? And do I really want to get deeply involved with either of them? What will happen with my career if I do? And on top of everything is the decision about moving.

I have some serious decisions to make, and I'd better make them soon before I do something I'll regret.

I finished lunch, got my visitor's pass from the reception desk, and went upstairs to see Betty, who was sitting in a wheelchair by the window, foot propped up.

"This is an improvement," I said.

"Come to gloat?" she asked, an angry edge to her voice. "Or is this your charitable deed for the week?"

"What?"

"I imagine it's hard to squeeze me in with all your front-page stories."

"Well, someone's got to cover the news now that the *Star*'s ace reporter is laid up," I said in a teasing way.

"Seems to me like *you're* the ace reporter now."

"Come on, Betty. Lou misses you, and so do I. Half the time, I have no idea what I'm doing. I've just been lucky that a few big stories fell into my lap, that's all. What did you expect me to do, ignore them?"

Betty looked at me, a sneer on her lips, and turned back to stare out the window.

"Just don't forget that *I'm* the lead reporter on the *Star*. As soon as I can manage it, I'll be back. And I don't plan on taking a backseat to anyone."

"I thought we went over this already. I didn't realize you felt this was a competition, but if you want to treat it like one, that's fine with me. I came here today for two reasons. One, to see you and bring you some books to read. And two, to ask you where I can go to dig up some news. But with your attitude, I doubt you'd be willing to help me out.

"I thought you'd be relieved someone's around to write the stories," I added. "At least they're getting reported. Lou can't do it all, you know. And I haven't seen hide nor hair of Joe, so he's no help. If you feel like I'm taking your job away, just remember, I wasn't given a choice."

She picked at imaginary lint on her hospital gown and said, "Maybe not."

"Here." I shoved the three books at her.

If she hates them, she'll probably think I deliberately brought her lousy choices. Just one more nail in my coffin.

"Oh, *Scaramouche*. I've wanted to read this ever since the reviews came out."

"Fine. Glad the librarian knows your taste. I've got to go."

"Wait a minute, Alex. I don't know what's come over me. Maybe being cooped up in here is driving me crazy. You're right. I should be thanking my lucky stars you're here. I apologize. Guess the green-eyed monster bit me."

I wasn't sure if I was ready to accept her apology, but what choice did I have? I could wage war with her and fight tooth and nail for every byline, or work with her, learn as much as I could, then leave this one-horse town for a real paper.

"Truce?" Betty asked, extending her hand.

Don't be a stubborn ass, Alex.

"Sure."

We shook on it and entered a new alliance, as fragile as a broken, but now mended, fine china vase.

"Oh, and thanks for the magazines. Why didn't you come up for a minute when you dropped them off? You couldn't have been mad at me then. I hadn't insulted you yet."

"No, I wasn't mad, but aside from the watchdogs at the desk, who guard this floor like it's Fort Knox, Adam was waiting for me."

"Adam? Pull up a chair and spill the beans about this new romance."

"It's not a *romance*. I wish everyone would stop thinking it is," I said, plopping down in the chair opposite Betty.

Or is it? I wish I could figure things out. Right now, my brain is like scrambled eggs.

"Sorry," Betty said. "I have no right to ask."

"Oh, I may as well tell you. I'd rather you hear it from me than from the local gossips."

I told her about my day at the ranch, leaving out the intimate moments, and answered her questions.

"Okay," I said, "enough about that. Now, where can I go to get some news?"

We spent the rest of the visiting time listing possible news sources, including some I had forgotten, like Dot in the mayor's office. I didn't know how I could have forgotten her.

By the time I left, we had established a working relationship.

"I'll try to get back tomorrow. But if you need anything, call the paper and leave a message with Pat."

"I will. Thanks for the books, Alex."

I waved goodbye and scooted out before Sister Marcus discovered I was still there after the bell that ended visiting hours had gonged.

CHAPTER 34

I spent the rest of the day visiting every civic organization in town. It surprised me to learn that the Chamber of Commerce had canceled any plans for a rodeo this year. The council decided there were still too many possible contestants now serving in the armed forces, or home recovering from war wounds, or missing or dead. The council suggested I talk to some of the bull and bronc breeders about their livestock and plans for future rodeos. We all believed when the rodeo cowboys returned, or were fully recovered, they'd be itching for a chance to compete.

I got the names of some local breeders and planned to see them over the next day or two. I had no idea about how they bred and trained these rodeo champions, and thought it would make an interesting series of articles.

Looked like I'd just about have time to get back to the paper, talk to Lou about my idea, and still get home to Edna's for dinner. It wouldn't do to miss dinner again, even if I did plan on moving out.

"I'm back, Lou," I said as soon as I hit the newsroom floor.

His grunt was his only acknowledgment.

I began organizing my notes.

"Whatcha got?" Lou asked.

"Thought I'd do a story on how broncs and bulls get bred and trained for rodeos. Since there won't be any competitions this year, at least it'll give our readers a look behind the scenes."

"Might work."

"I thought I'd visit some of the local ranchers tomorrow."

"Hmm. Okay. Get it to me as soon as you can. And drop this off with Phil, downstairs."

He handed me the high school graduation story I had finished after my discussion with the principal a few days ago.

"You got it, Chief."

"And don't call me Chief," he exploded, stomping back to his office.

I silently giggled at how that title riled him, which, of course, was why I decided to keep using it.

I took the story downstairs to Phil, and found him behind one of the giant presses.

"Lou said to give this to you."

"Front-page again?" he asked.

"Don't know, but don't think so. You'd better check with Lou on that."

The presses were quiet right now, but in a little while they'd start running, and you wouldn't be able to hear yourself think. As always, the pungent smell of ink and newsprint paper permeated the room.

Phil read the copy with hands that were stained black. I wondered if he was ever able to get rid of that ink.

"Anything else?" Phil asked.

"Nope. See you tomorrow."

Back upstairs, I asked Lou if he needed anything from me before I called it quits for the day.

"Guess that's it. Oh, by the way, Maureen's working out swell. Tell her I said that."

"Why don't you tell her yourself?"

He lay down the galley he was reading and leaned back in his chair.

"Because I'm the Chief and I told you to tell her."

I burst out laughing. "Okay, Chief." I gave him a quick salute and headed home.

When I got there, the door only opened enough for me to squeeze through.

What the hell?

"Your trunk arrived," Edna said, coming down the hall and standing behind it, arms crossed.

"So I see," I said. My large black steamer trunk lay on the floor between the door and the stairs. "Why didn't you have the delivery men bring it upstairs to my room?"

"They would have expected a tip to do that, and I don't have money to throw away on your behalf. Especially if, as I suspect, you plan on finding another place to live."

"I would have paid you back even if I didn't live here anymore. And yes, I am looking for another place to live. But there's still the problem of how to get this upstairs."

"I don't know, dear. I'm sure you'll think of something. Maybe one of your *gentlemen friends* can help."

"Speaking of them, I saw Jimmy today, and he told me he had called a couple of times and left messages for me. Why didn't you tell me?"

"I'm not your secretary, you know. I guess his calls just slipped my mind."

"If I leave a notepad by the phone, you think you could jot down any messages for me or Maureen in the future?"

"Maureen doesn't have all kinds of men calling here looking for her. She's not that type of girl."

"And what type are you implying I am?"

"I surely don't know. All I know is that you've only been in town a short while and you already have at least two men calling here. Goodness knows how many others you meet wherever it is you go. And since you never tell me where you'll be, I can only think they're not the type of places a decent young lady should be."

"Wait one minute—"

"Oh good, you're home," Maureen said, coming down the stairs. "Want help getting your trunk up to your room?"

I took a deep breath before I answered Maureen. I didn't want to offend *her*.

"Thanks, but Jimmy's coming over tonight. I'll ask him to help me."

"I don't allow men upstairs," Edna said. "I told you that before you agreed to rent here."

"Oh, for Pete's sake." My voice was reaching the screaming level. "He's only going to help me carry the trunk upstairs. He's not moving in."

"Well, I never . . . the very idea."

Bringing myself under control, somewhat, I said through gritted teeth, "If it would make you feel better, you can sit in my room to chaperone us."

Maureen covered her mouth in an attempt to hide the smile peeking out between her fingers. "I'll go set the table," she said. She wiggled between Edna, the staircase, and the trunk, and headed to the kitchen.

Edna's face was as red as a furnace, and I could almost see steam pouring out of her ears. Her eyes bored through me like an auger. "That won't be necessary. I can see you just as well from the bottom of the stairs."

"It's your house," I said. "Do what you like."

I went upstairs to wash up before dinner and splash some cold water on my face.

The situation was becoming more intolerable by the hour. How was I going to get through dinner with her? Why was she being so mean to me? All over one missed meal? There must be something else I'm not aware of. All I knew was that I was having a hard enough time trying to keep my head above water at work. I didn't need to come home to a war every day.

I went down to the kitchen, feeling a little calmer.

"Can I help?" I asked, not addressing anyone in particular.

"Sure," Maureen said. "You can get down the big vegetable bowls and the meat platter."

Edna stood at the stove, her back to me, never saying a word.

I got the dishes and brought them to the counter. Maureen spooned the beans and potatoes into them, and Edna placed pork chops on the platter. I carried each dish to the table, got a pitcher of water from the fridge, and waited for them to join me before I sat down.

Edna came to the table, filled her plate, and said, "I'll be in my sewing room if you need me."

"Edna," I said, "please don't. This is your house. If anyone should leave the table, it's me. I'd prefer it if we could forget all that's happened, but if not, I'll eat in my room."

Edna hesitated a minute, then sat down. I filled my plate and pushed my chair back.

"Stay where you are, Alex," Edna said. "There's no reason why you should have to eat in your room like an animal. We won't discuss what happened again."

I wanted to ask if that meant I'd get any future messages, or if Jimmy could help with my trunk, or both, but I decided not to rub salt in the wound.

"So," Maureen said, "what's the front-page story tomorrow?"

Thank goodness for Maureen, the peacemaker.

I told them about the cancellation of the rodeo and asked if either of them knew any ranchers who bred bucking horses.

"The Crazy Moose is in Rosebud, where I'm from," Maureen said. "But that's too far for a bike ride."

"Great," I said. "I wonder if Lou would let me use his car. Or maybe Joe. He's always visiting the ranches around here."

And he owes me after the Ferguson incident.

I decided to stop back at the paper that night and leave a note on Joe's desk. After all, he said I should do that if I needed anything.

"Oh, Maureen, I almost forgot. Lou said to tell you you're doing a great job."

"Thanks, Alex. But why didn't he tell me himself?"

"Because he's the Chief," I said in a deep voice, "and he told *me* to tell *you*."

We both laughed at my imitation of Lou.

That burst the uncomfortable bubble that had enveloped the table. Maureen told us about some of her teenage students' antics. I wondered if I'd ever been that silly. Probably, but at the time I'm sure I thought I was clever.

After dinner, Maureen and I cleaned up and chatted more about our day. Edna, as usual, retreated to the living room and turned on the radio.

"Have you thought any more about moving?" Maureen asked.

"I have, and I don't think I have a choice, especially after today. It's pretty obvious Edna doesn't approve of me, or my lifestyle. She just doesn't understand that a newspaperman has to go places and do things to get a story that might seem unseemly to some people. And I'm sure I'm not going to change her mind about that."

"I know," Maureen said. "I guess I'm not much help. I lead such a boring life I could be Edna's age. All I do is go to work, come home, eat, and grade papers. Talk about your spinster schoolmarm. That's me."

"It doesn't have to be that way, you know. You told me you had some friends here who are nurses. Why don't you go out with them?"

"Where?"

"I don't know. Where do they go? Movies? Dinner? A speakeasy?"

"A speakeasy? That would never do. Can you imagine one of my students' parents seeing me? It would be all over town that I was a drinker. And you know the unwritten moral code for teachers forbids that."

I stopped washing the pan. "Are you kidding? It's the twentieth century, not the eighteenth. Women are working and doing all kinds of things that society never imagined they were capable of doing. And I'm sure a lot of them stop for a beer on payday—in a speakeasy. Besides, if a parent sees you there, they have to be there, too. What's good for the goose . . ."

"Oh, Alex, I wish I could be as free and independent as you are. I guess I'm stuck in my ways. Small towns are gossip mills, and I can't imagine my principal would approve of me drinking in public."

"Well then, it's high time he got over his puritanical views. How about you and me go out for a drink together tomorrow after work? You'll be at the paper then and we can stop at Pete's speakeasy on our way home. He makes sure everyone is well behaved there. We'll sit at a table and have one drink. It'll get your feet wet, so to speak."

"I don't know."

"Think about it. You can let me know tomorrow."

I had just finished putting the dishes away when I heard the doorbell ring.

"Oh, hello," I heard Edna say. "Can you squeeze through?"

"I can manage."

"Gee, it's Jimmy, and I haven't combed my hair or fixed my makeup. I probably look a mess," I said.

"I'll keep him in the living room while you run upstairs," Maureen said. "Don't be long."

CHAPTER 35

"Be careful," Edna said. "I don't want my wallpaper torn."

"Don't worry, Mrs. Lynch," Jimmy said. "I've got an idea. Alex, do you have a blanket or towel?"

"This isn't my house, Jimmy. I only rent a room," I said, staring at Edna.

"I'll get a blanket," Edna said.

A minute later, she waddled down the hall carrying an old plaid blanket. "Here you are."

Jimmy draped it over the trunk. "There. That should pad the corners."

"How clever," Edna said, beaming her approval.

"Ready?" I asked, rolling my eyes. We each grabbed an end of the trunk and manhandled it up the stairs and into my room. Edna stood at the foot of the staircase and watched.

I thought about slamming the door shut, but then thought better of that idea. Jimmy didn't need the drama that would create.

"Where do you want it?" Jimmy asked.

"Right here is fine," I said. "I just need to be able to get in and out of bed and open the closet door. Thanks, Jimmy."

"Guess you're all set then. Ready to leave?"

"More than ready."

Seeing Edna still standing at the foot of the stairs made my blood boil.

I flew down the steps, grabbed my coat, hat, and purse, and was out the door before Jimmy was halfway down the staircase. I needed to get out of there before I exploded.

"Hey, hold on," he called.

I was three houses away before he hit the sidewalk. I waited for him to catch up.

"Where's the fire?"

"You have no idea what's been going on in that house the past two days."

"So, tell me. We came out to talk tonight, didn't we?"

"Yeah, but I think you wanted to talk to me. You didn't plan on listening to me moan and groan about Edna."

"We can do both. You don't have a curfew, do you?"

"Not that I'm aware of, but I'll hear about it tomorrow if I do."

"Then let's take advantage of our curfew free night tonight."

He took my hand and I slowed down to something less than a fifty-yard dash.

I asked him if we could stop by the paper, and explained why. "It'll only take a minute."

"Sure, then we'll go for a beer, okay?"

"Umm, could we also swing by the college? I didn't get a chance to go there today, and I want to check the bulletin board for apartments for rent, or see if someone's looking for a roommate. They have night classes, so there won't be a problem getting into the building."

"Whoa. This sounds serious. Maybe we should have left your trunk downstairs."

"Believe me, if I hadn't moved it, I think Edna would have thrown it away. It's safer in my room. For now, anyway. Thanks for helping me."

"That's what friends are for."

At the paper, I ran inside, scribbled a note to Joe, and we headed to the college. I scoured every notice on the bulletin board while Jimmy looked through their newspaper.

"Anything?" I asked.

"Nope. You have any luck?"

"Nothing. I can't believe no one's looking for a roommate."

"It's not the best time of year for that. It's March. The semester's almost over. Nothing's going to be available until May or June."

"Swell. What am I supposed to do until then? I can't stay at Edna's."

"Let's get a beer and you can tell me what's going on."

Jimmy grabbed my hand and led me away from the one place where I thought I might find a new home.

We went to Pete's place again. I didn't know if it was the only speakeasy in town, but it was comfortable there. I waved to Pete and headed for a table while Jimmy got our beers.

"Okay," he said, setting the glasses down, "what's the story with you and Mrs. Lynch."

I told him what had happened over the past two days. How I let her get to me, and how I told her I was looking for another place to live.

"Lost your temper, huh?"

"I sure did. And now I'm in a real pickle. I've got to find another place to live, and quick. Half the time I just want to throw something at her."

"You'd better rein in that temper or you'll wind up in jail for the night. And I don't think you'd like those accommodations either."

"Probably not."

Jimmy took a sip of his beer and stared off into space.

I realized I wasn't being fair. He had asked me out to talk and instead I was crying on his shoulder.

"Got it!" he said.

I jumped. "You scared the pants off me. What are you yelling about?"

Jimmy's shouts stirred up the men at the bar, and now they stared at us, mumbling complaints about young people not knowing how to behave.

"Sorry, fellas," Jimmy said. "Didn't mean to disturb you."

They grumbled some more, but went back to their drinks and their solitude.

"Now, what are you yelling about?" I whispered.

"I thought of a place for you. The Hamm's Tourist Court."

"Where?"

"You must know it. It's right down the street from Mrs. Lynch's house. You probably pass it every day."

"Oh, sure. I know the place. It looks kind of seedy, though."

"You're right. It's not fancy, but it's cheap, and you can stay there until something else comes along. I think the rooms have hot plates, so you can make coffee and something to eat. You won't starve, anyway. The bad thing is, I think there's only a community shower room."

"For men and women?"

"No, no. One for men, one for women."

"Oh. Well, that might be okay."

Jimmy grinned at me like he had discovered Utopia and laid it at my feet.

"I guess I can live with it for a few months. Anything is better than facing Edna at the end of every day. When do you think I should go see about a room?"

"I'd wait until tomorrow, when you don't have beer on your breath."

"Good idea." I took another sip of my beer. "What did you want to talk about?" I asked.

"Oh, yeah. I almost forgot. I spoke to a guy at the American Legion and he said since Cooper Union was tuition free, they'd pay for my books and fees, and I'd still get a stipend."

"That's swell, Jimmy."

"You bet it is. I filled out the school's application as soon as I got off the phone. Now I have to wait to see if Cooper Union accepts me. But I'm sure they will. I've got so many plans in my head, I know I'll be able to complete any project they send."

"Imagine. In a few months, you might be living in New York City, studying to be an architect. I wish I could live there. Imagine working for the *New York Times*. Boy, that'd be swell." Dreams of running around that big city, chasing stories, writing prize-winning articles filled my head.

"Alex? You still with me? For a minute, you looked like you floated away somewhere."

"Sorry, I was dreaming about what it'd be like to live in New York City."

"I can't think about anything else. I want this so much. Imagine seeing all those skyscrapers and museums. All the places you see in the movies."

"Gee."

For a few minutes, we both drifted off, imagining life in the biggest city in the world.

"You two want another?" Pete called over to us. "This ain't a public park, you know."

Jimmy's face turned red and I'm sure mine matched his.

"Sure," he said. "Okay, Alex?"

"Definitely. We have to celebrate, don't we?"

"We can't celebrate yet. I haven't been accepted."

"That doesn't matter. We can celebrate the fact that you've applied. You're on your way out of this one-horse town. I can feel it."

Jimmy glowed as he walked to the bar to collect our beers.

CHAPTER 36

The next morning, I awoke feeling better than I had in a couple of days. I had a plan, or maybe a couple of plans.

As I walked into the newsroom, Joe said, "Finally showed up, did you? I wondered how long I should wait."

"Guess you got my note."

"Sure did. I'm usually on the road about two hours by now," he said, flourishing his pocket watch.

"Sorry. I thought you'd let me know when I could go with you. I didn't expect it would be this morning."

"No time like the present. Ready?" he asked, striding to the door.

"Sure." I followed Joe to his car. "Where exactly are we going?"

"You said you wanted to talk to some bronc breeders, right? That's where we're headed."

"Anyone in particular?"

"Does it matter?"

"I guess not. I just want to be sure it's one of the breeders who raises rodeo broncs."

"They all do, Alex. The rodeo is their payday."

On our way to the first ranch, Joe told me about buyers who would come to the rodeo specifically to buy broncs. There was a lot more to it than I imagined. That day, we stopped at three ranches and I got an education on breeding and selling bucking horses.

"I bet a lot of people don't know what goes into raising these champions," I said to Joe on our way back to town.

"Probably true. Even a lot of cattle and bull ranchers don't know much about horse raising. You should ask your friend, Adam, what he knows. That'd give you an idea of what you could write about that's new. Not the same old stuff everyone knows."

"Does *everyone* in this town know I've had a date with Adam?"

"Probably."

Why can't I get a break like Jimmy and leave?

"That's infuriating."

"Nope. That's small town life. I'm sure it was the same in Jericho Flats."

"If it was, I don't remember it. Or maybe I never paid attention to the town gossip."

Joe chuckled.

Back in the newsroom, I wrote my first article on "What It Takes to Raise a Rodeo Champion." Even though Joe had aggravated me, talking about my date with Adam, I liked his idea about the differences between raising cattle and horses.

I'll call Adam tonight and ask if we can talk about it. It'll be a good excuse to see him again, too.

The click-clack of heels on the wooden floor pulled me back from my daydreams of Adam.

"Well, I'm game if you are," Maureen said, standing in front of my desk.

"Game for what?"

"A drink. Remember?"

"Gee, I forgot all about that."

"We don't have to go if you've changed your mind, or you're busy or something."

"No, not at all, especially since you got all gussied up today with high heels and everything. One minute while I get this copy to Lou and we can be off for a night of debauchery."

"You said one drink." The flush that had colored her face after my comments drained away, and she grabbed at the collar of her dress.

"I'm teasing. One drink it is."

I stopped at Lou's office and dropped off the first of my series, then Maureen and I grabbed our things and headed for the speakeasy.

"Fingers crossed there are no parents there today," Maureen said.

"If there are, just walk up to them and say, 'Shouldn't you be heading home for dinner?' Beat them to the punch."

"I couldn't do that! I'd never have the nerve."

"It'd be fun to see what they said back, though, wouldn't it?"

"Alex, you're a rabble-rouser."

"No. Maybe a little mischievous at times."

"A little?"

We laughed, and arm in arm, walked into the bar.

"Alex," Pete said, "nice to see you again. Brought a friend, did you?"

"Sure did. This is my friend and a fellow newspaperman, Maureen."

"Welcome," he said. "What's going on over there? You ladies taking over the paper?"

"Trying to," I said. "Just don't let Lou know."

"So, what can I get you to drink, or are you only here to brighten my day?"

"Maybe I'll have a martini today," I said.

"Going all fancy on me, are you, Alex?"

I shrugged, "Need a change of pace."

"And what can I get you, Maureen? The same?"

Maureen hesitated, then said, "Can I have a highball?"

"A highball it is," Pete said.

"We're going to sit at a table, okay?" I asked.

"Sure, Alex. You ladies make yourself comfortable and I'll bring your drinks over."

"Thanks, Pete."

I led Maureen to a table opposite the bar with a good view of the room.

"There's hardly anyone here," she said.

"We're too early for the evening crowd and too late for the lunch trade. Perfect time for a quiet drink."

Pete brought our cocktails over and Maureen started to relax. While we sipped our drinks, I told her about Jimmy's idea for me to rent a place at Hamm's Court.

"I think that place has a reputation for housing some less than desirable residents," Maureen said. "Are you sure you want to stay there?"

"Hopefully it will only be for a few months, but I'm not sure about anything anymore."

Especially Adam. I haven't heard from him in a while. Maybe he doesn't want to see me again. Gosh, I hope not. I think I'm falling for him.

"Alex?"

"Huh?"

Maureen laughed. "You're a million miles away. Anything you want to talk about?"

"No, just daydreaming. Would you come with me to see about Hamm's Court?"

"Sure, but we'd better make it after dinner. I don't think we'll have time before then."

"That's swell. Thanks, Maureen. You might be the only friend I have in this town."

We spent the rest of our time chatting about where, and what, we would like to do, and be, in the future. I could feel a real friendship growing with Maureen.

"We'd better get going," Maureen said. "Don't want to be late for dinner."

"Heaven forbid."

CHAPTER 37

That night, Maureen and I walked over to Hamm's Court. The run down cabins didn't look very inviting, but the atmosphere was a lot less hostile than Edna's place.

We met Mr. and Mrs. Forster, who managed the court, and their friendly attitude reminded me of my parents. They told me they didn't allow any drunkenness or rowdy behavior. They expected everyone who lived there to be "good Christian folks" who respected their neighbors.

Mrs. Forster showed us an available cabin and then left us alone to discuss it. While it needed paint and general sprucing up, it was clean and had its own bathroom, complete with bathtub with shower. Of course, that made it a little more expensive than the cabins without private baths, but I figured it was worth it. It had a single bed, a dresser with a hot plate on top, a table with two chairs, and a closet. At least I could make coffee in the morning.

"It's not too bad. What do you think, Maureen?"

She looked at me like I had just said the Huns were nice guys.

"You're not really considering moving here, are you?"

"Only until I can find someone who's looking for a roommate, or an apartment I can afford."

"Surely you can come to some kind of peace with Edna, can't you? This is horrid."

"Oh, come on. It's not *that* bad. At least it's clean. And Mrs. Forster provides linen and towels and cleans once a week."

"I don't know. What about the other tenants? Did you get a look at the men lounging around by the office? And the drifters who come and go? I get the shivers just thinking about staying here by myself. Would you feel safe here?"

"I'm not totally naive. I do know how to take care of myself."

Maureen nodded and looked around the room like she was expecting a monster to jump out from under the bed.

"I'll take it. At least I won't have to look at Edna's disapproving face every day when I come home. And I won't have to worry about getting home in time for dinner."

"What *will* you do about dinner?"

"I've been thinking about that. I could make lunch my main meal and eat at the hospital every day. The food's not too bad, and it's cheap. And we have a fridge at the paper so I can keep something there and make a sandwich to bring back here for dinner. I can make this work."

And it will give me an excuse to see Jimmy every day. Or at least a few times a week, depending on the stories I'm working on.

"You can always come to the school and meet me for lunch, too, you know. Well, I guess if you're determined to do this, you should let Mrs. Forster know you'll take the cabin."

"Right. Now, I have to figure out how I'll get my trunk over here."

"Maybe Mr. Forster has a truck you can borrow. I could help."

"That's a great idea. Let's go get this settled."

Back at the office, I paid for a week in advance. Mrs. Forster said she'd bring some fresh towels over and leave them on the bed, and Mr. Forster did have an old truck he said I could borrow. Everything happened so quickly it made my head spin.

In no time, Maureen and I had my trunk in the truck, I packed my valise, said goodbye to Edna, and handed over my key to her house.

"Here's your rent money for the remainder of the month," Edna said, giving me back the unused portion.

"Are you sure?" I asked. "It doesn't seem right. I'm leaving without giving you time to find another boarder."

"What's fair is fair. I don't want you thinking I charged you for room and board you didn't get."

"I wouldn't think that, Edna. I'm sorry it didn't work out. I guess a newspaperman's life is too chaotic to fit into what you're looking for in a tenant."

"Maybe so."

"Hope there's no hard feelings," I said.

"No. I'll just be more careful next time before I offer someone a room in my home."

I shook my head and sighed.

She truly believes I'm the only one to blame here. I don't know how Maureen tolerates her and her self-righteous attitude.

I spent the rest of the night unpacking. My clothes filled the closet and the top two drawers of the dresser. The bottom ones held extra linens and towels.

Mom had packed some of my favorite books, so I climbed into bed and started to read *Jane Eyre*, but fell asleep before the end of the first chapter.

When I woke the next morning, I looked around in a panic.

Where am I? Oh, that's right. I moved last night.

Jane Eyre had fallen to the floor during the night and the lamp on the night table was still lit. I jumped into the shower, then rummaged around trying to locate underwear, socks, and something to wear to work. Since my trunk took up most of the floor space, I had to maneuver around it to get dressed.

Maybe Mr. Forster has a shed where I could store it. I'll ask him on my way to work.

I stopped by the office and asked about storing my trunk. Mrs. Forster said I could keep it in the tool shed, but she didn't guarantee its safety. That wasn't very comforting, so I decided to stand it on its end and shove it into a corner.

CHAPTER 38

A few days later, I had settled into a new routine. After checking in with Lou, I would stop by the mayor's office, the sheriff's department, the city court, and the county court. There was always at least one interesting item I could develop into a story, even if they weren't front-page newsworthy. Then it was off to the hospital for lunch and a visit with Betty, who was still waiting to be discharged.

My lunch dates with Jimmy had become part of my routine. Soon after moving to my new home, on a day when I stopped by the hospital to visit Betty, I told Jimmy I'd be eating lunch there as often as possible.

"That's great. Look, if you can come later, we could eat together. I have to work the regular lunch shift, but I could ask to have lunch around two o'clock. If you can wait that long to eat, you could visit Betty before, or after lunch."

"Of course I can wait until two to eat. I'm not *that* obsessed with food, am I?"

"Seems to me you're always hungry."

"I'll eat a big breakfast."

And so, Jimmy and I started our daily lunch get-togethers. We talked about everything under the sun, but especially about our dreams for the future. He was still waiting for his assignments from Cooper Union, and I was still waiting for the one story that would bounce me out of Sunset Valley and into the big-time papers. We went to the movies whenever a new release interested us, always stopping for a beer afterward to wash the salty popcorn taste from our mouths. A quick chaste kiss ended the night.

No more steamy kissing sessions until I figured out where I wanted this relationship to go. For right now, I enjoyed having a male friend to talk to. I had lots of male friends in college, and I missed the easy banter and teasing that never seemed to happen with female friends.

But today I was having lunch with Betty. I had brought my meal upstairs so we could eat together, a special dispensation from Sister Marcus.

"I don't know why my doctor won't let me go home," Betty said.

"Maybe it's because there's no one to take care of you once you leave here."

"Maybe."

"Have you even started walking around on crutches yet?"

"A couple of steps, but this half-body cast makes it almost impossible to use them. I'm just sick of being here. I want to go home and eat a decent meal." She speared a green bean, looked at it, and tossed it back on the plate. "This food's disgusting."

"It's not so bad. Reminds me of my college cafeteria."

"Exactly. They're all the same. Institutional meals. Ugh."

"Have you heard from your family? Can someone come stay with you for a while?"

"My sister said she could probably come for a week, but that's it. I don't know what'll happen when she leaves. If I could walk, I'd manage on my own. Maybe I'll get used to the crutches. I don't know." She threw her fork down onto the tray, a disgusted look on her face.

"Almost forgot," I said. "I brought some new books. I left them at the reception desk. I didn't think I could carry them and my tray upstairs."

"Thanks, Alex. I do appreciate your visits and all, but don't feel you have to come by every day."

"I have to eat lunch somewhere, and this place is probably the cheapest in town. Besides, I enjoy talking to you."

"So, tell me, what's happening with Adam? Are you sweet on him?"

"I don't know what's happening. I haven't heard from him since my day at the ranch."

"Familiarity breeds contempt?" Betty asked with raised eyebrows.

I shrugged. *She doesn't have to be nasty about it.*

"I'd better go," I said. "I'm still working on my weekly series about bronc and bull breeders."

I pedaled back to the office thinking about my series.

Adam never called me back about that. Have I done something to make him mad? Other than proposition him, of course. He couldn't be mad about that, could he? He should be flattered.

Back in the office, I put a fresh sheet of paper into my typewriter to write up some local news. Before I'd finished the first paragraph, the newsroom door burst open and someone stomped across the floor and pulled me out of my chair. Strong arms wrapped around me in a vise-like grip. I smelled ranch dirt, cattle, male sweat, and aftershave before I realized it was Adam.

"What's the matter?" I asked. "Is everyone at the ranch all right?"

"Are you okay? Where have you been? Why haven't you answered my calls? Thank God you're all right. Don't ever do this to me again."

Our questions lapped over one another, and our eyes searched each other's faces until our lips pulled together, like magnets to an iron bar.

"I've been a wreck," he said.

"Adam, slow down," I said. "As happy as I am to see you, I don't know what you're yammering on about."

He held me at arm's length.

"You didn't return any of my calls. And when I called early this morning, hoping to get you before you left for work, Mrs. Lynch said you'd moved."

"I did."

"I asked her where you went but she said she didn't know. She told me you came home from work one night with whiskey on your breath and said you were leaving. And you didn't say where you were going. She wasn't even sure you were still in town."

"That witch. How could she be so mean?" I trembled with fury. "She knew where I went. I can't believe she's that spiteful."

"She knew?"

"Of course, she knew. I even asked her to give any mail that came for me to Maureen and I'd get it from her. I could wring her neck. Why, I could . . ."

I threw my notepad across the room and knocked the canister of pencils off Joe's desk and onto the floor.

"What the hell is going—oh, Adam, hello," Lou said. He stood at his office door and looked back and forth between the two of us.

"Hi, Lou," Adam said. "Sorry to cause a disturbance. Seems there's some confusion around here."

My face burned with rage. "No confusion. Just outright lies and vindictiveness."

"I'll leave you two kids to it," Lou said, and slunk back to his desk.

"Now he probably thinks we've had some kind of lovers' fight," I said between clenched teeth. I ran my fingers through my hair, exasperated at the way this day was going.

"Lovers?" Adam asked. "Is that what we are, Alex?"

Not sure what I saw in his beautiful blue eyes, I didn't know how to answer him.

"I think it's what I'd like us to be," I said, so softly Adam had to lean in to hear me.

He grinned an almost beatific smile. "Me too."

He strode across the room to Lou's office.

"Hey, Lou. Okay if I steal your ace reporter for a few minutes?"

"Sure, sure," Lou said, waving him away and never looking up from his typewriter. "Just make sure you return her."

"Promise, Lou."

Adam wove his way back through the empty desks, grabbed my hand, and pulled me out of the building.

"Where are we going?"

"For a walk. And you're going to tell me what this is all about. Then we'll get a few things straight between us."

"I see. Then, Mr. Caveman, will I be allowed to return to my job? To actually do what I get paid to do?"

Adam turned, and with a mischievous grin, said, "Maybe. Or maybe we can find a more enjoyable way to spend the afternoon."

My heart raced, and my face heated up.

We headed to Williams Park, found a bench, and I told Adam the whole sordid tale of my life with Edna, and where I was living now. He listened, and shook his head.

After a few quiet minutes, he said, "So, you went out with Jimmy again, huh? And you two have lunch together every day now?"

"He's my friend," I said. "And it's not every day. Just most days."

I bristled with the implication of Adam's question. Given his attitude, I had no intention of telling him about the occasional movies and beers we shared.

"Does *he* know you're just friends? I bet he thinks you're more than that."

"I don't think so."

Adam raised one eyebrow, pushed his hat back on his head, and sighed.

"Don't be a jerk, Adam. That night, he wanted to tell me about his VA benefits and applying to Cooper Union. That's all. I have to eat lunch somewhere, and the hospital is better, and cheaper, than eating alone at the café."

I crossed my arms and looked away.

"I doubt that's how Jimmy sees it, but I don't want to fight, so I'll drop it."

"Good."

I refused to look at him. Instead, I watched the first robins of spring hop around. I loved the way they tilted their heads to listen for underground sounds before poking their beaks through the dirt to catch a meal.

I felt Adam's arm snake across my shoulders.

"Hey," he whispered in my ear. "Mad at me?"

All I really want to do is grab you and kiss you, but I refuse to let you off the hook that easily.

"I'm not sure."

He pulled his arm away and stood. "Guess I'll go home then." He turned and walked away.

"Wait a minute."

He stopped and waited. I let out a deep breath and said, "I'm not mad." His smile made my heart skip. "But I have every right to see my friends whenever I want. And *you* don't have the right to say I shouldn't."

He walked back and sat down.

"Look, I know I can't get to town as often as either of us would like, but the ranch is very demanding of my time. Especially in the spring, when we have to get the cattle down from the winter fields, brand the new calves, and repair any buildings damaged during the winter. I don't expect you to sit home every night twiddling your thumbs, waiting for me. I wasn't trying to say you shouldn't see Jimmy, or anyone else you want to.

"But I know Jimmy. A lot better than you do. And I've never known him to have a girl as a friend. Hell, he hardly has any men friends since he came back from the war. But, he's *my* friend, and I don't want to see him get hurt. If you want to see him, that's fine with me. Just make sure he understands that you're his friend, not his girlfriend. Don't let him fall for you, Alex. Unless that's what you really want."

"No. I don't want that. And I think you're wrong. I'm pretty sure he only thinks of me as a pal."

"You don't think you might be leading him on just a tiny bit? Or maybe you're leading the two of us on. Is that it? Always keep one on the sidelines?"

I wanted to smack him, but instead I poked him in the chest with each word as I said, "You are the most infuriating and exasperating man I've ever met. How can you say that? How can you even think that? You're a first-class idiot if you can't see the way I feel about you."

His face changed from wide-eyed wonder at my tirade to a peaceful, contented grin.

"Are you done?"

"Oh, I'm done, all right—"

Before I could say another word, he enveloped me in his strong arms and kissed me so tenderly I felt my insides melt. I rested my head against his chest. I would have been happy to spend the rest of the day there.

"I guess you have to go back to work," he said, his words muffled in my hair, his breath grazing my cheek.

"Mmm. I guess," I mumbled into his chest.

Neither of us stirred.

"Look," he said, straightening up and lifting my chin to look at me, "how about this? You finish up at work and we'll go grab a quick dinner. I have a couple of things to do while I'm in town—Martha gave me a list—and I want to see where you're living. I don't like the idea of you staying at Hamm's Court, but," he held up his hand to stop my interruption, "I'll reserve judgment until I see it for myself."

"I haven't fixed it up yet or anything like that."

"I just want to see where you're living."

"Okay."

"Tell you what. You meet me at Pete's place when you're done with work and we'll go from there, okay?"

I nodded my head, gave him a quick kiss, and hurried back to the paper.

I didn't know what to think about anything. Had he, in his quiet way, told me he loved me? Had he hinted he didn't want me dating anyone else? What if he didn't like my cabin? What did he intend to do about it?

I walked away still confused about Adam and our relationship. And even more confused about what I wanted to do with the rest of my life.

CHAPTER 39

That night over dinner, we decided we would see each other as often as possible, given Adam's responsibilities at the ranch and mine at the paper. I had no idea how this would work out, but I wanted to give it a try. I knew I felt differently about Adam than any of the college men I had dated. Whenever he left me, an emptiness enveloped me. A lost feeling overcame me, and I felt like I was only half a person.

I agreed to make sure Jimmy knew we were pals and nothing more, although I wasn't quite sure how I was going to do that. My insides quivered with thoughts about the future of my newly formed relationship with Adam. But where did I want it to go? How could I become a lead reporter for a big city paper and be Adam's girl at the same time? Maybe neither would work out. Then where would I be?

"Ready?" Adam asked. He counted out bills to pay the check and stood. "Sure."

"Let's go see where you're living."

When we got to my cabin I hesitated for a moment, afraid he would hate it just like Maureen had. I took a breath, dug out my keys, and opened the door.

Adam stood on the front step and looked at the chipped paint around the door frame and windows. He ran his finger down the jamb and paint flaked off the splintered wood. He looked at me with raised eyebrows.

"Are you coming in or not?" I asked.

He took a step into the tiny room, glanced around, and shook his head.

"You can't stay here."

"Oh, really? Would you rather I sleep in the park?"

"Might be better than this dump."

I felt my temper rise.

"It suits my purposes for now. Toward the end of the semester the co-eds will be looking for new roommates and I can move. But this will do until then."

"This won't do for one more day. What were you thinking? Aside from the fact that this place is worse than the abandoned cabin on my ranch, did you happen to get a look at your neighbors? It's not safe here. Drifters like the guys hanging around the office have no qualms about what they do or say, or what anyone thinks about them. They're in and gone before anyone even knows their names. What are you going to do if one of them comes banging on your door at night, stewed to the gills? I guarantee you won't be able to fight him off."

"Mrs. Forster told me she doesn't allow drunks or rowdies to stay here."

"And you believed her? She'll let anyone stay who has the price of a room. And some of these traveling men seem fine until they get some whiskey in them."

"You might be right, but I can't go back to Edna's, and after my experience with her I don't know if I want to rent a room in anyone else's home again."

"Did you ask Pete about a place to stay? Saloons are great places to find out what's going on around town."

"I know that. But I can't keep running to Pete every time I'm in a jam."

"Why not? He knows more about what's going on in this town than anyone. And he doesn't blab it all over the bar. He's a stand-up guy."

"I know that too. But I should be able to take care of myself."

He patted the bed. "C'mere."

I plopped next to him, fighting to hold back my tears. He placed his arm across my shoulders. "Look, honey, you can't stay here."

He called me honey.

"I'd worry about you day and night, and I'd never get any work done. Come back to the ranch with me. There're plenty of bedrooms. You can have your pick. And Martha would love to have another woman to talk to. She likes you. She could be our chaperone."

"Oh, yeah. That's a swell idea. How do you think I'd get back and forth to work every day? It's too far to ride my bike."

Adam rubbed his chin, deep in thought. "You can use the car. That way, you can pick up supplies for Martha whenever she needs them, and we can see each other every day."

I leaned my head on Adam's shoulder. I didn't know what to do.

"Look," I said, "I'll talk to Pete tomorrow and see if he knows of another place, but until I can find something else in town, I'm staying here."

"You're awfully stubborn," Adam said, and kissed the top of my head.

"I know. But believe me, I can take care of myself."

Adam shook his head and sighed. "Fine. But I'm coming back tomorrow to put a better lock on that door. Even though a grown man could probably knock it down with one good shove. And I want you to call the house every morning and let Martha know you're okay. Deal?"

"Deal." We shook hands, then kissed to make sure we properly sealed our deal.

"I'd better go," Adam said, his voice husky. "This bed is much too inviting."

I threw my arms around his neck. "You sure you want to?"

"I'm sure I don't, which is why I have to." He kissed my forehead and stood. "Can you meet me at Pete's tomorrow after work so I can get that new lock on your door?"

"Okay. Want me to make a couple of sandwiches for us?"

He shook his head. "I'll ask Martha to make a picnic dinner for us. We can eat at your little table there, or maybe outside if it's warm enough."

"Gee, that sounds swell."

"See you tomorrow. Don't forget to call in the morning."

He grabbed his hat from the top of the dresser, gave me a quick kiss, and was out the door.

I had to watch myself. I was really falling for him. I couldn't imagine him wanting to live in a city. And that's what I wanted more than anything. I didn't want to have to choose between love and everything else that mattered to me.

This was becoming messier every day, but I knew I'd have to make some decisions about my life sooner rather than later.

CHAPTER 40

The days went by, one after another, with boring regularity. This little town began to suffocate me. My daily trips to the courthouses became an exercise in futility. My Police Blotter column became more mundane every day. I found it hard to believe that someone was arrested for yelling. Obviously the local deputy took disturbing the peace very seriously. I didn't remember Jericho Flats being this provincial. Maybe I just hadn't noticed.

Adam stopped by a couple of times a week, usually with a basket from Martha, and we ate in my cabin, or walked over to the park if it was warm enough. One Saturday, Adam drove me to Billings where I picked up a few things to make my room homier—some throw pillows and pictures, even an old radio from a pawn shop. Mom had packed an afghan, which now lay at the foot of my bed, and I bought a plant for the windowsill. The room started to look fairly nice. Adam still thought it was a hovel and cringed a little every time he visited.

Pete didn't have any ideas about another place to stay, and there was still a ways to go before the end of the semester. So, for now, I stayed where I was. Maureen and I stopped for a drink about once a week, and she began to feel more comfortable in a bar. She even made plans to meet one of her nurse friends for cocktails one night. A few times, I noticed some men looking her way, but didn't say anything to her. I didn't want to spook her.

One Saturday, Adam and I went to the Palace Theater to see *The Four Horsemen of the Apocalypse* starring Rudolph Valentino. Afterwards, we stopped at Pete's for a beer. The Montana's High School Basketball Tournament, scheduled for the next weekend in Great Falls, was the main topic of conversation.

But the next night, everything changed. It was ten o'clock and I had just turned my radio to the local station, KRJF. I planned on listening to some music while I read, or maybe catch one of the regular radio programs, like "Pioneer Women of Montana." But when the station came on, I heard the following announcement:

"This is a news alert. Mayor Kerns has just issued an evacuation notice to anyone living on the south side of town. Ice jams on the Yellowstone River are causing the water to rise. Flooding has already started in some places and is imminent for the whole town. The mayor has called in all state police, fire, and sheriff department personnel to work overnight to keep track of the rising water."

I shut the radio off.

I was still trying to digest the information from the news bulletin when there was a knock on my door.

"You have a phone call, miss," Mr. Forster said through the closed door.

"A phone call? Okay, just let me slip on my shoes."

"Better make that your galoshes."

I couldn't imagine why I would need them, but I shoved my feet into my rubber boots and walked out of my cabin. Ice-cold water covered my feet and ankles. The courtyard was flooded.

I sloshed over to the office, picked up the phone, and said hello.

"Alex? It's Lou. Better get over to the office right away. It looks like this might get bad. We'll probably have to work all through the night, and maybe tomorrow night as well. Bring whatever you think you'll need for a couple of days. I'm on my way in now. I just hope they haven't blocked off any of the roads yet. Phil's on his way in, too."

"You think it'll get that bad, Lou?"

"That's what the sheriff thinks."

"Okay. I'm on my way." I hung up the phone, thanked Mr. Forster, and headed back to my cabin.

A couple of days?

I wasn't sure what to bring.

Maybe just a change of clothes? Definitely some socks. Oh, and my waders. In fact, I'll pull them on over my dungarees.

I gathered everything together and threw them in a small travel bag. I grabbed a comb and brush, my notepad, pencils, and my purse, and headed for the door. Then I remembered my bike. Since it would be useless as a way to get around, I lifted it into the bathtub in case my room got flooded. I hoped that would keep it from getting completely rusted. I didn't think Adam would appreciate it if I returned a rusted hunk of metal to him.

I headed for Main Street. Even though the water was only a little past my ankles, I could feel the current pushing against my legs and I struggled to keep my balance. At this hour, the streets remained empty. The stores wouldn't open until tomorrow morning, if any of them opened at all.

As I walked, I heard distant rumbling. It didn't sound like faraway thunder that comes in waves. This was constant, only the intensity changed.

When I realized the noise I heard was the ice breaking up, the huge floes smashing into one another, a shiver passed through my whole body. We had small jams once in a while in Jericho Flats, but the last one was a long time ago, and I had forgotten how they sounded.

I reached the building sometime before 11:00, and saw it looked fine above the third step, but I knew the basement would be a mess. Once inside, I pulled my waders off and took a look around. No one was there yet. I decided to call Adam and let him know where I'd be for the next couple of days. He lived far enough away that he wouldn't be affected by this, I hoped.

As soon as I got him on the line, I told him what was going on in town. Of course, he had a plan to bring me back to the ranch and out of danger.

"I'll hitch up the horse trailer and drive in as far as I can, then ride the horses the rest of the way," he said. "I'll bring Midnight for you."

"I don't know if that's such a great idea," I said. "The current's pretty strong, and you won't be able to see any holes in the road. And there's going to be lots of things floating around, too. Walking over here I saw some trash and items left outside the shops bobbing past me in the water. You don't want one of your horses going lame."

"Hell, no."

"Then stay where you are. I'm fine. I'm at the paper and it's dry here. The presses may be underwater, but I'm not going down there to check on them."

"Promise me you won't do anything stupid."

"Like what?"

"Like decide to tramp around town to get this story."

"That's my job, Adam. I can't promise I won't. Stop worrying. I can take care of myself."

I could hear him push his breath out. "You are the most stubborn, frustrating woman I have ever met."

"I'll take that as a compliment."

"It wasn't meant as one."

"I know. Oh, the other phone's ringing. I've got to go. I'll call you later today, if I can."

I hung up before he could issue any more orders that I would ignore.

I fielded the incoming calls as best I could. Pat called to say she wouldn't be in; she didn't want to risk it. Joe called and said he'd try to get in, but wasn't sure he could make it.

Phil was the next to call. He wanted to reassure me he'd definitely be in, even if he had to row a boat or swim the whole way.

"Meantime, Alex," he said, "there's a red switch to the basement pump at the top of the stairs. Go see if you can find it and turn it on. I'll wait."

I hurried to the staircase, found the switch, flipped it, and heard the pump motor come to life. The noise was as bad as the ice breaking.

"Got it, Phil," I said when I got back to my desk.

"Terrific. That's all you can do for now. I'll turn the fans on as soon as the water goes down. Lou on his way?"

"I hope so. He said he'd figure out some way to get in."

"He lives on the other side of town, but if he's not in by the time I get there, I'll go get him."

"Okay. See you later."

I hung up, not sure what to do with myself.

I called the mayor's office to find out what was going on. Nothing but a busy signal. I didn't really think I'd be able to get through. Everyone in town was probably trying to talk to him.

I started to write the first paragraph of what I knew would be the front-page story, mostly guesswork, since I didn't have all the facts.

"Oh, well, it's a start," I said out loud. I wanted to hear something besides the sucking noise from the basement and the occasional crash of debris hitting the building.

I went to the window to see if anything had changed. That's when a wooden crate the size of a car floated past.

"Geez! I hope this building's solid," I said out loud, hoping the sound of my own voice would help calm my jitters.

With nothing else to do, I wrote down everything that floated past. Somehow, it could all become part of my story.

I paced the office. I looked out the window. I checked the water level in the basement. It looked like it was going down a little. I called City Hall, again. Nothing but a busy signal. I read yesterday's newspaper. I scoured every nook and cranny, looking for something to read. At last, success! I found an old copy of *The Sea Hawk* buried under a pile of newspapers in Lou's office. It wouldn't have been my first choice, but it was better than staring at the wall. As it turned out, the adventure story captivated me completely.

"Anybody here?"

I jumped from my chair, dropping the book on the floor.

"Sorry, Alex. Did I scare you?" Phil asked.

I took a deep breath. My hands trembled as I picked up the book.

"Scared me to death," I said, my voice quivering voice. "How'd you get in so quietly?"

"Don't know. Must be these boat shoes. How's the basement look?"

"Last time I checked, the water seemed to be going down, but not by much. I don't know how effective the pump will be since the water level outside keeps rising."

"You're right. Of course. I don't know why I thought I could drain the basement when the water's still coming in. I might as well shut the pump off before it burns itself out."

"Where will we print the paper?"

"Hmm . . ." Phil rubbed his hand up and down his face. "I'll call the *Forsyth Independent* and see if they'll run a special edition for us. The logistics of how we'll do that, and get the paper distributed, will be tricky. But, hell, we've got all night to work that out. What'd you write so far?"

My jaw dropped. "Uh, nothing."

"Nothing! Why not? This is a big story, Alex."

"I know that, but I don't know any details except that the ice jam is causing the flood."

"Well, get the lead out and find out what else you can about it."

"How do you suggest I do that?"

"I don't know. Maybe get a boat and go somewhere where you can see what's going on. Use your noggin, Alex. This is no time to sit around with your feet up, reading a book."

Phil stomped off to the basement.

Who does he think he is, ordering me around? He's not my boss.
And I didn't have my feet up.

I thought about where I could see the river without going right to the water's edge.

I had it. The high school! I phoned Edna's house.

CHAPTER 41

"Hi, Edna. It's Alex Lawson."

"Hello, dear," she said, a chill in her voice.

"Sorry to call so late. Hope I didn't wake you. Everything okay at your house? Not flooded, are you?"

"No, Alex, we've been listening to the reports of the flood on the radio. We're all right for now. Although we won't be if the water gets much higher."

"Hopefully, that won't happen. Can I speak to Maureen? Is she there?"

"Of course, she's here. Where else would she be at this hour?"

"Of course."

I waited for Maureen to get on the line.

"Hi, Alex. Are you all right? Is there something I can help you with?"

"Do you have a key to the school?"

"Sure, all the teachers do."

"That's swell. If I can get a boat over to you, will you let me use it? I want to get on the roof and see what's happening."

"Oh, gee, I don't know. I've never been on the roof. I don't even know if I'm allowed to go up there."

"Who's going to know? Please, Maureen. This is for the town. It's the only way we'll know exactly what the situation is."

I clenched my fist and tapped my foot, waiting for her decision.

"Okay, but I have to come with you. And I think we'd better wait until morning. You won't be able to see anything in the dark."

"You're right. Okay, as soon as it starts to get light, I'll see if I can grab a boat, and come over and pick you up."

I hung up before she could have any second thoughts about this escapade.

I went to the basement stairs to let Phil know my plan. He nodded and waved me off, his eyes glued to his presses, their legs covered in water.

Before long, Lou showed up with a basket of food his wife had prepared for us.

I told Lou my plan and he nodded, saying, "Good, good."

Meanwhile, we listened to KRJF. They had a direct feed into the mayor's office and were providing us with the most up-to-the-minute news.

I walked back to my desk, not knowing what I should do. Phil and Lou were discussing how to get the paper printed and what state the presses were in, given the flooding in the basement. For the first time, I felt like an outsider. I wasn't contributing anything to what was going on.

Oh, what the hell. I may as well walk over to City Hall and see if I can get any information that's not being broadcast over the radio.

"Lou," I yelled across the newsroom while I pulled on my waders. "I'm going over to City Hall. Depending on what happens there, I may go straight to the high school before I come back."

"Wait a minute, Alex." He talked quietly to Phil for a minute, then said, "Maybe I should send Phil or go myself."

"Phil? But I'm your lead reporter. You said so yourself."

"Look, Alex, this is probably the biggest story of the year, and you're still green around the gills. Phil was writing lead stories before you were born. I don't know if you can handle a story this big. Reporting on a local shooting and trial is one thing, but this affects the whole town. We could all be wiped out. I think maybe I'd better cover it myself."

"Don't take this away from me, Lou. I can do it. I know I can. I'll call from the mayor's office." I grabbed my notepad and a bunch of pencils and ran to the door.

"Alex, wait! If you're going to be so pigheaded about it, at least take the camera with you and get some shots of the destruction. Bob, our photographer, has already been evacuated, and he's got his family to take care of. We won't be seeing him for a few days." Lou raked his fingers through his sparse hair.

"And don't bother coming back unless you've got a blockbuster story under your belt. I'm not trying to be funny. This is your one shot at staying here. Screw this up and you're on your way back to Jericho Flats."

"It's a deal."

It's do or die, kiddo.

This was the chance I'd been waiting for. I hoped Lou didn't really mean I'd be fired if I messed up this story. But I knew I'd be back on the Community News desk, at the very least. I made a wish to newspaper gods everywhere, grabbed the camera, and headed for the door.

My legs trembled so much I wasn't sure I would get there without falling down. Why did he have to throw in the camera? I didn't really know anything about photography, but, what the hell. I'd taken pictures at home with my Kodak box camera. How different could this one be?

I waded through the muck and mire that swirled through the streets. The water had risen a lot since I'd walked to the paper. It was up to mid-thigh now and the current was stronger. Porch furniture from homes and basket displays the storekeepers left outside floated past. The possibility of any store opening in the morning became more and more unlikely.

"Hey, miss. You okay?" A rowboat pulled up alongside me. "Can I take you somewhere?"

"Am I glad to see you. I was beginning to think everyone had disappeared."

The man chuckled. "'Fraid most people are tucked away and asleep by now. I'd be glad to take you somewhere dry."

"I'm headed to City Hall. Do you know if it's flooded?"

"Should be okay. Don't think the water's gone that far yet. Hop in and we'll see."

"I appreciate the ride."

"Guess that's where all the big bosses are tonight, huh?"

"That's what I'm hoping. I'm a reporter for the *Star*. Maybe somebody there can tell me what's going on. I couldn't get through on the phone."

I stepped into the boat, trying not to capsize it. "I'm Alex Lawson. Want me to row for a while?"

"That wouldn't be very gentlemanly of me, now, would it? I'm fine, and my name's Hank. Actually, it feels good. Been a while since I did this."

"This flood looks pretty serious. I'm from Jericho Flats, and we get ice jams sometimes, but never enough to flood the town."

"You're lucky. Been a long time since we had one like this. Not since 1881."

"From an ice jam?"

"Not sure about that. Before my time. But my dad used to tell stories about it. How all the streets flooded out. 'Course, back then, the raised wooden sidewalks meant most of the shops escaped any serious damage. But you needed a horse or a rowboat to cross the street."

"Gee, that must have been something."

"Seems like nothing compared to this flood. Lots of businesses are going to lose most everything, especially if they use their basements to store goods."

"I never thought of that."

"Here you are, Alex."

Hank pulled the boat as close as he could get to City Hall's front steps.

"Thanks, Hank."

"I'll be around, so if you see me and need a ride, just wave me over."

"I will." I scrambled out of the rowboat, up the stairs, and into City Hall.

The deserted downstairs, quiet as a graveyard, contrasted with the uproar I could hear coming from the second floor. I plodded up the steps. Waders were obviously not meant for indoor walking.

The conference room next to the mayor's office looked like a scene from old newsreel films of the Army's War Offices. Men scurried back and forth with maps and charts tucked under their arms, laying them out on the conference table, one on top of the other. A radio reporter sat at the only desk in the room, talking to someone who, I assumed, was the on-air announcer at the other end.

I grabbed Dot's arm as she hurried past.

"Hey, Dot, any new information for me? Anything other than what KRJF is broadcasting?"

"Alex, I have no idea what they're saying on the radio. If I were you, I'd find an out of the way spot and just listen. That's probably your best bet for hearing anything new."

"Thanks, Dot."

I tucked myself into a corner and tried to decipher what everyone was talking about.

Some of it was engineering stuff I didn't understand, so I decided to ask the radio reporter what he knew. He filled me in as much as he could, but he got lost too when the city engineers started discussing dikes, hydraulic excavators, and other engineering marvels. I tried to ask one of the engineers a few questions, but he wasn't very receptive.

I decided my best bet was to listen, take notes, and bring them back to the office. Maybe Lou or Phil would have a better understanding of what everything meant.

Time passed quickly, and before I knew it the sky was beginning to get light. Even though I hadn't had any sleep, the electric energy in the room kept me wide awake.

I hoped Maureen hadn't changed her mind about letting me into the high school. I said goodbye to Dot and my radio colleague and left the conference room.

Outside, I looked for Hank, or anyone willing to take me on my mission.

"Looking for me?" Hank asked, rowing around the corner of the building.

I grinned like the Cheshire Cat. "You're my knight in shining armor today."

"Jump in."

I settled in and told Hank where I wanted to go.

"The high school, huh? That's a good idea. Mind if I go with you? I'd like to see the river myself."

"It's okay with me."

We chatted while Hank rowed me to Maureen's. On the way, I took pictures with the newspaper camera. I didn't know if I was doing it right, but it didn't seem all that different from my box camera.

Here's hoping.

We passed the "7th Street Auto" garage. Water covered the bottom half of the bay door. The end of Pleasant Street was submerged, and some of the smaller bungalows were already filling up with water. Waves sloshed against the elementary school's front door.

I spotted Maureen on the porch at Edna's house.

Hank pulled up as close as he could, she climbed in, and we headed for the high school.

CHAPTER 42

Luckily, when we got to the school, water covered only the first two steps leading up to the front door. Hank tied the boat to the banister, and we climbed out.

It's amazing how quiet a high school can be when it's empty. It takes on the feel of a ghost town. Deserted desks waiting for someone to sit in them. Silent metal lockers that normally slam and bang with ear deafening regularity. Empty hallways usually teeming with whispered secrets and bravado shouts.

Today, only the squishing sounds of our waders echoed through the building.

We climbed three flights of stairs before reaching the door to the roof.

"I've never been up here before," Maureen said as she opened the door.

"Is there something we can use to prop this open?" I asked, pushing on the outside handle. "Seems it automatically locks once it closes. We don't want to get stuck out here."

We looked around, but didn't see anything.

"I'll go downstairs and get a garbage can or something," Hank said. While he did that, Maureen and I walked to the eastern edge of the roof.

"My God, look at that," she said.

Overnight, the ice had backed up on the Yellowstone River and created the jam. Giant chunks piled on top of each other, and wedged themselves against the bridge. The ice flowing from the Tongue River only made the water rise more, a terrifying yet somehow beautiful sight. The sun, just beginning to rise, cast a silvery blue glow on the ice and made it appear otherworldly. It took a minute for me to snap out of the fascination it held. I never stopped clicking my camera.

Hank returned and the three of us walked around the roof and watched the water swallow up more and more of Sunset Valley every minute. As the sun rose higher in the sky, so did the water on the ground. In a matter of minutes, men could no longer wade through the streets. Boats became the only safe way to get around.

We watched as neighbors climbed out of windows from their flooded homes into rowboats that took them to a safe place. Or, at least, safe for now. Other families, not so fortunate, huddled on their roofs. Houses kept disappearing under the rising waters. It made me wonder if any part of the city would stay dry, or even survive this flood.

"I'd better check on my boat," Hank said. "I'm not sure I left enough slack in the line for it to rise above the water. Didn't expect it to come up this quick."

He hurried downstairs and Maureen and I watched over the roof's edge as he reached the boat and let out more rope. We also noticed a number of boats filled with what looked like evacuees headed for the school.

"Seems we'll have company soon," I said, pointing to the flotilla rowing our way.

"They're smart," Maureen said. "Between this building and the County Courthouse, there should be room for everyone."

I made another tour of the roof, snapping as many pictures as I could. I wished I had brought more film. I had never been in a flood before, and the water's power both excited and terrified me. I knew I should get back to the paper, but I couldn't pull myself away from watching the river invade the town. I saw the water rush over Hubble Street and across 7th Street North. One escape route out of town eliminated.

Hank came back looking dazed.

"I can't believe the way the water's rising," he said. "My truck's gonna be flooded if I don't get back to it soon."

"Gee, I didn't even think about how you got here," I said. "Come on, Maureen, let's go and let Hank rescue his truck before it's washed away."

A horrified look passed over Hank's face. "Washed away?"

"I saw a crate the size of a car float by earlier," I said.

We headed for the stairs. People trickled into the school looking confused, scared, and eerily quiet, except for the stifled sobs behind handkerchiefs. Some still dressed in their pajamas; others had thrown dungarees right over them, not bothering to get properly dressed. Children clutched dolls, trucks, teddy bears, and other assorted toys and looked around in wide-eyed wonder. It was hard enough for adults to comprehend. I couldn't imagine what those kids must be thinking.

I tried to interview some of the people, but most shook their heads and kept climbing to safety. The ones who did stop to answer my questions spoke of everything being ruined, water rising two to three feet up the walls, some even higher. All looked dazed and in shock.

We continued to work our way against the tide of people going up the staircase and made it back to the front door, now at the water's edge.

"Stay here," Hank said. "I'll bring the boat as close as I can."

He waded through the water to the top of the steps leading down to the street. He held on to the banister, the water rising up his body with each step.

As he reached the boat's rope, he pulled it toward him.

"Okay," he yelled, and waited for us to join him.

Maureen and I pushed through the rushing water. Hank helped each of us get into the boat, then untied the rope and jumped in. I had grabbed the oars and began rowing as soon as he pushed off.

"Better let me do that, Alex," he said.

"I've got it," I said. "If we try to change seats, I'm afraid we'll all wind up in the water."

Hank nodded, but didn't look very happy with the arrangement.

"Say, Hank," I said, "I've been thinking."

"Always a bad sign with her," Maureen said, smiling at Hank. But he looked away and squirmed a little in his seat.

"How is it that you appeared exactly when I needed to get around?" I asked.

"I knew this would happen," he said.

"What would happen?"

"I told Adam you'd never believe it was just luck if I kept showing up wherever you were."

"So, Adam sent you to rescue me?" My voice reached a screaming level much louder than necessary to be heard over the rushing water and breaking ice.

"Not rescue, really. Just keep an eye out in case you needed help or anything."

I rowed harder and faster, my temper rising as fast as the water.

"He was only trying to help," Maureen said, always the peacemaker.

"Don't try to placate me, Maureen. Why can't he accept the fact that I can take care of myself? What gives him the right to think I need his protection every time I'm faced with a difficulty? He just had to install his own new lock on my cabin because, obviously, I couldn't protect myself. Or wasn't smart enough to put one on myself. And now, he sends Hank in to help even though I told him I'd be fine. But no. He knows what's best for me."

I took a few deep breaths and tried to calm down.

"Hank, I'll take us to City Hall, then you can row Maureen to the paper and get yourself back to your truck. And tell Adam he can stop sending rescue teams to take care of me. And to not even think about coming to town himself, because I won't be responsible for what I say when I see him."

Hank pulled his hat down further on his forehead and looked away.

Maureen gripped the edge of her bench seat and stared into the puddle at her feet.

Thanks to my feverish rowing, we arrived at City Hall in no time, although it actually wasn't that far away from the school.

"Okay. I'm getting out here. Maureen, can you go back to the office and take the camera with you? I'll call from the mayor's office with the latest developments. Then you or Lou, or *Phil*, can write them up."

"Are you going to be all right?"

"Right as rain," I said, "and Hank?" He looked up from under the brim of his hat. "Thanks for all your help today. You're still my knight in shining armor, even if you were sent by an evil king."

Hank grinned, a little sheepishly, and his face turned rosy red.

"You're welcome, Alex. It was my pleasure. Glad you're not mad at me."

"Mad at my knight? Never."

I climbed out of the rowboat right at the door of City Hall, the steps now underwater.

"See you back at the paper at some point, Maureen."

"Okay. Stay safe, Alex."

I watched as Hank took over the oars and rowed them away.

Now I'd go see how chaotic the situation upstairs had become.

CHAPTER 43

I walked into the kind of pandemonium that only bureaucrats can produce. Everyone issuing directives which no one paid any attention to. Voices talking over voices to rival the Tower of Babel. And amid the chaos, Dot brought fresh cups of hot coffee to replace the cold ones neglected on the conference room table. Between the overpowering smell of coffee and the veil of cigar and cigarette smoke, the room suffocated me.

"How goes the battle?" I asked Dot as she walked by, carrying a tray of cups.

"Oh, Alex, it's a nightmare. I don't know if anyone has a real plan. They all seem to think they do, but so far, nothing's been done."

"Isn't that how government works?"

Dot gave me a half smile and shook her head. A phone rang in the adjacent office.

"Excuse me, Alex," she said, running to answer it.

"Mr. Mayor," Dot called into the conference room, "Frank Cullen's on the line. He says it's urgent."

The Mayor walked to the desk and grabbed the phone. "Frank, what is it?" He listened, nodding his head, then said, "Thanks, Frank. I'll get back to you."

I watched him rub his hand over his face and look out the window for a minute.

"Well, gentlemen," Mayor Kerns said, his voice rising above the clamor as he reentered the conference room, "it's time for some decisive action before Sunset Valley is washed away. It's too late to discuss levees and dams. We need to stop the flooding now, not worry about what we should have done or what we will do in the future. I have more than seven thousand people who live in this city relying on me.

"That was a call from one of our town's flyboys. He just flew his private plane over the area and told me the water and ice floes have crested the Tongue River Dam. That's twenty miles south of here, and upstream. For those of you who don't know, the Tongue River flows north. Frank says from what he could see, the south end of Sunset Valley is already lost. People are sitting on their rooftops, hoping to be rescued. Drowned livestock are floating downstream. We have no choice. We have to bomb the river."

The room erupted. Everyone shouted instructions, praise, questions, doubts, the full gamut of possible responses to his announcement. He ignored them all, walked back into his office, and asked Dot to get Frank back on the line. He spoke to him for a few minutes, then returned to the conference room, now silent as a graveyard. I held my breath, waiting for the mayor's report.

"Frank Cullen says he'll get together with Bob Forest and Tom Flynn. If they can get help from the explosive experts over at the Colstrip mines, they'll load up their private planes, bomb the Yellowstone, break up the jam, and this will all be over."

A round of applause and cheers greeted this announcement.

Now the waiting began. Waiting for the explosive experts to decide on the type of bombs to use. Waiting for the results of the pilot's reconnaissance flight. And while we waited, the water rose.

The phone rang, shattering the funereal atmosphere of the room.

"Frank's got the go ahead," Mayor Kerns said. "They're going to drop 1,500 pounds of dynamite. It won't be long now."

The waiting began anew. Some men paced, others settled in chairs. Dot, with her bottomless urn, continued to supply everyone with coffee. I phoned in the latest happenings to Maureen and Lou, each on an extension, each shouting questions at me. A stark contrast to the stillness of the conference room.

This time we didn't have to wait for the phone to ring. The explosive blast rattled windows. Coffee sloshed over the rims of cups. Everyone cheered.

And we waited. Waited to see the water recede. Waited for the pilots' reports. Waited. Waited. Waited.

But nothing happened.

The massive bombing had cleared a small portion of the ice floe, but not enough to make a difference. The dire situation that everyone thought would end with the blast hung over the town like the sword of Damocles. The below freezing water, slush, and ice still flowed through the city nonstop.

"It's time," Mayor Kerns said. "Dot, get the Governor on the phone."

I had no idea what the mayor had in mind. I snuck over to the doorway to listen in to his conversation.

When the Governor got on the line, Mayor Kerns explained the situation to him, then said, "Send in the Bombers."

With the Governor's approval, the Mayor called the Rapid City, South Dakota, US Army Air Base to ask for their help. Unfortunately, fog enveloped the base, and grounded all flights in the Black Hills area.

Once again, we waited and watch the river rise.

CHAPTER 44

Mayor Kerns told us the US Army Air Force Service's Martin and DH-4 bomber crewmen stood ready to take off as soon as the fog lifted. Although now, a sudden blizzard made flying impossible.

"They're busy loading the planes with as many bombs as they'll hold," the mayor announced to the roomful of people who had worked through the night. Shoulders relaxed. Chain-smoking eased up. Deep breaths echoed throughout the room.

I tiptoed over to a window and opened it a crack, hoping a little fresh air would clear some of the smoke and coffee stench, as well as the odor of nervous sweat.

A few hours later, the ringing phone snapped the tension hovering in the room. The bombers, with full crews, were ready. The planes would drop their cargo over the Yellowstone River and make as many passes as needed until the jam cleared. The Mayor stayed in contact with the Rapid City base and kept us informed of their progress.

At 7:30 that night, Mayor Kerns got word that the planes had taken off.

In minutes, we heard the planes overhead. Everyone rushed to the window. I decided the roof would make a better lookout post. I raced up the stairs in time to see the first plane drop two bombs. I looked around and saw the high school and courthouse roofs packed with people. Soon, men from the conference room came upstairs and joined me. Everyone wanted to watch this unique spectacle.

The second plane flew over and dropped two more bombs. I found out later these were test bombs. They seemed to explode right on target, but nothing else happened. Both planes made two more passes. On each pass, they dropped more bombs. The entire town watched, silently. Their homes, their families, their futures rested on those bombs.

Then, just as I began to lose faith in this experiment, a geyser that would put Old Faithful to shame erupted. Ice, mud, and water exploded 150 feet into the air. A cheer rose from the crowds.

Within an hour, the ice began to loosen and the water began to flow again. Huge chunks of ice crashed into one another, louder than any thunderstorm I had ever heard.

Mayor Kerns and some other city officials made their way to the 7th Street bridge to watch the river's progress.

And the residents of Sunset Valley breathed a collective sigh of relief.

That night, the bomber crew stayed at the Sunset Hotel, and the town treated them to a steak dinner at Range Riders, which miraculously had escaped serious flooding. A mass of people gathered there to thank them.

I squeezed through, trying to find someone to interview.

"Hi," I said, sidling up to one crew member, "I'm Alex Lawson. I'm a reporter for the *Daily Star*. Can I ask you a few questions?"

"Sure. I'm Staff Sergeant Earle."

"Nice to meet you. You guys did a great job today. Thank you for saving our town."

"We were happy to help. You said you had some questions."

"Right. We all expected to hear a huge explosion, but, well . . . nothing. No noise at all. What happened?"

Sergeant Earle chuckled. "We set them to detonate underwater. That way, the only sound you heard was the ice breaking up."

"Gee."

"You know, the jam extended about two miles on either side of the river bend." He looked around the crowd and started to laugh.

"What's so funny?"

"Who's that guy over there talking to Major Cooper?"

"Major Cooper?"

"Our pilot. The one in the middle of all those civilians."

"Oh, the mayor. Mayor Kerns. Why?"

"We watched him and some of the other guys at that table walk onto the bridge. Some really big chunks of ice kept slamming into it. It looked pretty shaky to me, and they scooted off like jackrabbits."

I laughed at the image of the mayor and his entourage running to safety. I asked him a few more questions about the planes, the Army Air Service, and the bombs they used to free up the jam.

I couldn't wait to get back to the paper and write this up. I felt like a little kid on Christmas morning. This could be the scoop I needed to get national attention. The first, and hopefully the only, time the US Army bombed a US city.

I spent a little more time with the crew, then left to get back to the paper. The water had already receded a lot, but I still had to wave a boat over to get back to the office.

"Thought maybe you got swept away in the flood," Lou said when I burst through the newsroom door.

"Just getting all the facts, Lou."

I sat at my desk and started typing furiously. Maureen had written up the background, so all I had to do was pick up from the time the plane took off from Rapid City, South Dakota. Lou left me alone and instead, he haunted Phil, now trying desperately to get the presses working.

By that night, everything seemed to be back in working order, and there was no need to ask another town to print the paper. Although we did have to send to our warehouse for dry newsprint.

Lou decided to put out a special "Midnight Edition." With all of us working together, including a few other employees who straggled in, we pulled it off. The first ever "Midnight Edition" of the *Sunset Valley Daily Star*. Even though everyone had contributed to it, Lou decided I should have the byline, since I had done most of the work, and Phil and Maureen agreed.

My headline spanned four columns:

Flood Waters Reach into City

Lou called it into the wire services as well. This was national news, after all.

CHAPTER 45

As soon as the paper was put to bed, we all crowded into Lou's office for a celebratory drink. Then, one by one, we found places to curl up and catch a nap. Lou stretched out on one of the sofas in his office and I claimed the other one. No one challenged me. Soft and comfortable, I fell asleep right away.

A few hours later, I woke, achy and stiff. I stood and stretched, trying to work out the kinks in my back and neck.

By sunrise, the water level had dropped ten feet and people began returning to their muddy homes. The planes flew a low victory pass over the town and tipped their wings in a silent farewell.

With the water receding, life started to return to the town. I wondered if anything would be salvageable from my cabin. It probably had a couple of feet of water in it before the ice jam broke.

Nothing to do but go and see the damage.

Lou came into his office, wiping a towel across his face.

"Finally awake, Sleeping Beauty?"

"Please don't tell me you've been awake for hours."

Lou chuckled. "Nah. Just woke up myself a few minutes ago. Maureen's still conked out at her desk, and Phil's still downstairs. I have an idea he has a bed hidden away somewhere down there."

"I would have killed for one of those."

"You may have had to do that under other circumstances. But if he does have one, it was well underwater last night. Don't think you would have wanted to sleep in a waterlogged bed."

I shivered a little and grimaced at that image. Lou went to his desk and plopped into his chair. "Alex, much as I hate to say this, we still have a paper to get out, and we need to see how badly this flood has damaged the town."

"I know, Lou. But I'd like to go home and see what my personal damage is first. I have no idea if I'll even have clothes to wear or if they all washed away. And I'd like something to eat."

"We all need that." Lou lit a cigar, stood, rubbed his neck. and began pacing. "You know, considering the circumstances, I think we can skip publishing for a day, especially since we just put out a midnight edition. In all likelihood, everyone's going to be too busy cleaning up to sit and read the paper anyway. Go home, Alex. You did a yeoman's job yesterday. You deserve a break."

"Thanks, Lou. I appreciate it."

"But take the camera with you and snap some pictures of the aftermath, okay? I haven't heard from Bob yet. Who knows what's up with him and his family."

"Sure, that's not a problem. My biggest problem will be finding a place to eat. I'm starving."

Lou shook his head. "Better take Maureen with you." Then he reached into his pocket and grabbed some bills. "My treat," he said, throwing a few dollars on the sofa.

"You're a prince among men."

He waved me out of his office and shuffled through the papers piled on his desk. I headed over to Maureen, still asleep, her head cradled on top of her arms, but stopped dead when the newsroom door burst open.

"There you are!"

Maureen's head popped up, and Lou stood from behind his desk. "Jimmy! What's the matter? What's happened?"

"Nothing's the matter now that I know you're safe." He grabbed me and pulled me close. "I've been worried to death about you." He lifted my chin and kissed me.

He tasted of coffee and something sweet. But when I realized my arms were laced around his neck and my lips were kissing him back, I pulled away.

"Jimmy, wait. I . . . I can't do this. *We* can't do this."

"Why? Because this is your office and it's not a proper place to kiss you? I don't care about all that. I haven't been able to stop thinking about you since the flood started. Now that I know you're okay, I'm not ever going to let you go again."

"Jimmy, we need to talk." I pulled him over to the far side of the room where a few chairs and a table served as our conference room. "Sit down. I'm not sure how we got here, but I don't feel the same way about you that you seem to feel about me."

"What do you mean? We've spent hours together and shared all our thoughts and dreams. Things you only tell people you care for, and who care about you."

"Jimmy, I *do* care about you. As a friend. But that's all. I thought I had made that clear."

Jimmy landed his elbows on the table and held his head in his hands.

"I thought as soon as I get accepted into Cooper Union, because I know I will, your feelings would change. Think of it. We could both move to New York City. I want you to marry me and come with me. You could get a job at one of the big newspapers there. Between my stipend and your salary, we'll be able to have a good life. We wouldn't be rich, not at first anyway, but we'd be married and happy, living in the greatest city in the world. You always said that's what you want, isn't it?"

"Oh, Jimmy. How can this sound so right and be so wrong?"

"Why is it wrong? Marry me, Alex."

By now, tears streamed down my face. I'd never met anyone as sweet and gentle as Jimmy, and I wondered whether I had made the right choice when I chose Adam.

Although probably only a minute or so went by, the silence between us seemed to last for hours.

"At least think about it," he said. "Please."

I nodded my head. "I'll think about it. But I need some time. This flood knocked me for a loop. I don't even know if I have a place to sleep anymore."

"*That* I can solve. You can bunk with my sisters."

"Oh, I couldn't."

"You could. Problem solved."

He stared at me, his eyes begging me to say yes to everything. Like he had solved all the problems in the world, or at least in my world. Maybe he had.

Once again, I was more confused than ever. Jimmy was beer and ball games. Adam was bourbon and business. And in my own way, I loved them both.

"Let me go see what my cabin looks like first."

"Okay. But promise you'll let me know." He grabbed a piece of paper off a nearby desk. "Here's my phone number at home. You know the hospital's number. Call me at one of them and I'll come get you."

I folded the paper and stuck it in my pocket. I didn't think I could talk anymore, so I nodded.

Jimmy stood, gave me a kiss on the forehead, then walked across the room and out the door.

"Wow," Maureen said. "That may be the sweetest guy in Sunset Valley."

"He is." I couldn't tear my eyes away from the door.

This is a fine pickle I've gotten myself into.

"Let's scour up some breakfast. Lou's treat." I said fanning the dollar bills in Maureen's face.

Maureen and I left the building, surprised to see the water levels had gone down a lot. But we still needed our waders.

"Think we'll find anything to eat around here?" I asked.

"Probably not. I imagine all the stores and cafés are still cleaning up. And to be honest, Alex, I should go home and help Edna," she said, as we sloshed through the knee-deep water. "I'm sure she's having conniptions about this flood."

"I'll go with you to Edna's," I said. "I'm sure she could use an extra pair of hands."

"That'd be swell, but don't you want to see about your things first?"

"They won't run away, if they haven't already been washed away. I can at least lend a hand before I go face whatever disaster awaits me."

Maureen threw her arm around my shoulders and gave me a hug.

A few pickup trucks inched their way through the streets, some filled with water-soaked furniture and boxes. I assumed they wanted to get to higher ground where they could spread things out to dry in the sun. Or maybe they planned on unloading them at the town dump. Everyone who passed honked their horns at us and we waved back. The sense of community that comes after surviving a disaster abounded throughout the town that day.

"Alex!"

I heard Adam's shout before I saw his truck.

"Damn." I hoped I could avoid him for a day or two.

His old blue truck crawled through the debris filled street.

"Isn't that Adam?" Maureen asked.

"Yep. Just the person I *don't* need to see right now."

Maureen shook her head and frowned. "You can't put him off forever, so might as well get it over with now."

He pulled up alongside us. "I've been looking for you. Are you okay?" He jumped out of his truck and wrapped me in a bear hug.

"I'm fine. Didn't Hank give you a full report?"

"Yeah, well, about that . . ."

"Yeah, well, nothing. I told you I could take care of myself, but you didn't believe me. No-o-o. You just *had* to send someone into town to watch over me. I'm neither a child nor a feeble old lady, and I don't need a guardian angel. And did he forget to mention that I didn't want to see you? Or did you choose not to believe *that* either? Because, of course, you would know better than me. After all, I'm just a stupid woman, whereas *you* are the brilliant, brave, all-knowing-what's-best-for-everyone man."

Maureen's eyes bulged out of her head and Adam looked shell-shocked. In fact, my vehemence surprised even me. Now that the dangerous floodwaters had receded, I realized I truly resented Adam ignoring my assertions that I'd be all right. After all, I had a job to do. He had to understand that sometimes my career might put me in dangerous situations. I didn't need him, or anyone else, thinking I needed a bodyguard.

"I guess I should have left you alone and maybe let you drown in the flood, huh?"

"Nobody drowned, Adam. Don't be so melodramatic."

"Look, you two," Maureen said, "it's been a long day and night for everyone. Why don't you wait a day before you both say something you'll regret?"

As angry as I was, I knew Maureen was right, even though I didn't want to hear it.

Adam blew out a breath and said, "She's right. We can talk this over tomorrow after you have something to eat and some rest."

"Hah! I don't even know if I have a bed anymore. Or where I'll get something to eat, so I'm not sure *when* we can talk about this."

Adam looked at me like I had just landed here from Mars. "We'll fix all that as soon as we get back to the ranch, of course. What else did you think I meant?"

Now it was my turn to gape at him. "The ranch? I don't think so. I don't want to be stuck out in the middle of nowhere—"

"Oh, so that's what you think about my home?"

"It's not exactly in the middle of town."

"Stop it. Right now. Both of you," Maureen said in her best schoolteacher voice. "Adam, go home for now. You've seen Alex. She's safe. No need to worry. And Alex, we're going to Edna's to help her clean up, then we'll go to your cabin and see what's what there."

Adam looked ready to burst a few blood vessels, and I wanted to continue my barrage, but Maureen's look said she wouldn't brook any dissent. She grabbed my arm and led me down the street. I heard Adam's truck door slam so hard I imagined the old rusty thing crumbling to a dust pile and disappearing.

CHAPTER 46

When we arrived at Edna's house, she was in a tizzy, as I expected. She flitted around from room to room, moving knickknacks from one place to another. Amazingly, her house had escaped serious damage. Raised on stilts, the water level had stayed below the first floor. She'd have to have the stilts and front steps replaced in all likelihood, but that was nothing compared to some of the devastation we had seen on our walk from the paper. Water lines and mud, from one foot to a few feet off the ground, remained on the outside walls of stores and homes. I could only imagine what they looked like inside. And they were further away from the river than Edna.

When Maureen and I told Edna about her neighbors' difficulties, she didn't want to hear it. Instead, she babbled on about her limited finances and how "those people in their big houses" could afford to replace furniture and make repairs.

I rolled my eyes at Maureen and waited for a break in Edna's tirade before saying that I should go and see what my cabin looked like.

"Want me to come and help?" Maureen asked.

Knowing she wanted a reprieve from Edna's monologue about all the upset the flood had caused her, I said, "That would be swell." "Edna," Maureen said, "I'll be back as soon as I can, but would you like me to make you a cup of tea before I leave?"

"Oh, do you have to go? There's so much to do around here."

"Edna, you know perfectly well there's nothing to do here. We both came here to help, but you'll need to get a carpenter to replace the porch steps and someone to look at the foundation stilts. Neither of us can do that. The rest of the house is perfect."

Edna looked around as if to confirm Maureen's assessment or to prove her wrong, I wasn't sure which.

"Edna?" Maureen asked. "Tea?"

"That would be nice," Edna said. She sank onto the couch as if she had just finished a day of hard work in the fields. Maureen pushed me into the kitchen.

"Edna," Maureen called as she filled the kettle, "Alex and I haven't had a thing to eat. Would it be all right if I made us a peanut butter sandwich and a cup of tea?"

Not a peep came from the living room.

"Maybe I should sneak out the back door and be on my way," I whispered to Maureen.

"No need to sneak anywhere," Edna said, appearing in the kitchen and tying on her apron. "I don't know what I was thinking. Sit down, both of you. I'll make breakfast. I think there's some leftover ham in the fridge. I'll fry that up with some eggs and make toast. I'm afraid that will have to do."

"Please don't go to any trouble on my account," I said. "Peanut butter is fine."

"You came here to help me after the way I treated you," Edna said, standing with her hands on her hips. "The least I can do is make you a decent breakfast. Now, I don't want to hear another word."

Maureen grinned and waved at me to sit while she made toast. Needless to say, Edna's behavior amazed me. I sat like a docile child and waited for my meal. At the first whiff of ham frying on the stove, my stomach growled loudly. Edna and Maureen looked at me and laughed. I felt my face heat up, but I laughed too. After the last day or so, it felt good to laugh.

We ate and chatted away with the same comfortable camaraderie we had enjoyed during my first days at Edna's house.

"Thank you, Edna. That was wonderful."

"You're very welcome, dear." She started to clear the table, but I insisted she have another cup of tea while I did the dishes.

"Why don't you go inside and turn on the radio? There might be some news about the flood," I said.

As soon as she left the kitchen, Maureen said, "Alex, I think this may be the solution to your problem."

"What problem? Or rather, which problem?"

"Where to live, of course."

"Maureen, what are you getting at?"

"Look, Edna seems to have forgiven you for whatever she thought was so terrible, so maybe you can come back here."

"Are you crazy? She'll never go for that, and I'm not sure I want to."

Maureen threw the dishtowel over her shoulder, and grabbed my arm.

"Listen, Alex, this may be the best, if not the only, solution for you. You don't want to live at either Jimmy's or Adam's houses, so where else are you going to go? I'm sure that rat trap you call home will be a mess, if it's still standing. And I'm pretty sure Edna will be willing to take you back.

"She's mentioned you more than once and commented on how she didn't like to think about you living in Hamm's Court. And I think your coming here today meant a lot to her. Leave it to me. I'll put a bug in her ear before we leave, and I bet she'll ask you to come back."

"She'd never ask."

"Well, she might *offer* you the opportunity. You know, make it look like she's doing it because it's the 'Christian thing' to do."

"Let's go see what my place looks like first."

"All right, but I'm still going to say something to her."

I rolled my eyes and shook my head. There was no use arguing with Maureen. She'd do what she wanted, no matter what I said.

The dishes done, I went to the bathroom to wash my face and Maureen headed to the living room.

"Thanks again for everything," I said to Edna before we left.

"Alex," Edna said, "if you find your place is not livable, you can come back here. For a while, anyway."

Maureen stood behind Edna and winked at me.

"Thanks, Edna. I appreciate the offer. If my cabin's as bad as I think it will be, I just may take you up on that."

"Well, plan on coming back here for dinner, at any rate."

"Thank you, Edna. Ready, Maureen?"

Maureen couldn't wipe the grin off her face.

She's really a good friend.

Once again, we sloshed through the muddy water to get to Hamm's Court. To call it a disaster area would be putting it mildly. Mattresses and random chairs lay scattered everywhere. Shoes and clothes hung from doors or were draped over dressers sitting in the middle of the muddy courtyard. Screen doors hung askew from one hinge. People wandered around aimlessly.

"This is terrible," Maureen said. "I thought this place was bad before, but now it's a complete junkyard."

We walked through the tangle of furniture, bedding, and fires, presumably set to burn items ruined beyond repair, and arrived at my cabin.

I opened the door to chaos. A deluge of water flowed out, but even that release still left some deep puddles on the uneven warped floor. The dresser had toppled over and the top half lay across the bed, the bottom half still in murky water. Various small items and my trunk floated around the room, including my much-loved radio.

In the bathroom, Adam's bike stood proudly in the tub, gleaming in the sunbeam that filtered through the window. Fortunately, most of my clothes still hung in the closet, high above the water. I assumed the items in the top drawers of the dresser escaped damage, but I wouldn't know for sure until I could get that righted.

I ran my hand through my hair and sighed.

"Guess I'll see if Mrs. Forster has a push broom I can borrow to sweep out the water," I said.

"Okay," Maureen said, still staring at the devastation.

A while later, I had swept most of the water out of my room and we were able to stand the dresser back on its four feet. As I suspected, the items in the top drawers were fine. Fortunately, the bottom drawers held extra blankets and linens that belonged to the management, so not my concern. We lifted my trunk onto the bed and opened it, hoping for the best.

"Well, what do you know," I said. "When my dad bought this, the salesman said it was waterproof, and it is." The inside was completely dry.

We packed up my clothes and the afghan from my bed, and I retrieved the bike from the tub.

"Looks like you've got a roommate again," I said to Maureen.

"Welcome home," she said, and gave me a hug.

Mr. Forster loaned me his truck for the quick ride to Edna's, and within an hour I had reestablished myself in my old room.

Edna fussed over me a little, and I reminded her that I knew the rules and would obey them to the letter this time.

"Maybe I was a little too harsh," she said. "I guess I'll have to adjust to a newspaperman's irregular schedule."

With that semi-apology, we lay the foundation for a truce to our hostilities.

CHAPTER 47

Over the next few days, city crews pumped out flooded basements for residents. The mud remained, but at least the houses were livable. Some people had problems with their wells, or health problems brought on by waterlogged walls and furniture, but considering the enormity of the flood, the Sunset Valley residents felt fortunate. To some, the bigger disaster was the fact that the Sunset Valley High School basketball team, the Mustangs, lost the tournament by a slim margin.

Everything at the paper was back to normal, meaning I had returned to making the rounds of courthouses, the sheriff's and mayor's offices, and the hospital.

Betty had come through the flood no worse for wear. The doctors weren't releasing anyone until they could show that their homes were safe and livable. The hospital sat on high ground, and only sections of the basement had water damage.

I saw Jimmy most days for a few minutes, although I stopped having lunch with him every day. He didn't mention his proposal and neither did I. I hoped it had died a quiet death.

Or maybe I didn't. It had taken me by surprise, and I honestly didn't know how I felt about it. His invitation was tempting. It was everything I'd ever dreamed about: a job at a big city paper, a life in New York, access to museums, theaters, concerts, and, on top of all that, a man who loved me. Of course, it all hinged on Jimmy's acceptance into Cooper Union. Although he seemed confident it would happen, I refused to allow myself to make future plans based on a possibility. After all, I took this job based on the possibility of it leading to great things, and that seemed to be a far-fetched dream at the moment.

From now on, I was going to rely on concrete facts, not possibilities.

"Hi, Betty," I said as I entered her room.

"Hello, stranger. Gosh, it's been ages since you've visited."

"Oh, it hasn't been that long. I have been a little preoccupied with the minor annoyance of a flood."

"Yeah, that," Betty said, waving her hand in dismissal. "Great reporting, Alex. You've become an ace reporter in my book."

"I'm only filling in on the big stories until you're back on your feet."

"Don't kid yourself. You're not the only visitor I get, you know. People respect you and think you're doing a great job."

An inner glow spread warmth from my toes to the top of my head. "Thanks, Betty."

She looked at me and seemed to be appraising me. "Well, we'll work something out when I get out of here. I guess there's room for the two of us."

"Sure." I thought about that possibility and didn't know if I agreed with her or not. But I knew I wasn't going back to reporting on bake sales.

How can we both be lead reporters?

"What does the town look like now?"

"Huh? Sorry. Guess I was daydreaming."

"You know, you don't have to visit if I bore you."

"No, it's not that. I . . . I just have a lot on my mind. It's been kind of rough these past few days. The town? Fortunately, no people were hurt, but some livestock were. Joe and I have joined forces to see how the loss has affected the ranchers. The economics of ranching is something I know nothing about, so there's a lot to learn."

"Sounds interesting."

"It is, just tiring."

The bell rang for the end of visiting hours.

"Anything I can bring next time? Or are you still working your way through the books I dropped off?"

"I'm almost done with them. Maybe some light reading? Something that my brain doesn't have to struggle with. I'm having a hard enough time struggling with negotiating crutches and these casts. I don't need my brain to get worn out too."

"I'll see what I can do." I gave a little salute and headed out.

I wondered what *would* happen when Betty came back. She was Lou's fair-haired gal, but I'd be damned if I'd go back to doing community news.

Maybe I should give Jimmy's proposal some serious consideration.

Back at the paper, I stowed my bike in the reception area and walked into the newsroom, mulling over possible options for the day Betty returned. Of course, I had no idea when that would be, but I wanted to be prepared in case there weren't enough stories for two reporters.

No more hoping things would turn out the way I dreamed. I was determined to make sure things turned out the way I wanted. Wasn't that what Dad said I should always do? I could hear his voice in my head: "Proper prior planning prevents piss poor performance."

"Alex, there's a letter here for you," Lou bellowed from his office.

"A letter? For me?"

"Am I not speaking English?"

Lou sounded unusually harsh. We'd been getting along great since the flood. He no longer treated me like a kid. Instead, he gave a certain amount of respect to my ideas and stories. But right now, he sounded angry and a little disgusted that he had to talk to me at all.

I walked into his office not knowing what to expect.

"It's there, on top of the file cabinet."

I reached up for the cause of his annoyance, pulled it down, shoved it into my pocket, and retreated to my desk, or started to anyway.

"Did you look at the return address?" he asked.

I pulled the offensive envelope out of my pocket. There in the upper left-hand corner in bold print:

San Francisco Chronicle.

What? Why would they write to me?
I ripped the envelope open.

Dear Mr. Lawson,

We have been following your excellent reporting of the Sunset Valley, Montana, flood, and the subsequent bombing of the ice jam on the Yellowstone River.

In our opinion, your attention to detail while addressing the effects of this disaster on the residents of Sunset Valley is exemplary.

We would like to offer you a position on our staff.

Please contact us at your earliest convenience.

Regards,

George P. Clark

George P. Clark
Publisher

I stood there in stunned silence. My hands trembled, and my legs turned weak and wobbly.

"Well," Lou thundered, "what does it say?"

I handed him the letter, unable to speak.

"Figured that's what this was all about." He rubbed his hand over his face and chewed his cigar to a pulp. "Well, what are you going to do?"

I heard Lou's voice through a foggy cocoon. My vision distorted. My hands clammy. My mouth dry. Lightheaded, I stumbled to the sofa and fell onto it.

"Humph. Suppose I should have expected someone would try to steal you," Lou said. He looked up from the letter, which he was reading again. "You all right, Alex? You look a little pale."

272

"I'm in shock. I think. Oh, Lou, this is the most wonderful thing that's ever happened to me. I feel like I'm in a dream."

"It's not a dream. It's real. Much as I wish it wasn't."

He plopped down next to me and handed me a glass.

"This calls for a drink."

I took a sip and realized Lou had handed me a glass of bourbon, not water.

"Kind of early for this, isn't it?"

"Nah, not when you get news like this."

He took a healthy gulp of his drink and so did I. The liquor shot through me and woke up all my senses. I bolted out of my dream world and landed back in reality.

"Guess you'll be leaving us, huh?" Lou asked. He leaned over, his forearms resting on his knees, and swirled the remaining bourbon around in his glass. "Damn. Just as I was getting used to you."

"Really, Lou? You were? Well, it's all your fault, you know."

He looked at me like I had just made the most idiotic statement ever.

"If you hadn't sent my stories to the wire services, the *Chronicle* never would have read them."

Lou nodded. "The story needed to be told, and you did a bang-up job. You've earned this."

"Now that what I've dreamed about, and hoped for, is really happening, I don't know if I can do it. I don't know if I'm good enough for something as big as the *Chronicle.*"

"You're a talented reporter, Alex. You're ready."

"Thanks, Lou. I'll never forget what you've done for me."

"You can mention that when you accept your Pulitzer."

"I'll do that."

"Meanwhile, better write back before they change their mind," he said, going back to his desk. "Or better yet, why don't you call them? I guess we can finance one long distance call."

"Really, Lou?" I leaned over and gave him a hug.

"Now don't go getting all sappy on me. Go ahead and call them, then let me know how long you'll be here."

"Thanks, Lou."

I flew to my desk, my feet never touching the ground. My hands were shaking so much, I wasn't sure I could dial the phone. I picked up the receiver. "Pat, can you get the *San Francisco Chronicle* on the line? Here's the number."

"Sure, Alex. I'll ring you as soon as it connects."

I reread the letter while I waited for Pat to make the connection. Before I knew it, I was talking to Mr. Clark. After we cleared up the confusion about me being Miss Lawson, not Mr. Lawson, he repeated the offer he had made in his letter at a salary that was impossible to resist. I accepted the job, though I would have said yes if it meant eating peanut butter sandwiches and living in a hovel for the rest of my life.

"Better take the rest of the day off, Alex," Lou said, standing in his office doorway. "I can see you'll be no use to me today."

"Thanks, Lou." I grabbed my hat and purse, and retrieved my bike.

Riding home, I thought about Jimmy and Adam. I needed time to think about what I should do. Of course, I still hadn't heard a word from Adam, so maybe I didn't need to worry about him. But I knew I had to let him know I was moving.

As soon as I got home I told Edna my news, then phoned my parents. Dad was thrilled and told me he'd always known I'd be a big success. I think he was already planning his trip to the Pulitzer Awards. Mom seemed genuinely surprised that I had achieved my dream. It saddened me a little when she commented about getting above my station in life. I wanted both of them to be happy for me, but realized I'd have to settle for just one. Although Mom did get a little teary thinking about how far away I'd live. But Dad said they could make a vacation out of visiting me. I thought that was a swell idea.

We stayed on the phone for a long while, so I left a few dollars under the message pad to pay Edna for the call.

I walked out onto the porch and took a deep breath. It was time to call Adam. With firm resolve, I dialed the ranch. Martha answered and told me he was out, but she'd let him know I called.

Now I didn't know what to do. Wait for Adam to call back, or go to the hospital to see Jimmy? Maybe I could catch him before he left for the day.

I also wanted to tell Betty my news. I felt sure she'd be thrilled, if for no other reason than that her old job would be waiting for her, now that I was out of the picture.

Jimmy, however, was something else entirely. He had proposed. This wasn't going to be easy.

I decided to call the hospital and ask him to come to Edna's after work. That way, we'd have some privacy. I could explain things better in person.

CHAPTER 48

Jimmy arrived at Edna's house that night after his shift ended. I took him into the kitchen and told him about the offer from the *Chronicle* that I had accepted.

His head dropped to his chest. "Guess you won't reconsider, will you?" His gaze stayed focused on the floor as he swept his fingers through his hair.

"No, Jimmy. I want us to stay friends, though. If I write to you, will you write back?"

"'Course I will." He looked at me, his eyes watery. "It'll never be the same as seeing you almost every day though. I thought we had something special, Alex."

"We do. A friendship that I never want to lose." I placed my hand on his forearm and squeezed. "You're probably closer to me than anyone else in my life has ever been. And I don't want to lose that closeness."

"That'll never happen." He put his hand on top of mine and sighed.

We sat there for a few minutes, looking into each other's eyes. Neither of us spoke.

"Want a cup of tea?" I asked, in an attempt to break the tension that buzzed around the room like static electricity.

"No. I should go."

"See you tomorrow?"

His lips curled in a half smile. "Sure, why not." Then he stood, gave me a quick kiss on the top of my head, and left.

An incredible veil of sadness enveloped me. I crossed my arms on the table, let my head drop onto them, and cried. Edna and Maureen left me alone to deal with my grief in my own way, and I was grateful for that. I knew I would miss him terribly.

After I cried myself out, I walked to the kitchen sink and splashed water on my face. All I wanted to do was curl up in my bed and throw the covers over my head. But that luxury would have to wait.

"Alex," Maureen said from the doorway, "phone call."

I walked in a trance to the phone.

"Hello," I mumbled.

"You sound awful. Are you okay?" Adam asked. "Is everything all right?"

"Hold on a minute." I blew my nose and took a deep breath. "Hi, Adam. I called because I have some exciting news."

"I didn't think you wanted to talk to me again."

"How could you think that?" I sighed. "Adam, I was tired and hungry and angry, yes; but that didn't mean I didn't want to see you or talk to you ever again."

Silence.

"Adam? You still there?"

"I'm here."

Gripping the receiver so tightly my knuckles turned white, I murmured, "Don't you want to see *me* again?" My world was crumbling before my eyes while I waited for his answer.

"Of course, I do," he said in a leaden voice, "but you don't make it easy to love you."

Love me? Does he love me? Why is he saying this now?

"Adam, we need to talk, and I don't want to have this conversation over the phone."

"I'll come into town tomorrow after supper, if that's all right. Wait a minute. What's your news?"

"I'll tell you tomorrow."

I hung up before I blurted everything out. If he really did love me, would it change everything? Just when I thought things were going great, a monkey wrench was thrown into my plans.

"Everything okay?" Maureen asked.

"I don't know anymore. I don't think I can think straight right now."

"Want to talk about it? I can make us a cup of tea."

Later, after spilling my guts to Maureen, I didn't feel much better or any surer of my decisions.

"I think you should wait to see what Adam says tomorrow," Maureen said.

"Maybe I should just marry Jimmy and hope everything works out."

"Alex, you know you don't love him that way. It wouldn't be fair to Jimmy. And you already accepted the position at the *Chronicle.*"

"You're right. Of course, I could always call them and tell them I changed my mind. I'm so confused. My heart and my head are splitting me in half."

"What you need is a good night's sleep. Things always look clearer after you sleep on them."

The next morning I woke after a restless night, and hoped I'd feel better about everything. But I didn't.

I felt like a heel about Jimmy. I pictured his face, the look of despair and broken hopes. I mentally replayed the conversation with Adam and dreaded my meeting with him later that day. Overnight, I had come up with what I thought might be a reasonable solution. I just didn't know if Adam would agree with it. I remembered Lou's look of resigned acceptance of my decision, coupled with one of frustration over producing a newspaper with no reporter on hand. Not only had I created havoc for my own life, I'd let my decision affect three other people.

I dragged myself down to breakfast.

"Good morning." Edna sounded more chipper than usual. "Sleep well?"

"Morning," I mumbled. "Sleep wasn't great, but waking up's even worse."

Edna chuckled. "You'll have a lot to do over the next few weeks, won't you?"

"I guess."

"It's so exciting. Imagine. Our little town producing a big-time city reporter. I couldn't be prouder." She cackled over me like a mother hen, fixing my coffee, getting me toast, pouring cereal into my bowl.

Guess I'll be grist for the gossip mill today.

I managed to eat breakfast even though everything tasted like sawdust. "Where's Maureen?" I asked.

"She went to work early. Something about wanting to talk to the coach about next year's basketball schedule."

I swallowed the last of my coffee and said, "I'm off."

"Have a good day, dear," Edna said. "Maybe I'll see you at the courthouse."

I gave her a weak smile, nodded, and headed out the door.

As I walked alongside my bike to the office, I tried to work out the logistics of this move. I'd have to arrange shipping for my trunk, get a bus ticket, and find a place to live in San Francisco. I thought maybe the personnel department at the *Chronicle* could help. In college, I had heard that some companies had relocation packets for future employees. If Lou let me call them again today, that might solve my housing problem.

"Hey, watch it, Alex."

The shout knocked me out of my daze.

"You almost ran me over." Joe stood in front of me, grasping the handlebars of my bike, the front wheel between his legs.

"I'm so sorry, Joe. Guess I was daydreaming."

"I'll say. You look like you're sleepwalking."

"Just got a lot on my mind."

"I heard. Got time for coffee?"

"I should check in with Lou."

"He can wait. I want to talk to you."

I shrugged my shoulders and propped the bike against the nearest lamppost. Inside the café, the usual enticing aromas of bacon, coffee, and freshly baked pastries assaulted me.

Joe headed to a table in the back, away from the counter.

"What's on your mind?" I asked.

"I heard you're moving on."

"Yep. I got an offer from the *San Francisco Chronicle* yesterday."

"Congratulations, but I've got to say . . . I've seen happier faces at a funeral."

A brief smile crossed my face.

"What's the matter, Alex? Having second thoughts?"

"Not really. It's what I want, but I didn't figure on how it would affect everyone else."

"I wouldn't worry about Lou. He'll find a replacement."

The waitress came over and took our order. I only wanted coffee, but Joe insisted I have a sticky bun with it. He ordered the breakfast special, pancakes and bacon.

"I just feel bad about Lou. If he hadn't sent my story out to the wire services, I never would've gotten this offer."

"He knows that. And between you and me, he's thrilled that you did. He was like a proud papa last night, telling me all about you. Even gave me a cigar and a drink to celebrate."

"Really? That makes me feel a little better." I took a sip of coffee. "Do you know what he plans on doing when I leave?"

"Well, I'll pick up some of the slack, but I think until Betty's back on her feet, and no one knows how long that'll be, he's going to ask Maureen if she'd like a full-time job."

I almost choked on my coffee, sputtering some out my nose.

Joe pounded me on the back. "You okay?"

"Yeah, sure," I said between coughs. "Maureen? Really? She's a teacher."

"Yeah, well, she's done a great job on the community news, so Lou wants to offer it to her first. And considering the abysmal teacher salaries, I'm sure she'd make more at the paper. That's kind of what I wanted to talk to you about. I was wondering if you'd feel her out about the job. If she doesn't want it, I'd like to throw my hat in the ring. I don't know how Lou would feel about that. I've made my own niche with the ranchers and all, but it's worth a try. And if Maureen says no and Lou nixes my overtures, well . . . college graduation will be here soon. Maybe we'll luck out and get another Alex."

The waitress brought our meals just in time for me to avoid commenting on Joe's last remark.

We dug into our food, each lost in our own thoughts. The sweet sticky bun tasted delicious, so much better than the cardboard corn-flakes I had shoveled down earlier.

I asked Joe about the ranchers affected by the flood, and he gave me the latest news on the ones we had visited together.

When the waitress landed our check on the table, Joe grabbed it. "My treat. A little farewell gift."

"Thanks, Joe."

Outside, we went our separate ways, Joe to the farmers and ranchers, me to the office.

Inside the newsroom, all was eerily quiet. Pat gushed over me for a minute before the phone started ringing; Lou pored over some copy, red pencil in hand. I put my purse and hat away, then stepped over to Lou's office to ask about making another phone call. He nodded and waved me off, absorbed in whatever had come in overnight from the wire services.

The head of personnel at the *Chronicle* said she'd be happy to send me a package with the names and locations of some single women's hotels and reputable boardinghouses. I wasn't going to make the same mistake I'd made when I moved here. This time I wanted to have my living arrangements all set before I got to San Francisco. We also settled on the start date—one month from now.

I typed my formal resignation letter stating my last day, three weeks away. That gave me a week for any final preparations. Making definite plans calmed some of my anxieties, but there was still a lot to do.

I poked my head into Lou's office and told him I was off for my usual rounds. He grunted and nodded.

On the way to the courthouse, I stopped at the Sunset Hotel to pick up a bus schedule. The bus company kept a rack there for the different destinations on its routes.

The morning flew by. Before I knew it, it was time for lunch. I wondered if I'd see Jimmy today. He'd become a true friend and I knew I'd miss him.

When I got to the hospital cafeteria, I saw Jimmy at our usual table. I filled my tray and joined him.

"Hi, Jimmy. I didn't know if I'd see you today."

Jimmy smiled. "I wanted to talk to you. And congratulate you. I realize you have to go after your dream just like I'm going after mine. I wish they could be in the same place, but . . ."

"I'm so glad you said that. I'll miss you terribly."

"You'll be so busy, you'll never even notice I'm not there."

"Never."

Jimmy asked about when I'd leave and I filled him in on the plans I'd made.

After we finished lunch, he gave me his address and a quick kiss on the cheek. Then I went upstairs to see Betty.

When I told her my news, she said she was thrilled for me, but I sensed a tinge of insincerity.

"Now you have to get better quickly," I said. "Lou needs his ace reporter back."

She gave me a halfhearted smile. "We'll see. Any idea what he plans to do in the meantime?"

"No. He hasn't said a word to me."

Technically, not a lie. He told Joe, not me.

"Well, thanks for sharing your news. It must be very exciting for you."

Her words conveyed a definite dismissal, which was confirmed when she picked up her book and began to read. So much for the old team spirit. More like sour grapes.

Now I just had to get through the day before I faced Adam with the plan I had hatched overnight.

CHAPTER 49

At supper, I pushed my food around on my plate, afraid if I ate anything, it wouldn't stay down. Edna cast a few admonishing glances my way, but didn't say anything. Maureen tried to lighten the mood by telling some funny anecdotes from her day. I only half listened. My stomach was twisted into a mangled mess, and my brain was doing cartwheels, imagining what Adam would say.

I helped Maureen clear the table and had started to wash the dishes when the doorbell rang.

"Go," Maureen said. "I'll finish up."

I untied my apron and ran to the door, beating Edna by seconds.

Adam stood there, hat in hand, looking more handsome and vulnerable than ever. I grabbed his hand and pulled him over to a couple of chairs on the porch. But before we could sit, he wrapped his arms around me and kissed me hard. No gentleness anymore, this was pure passion. My knees buckled. We stood clinging to each other for a long time, his heart pounding next to mine. I never realized I could feel so much a part of another human being, like we had merged into one person. I was lost in Adam, and didn't want to be found.

He finally pushed me back a little, kissed me gently, and asked in a husky voice, "Now, what do you want to talk about?"

I could hardly breathe, much less speak. I cleared my throat. "Let's sit. I can't concentrate when you're holding me like this."

"Before you say anything," he said, "I owe you an apology. I know you can take care of yourself. I was just worried that you'd be so caught up in getting your story that you'd forget to be careful. I only wanted Hank to keep an eye on you, but it seems I didn't make that entirely clear."

His worried frown made my heart jump.

"I know. I shouldn't have exploded like I did. Dad always said I had the shortest fuse of anyone he'd ever known. I'm sorry too."

He breathed a sigh of relief. "Glad we got that settled. Now, what's your big news? You get promoted?"

"Something like that."

I told Adam that Lou had sent my stories out to the wire services, and papers across the country printed them. He was thrilled to hear my reporting had gone nationwide.

Then I told him about the offer from the *Chronicle*.

"Bet that made you feel good. Imagine, a big city paper offering you a job. That's something you can brag about around town in your old age."

"That'd probably be true, if I stayed here."

Adam looked at me and started to speak, but I held my hand up to stop him.

"Believe me, Adam, I've thought long and hard about this. I've wondered if I'll be able to make it in a big city. I've doubted my abilities as a reporter. I've wondered about us and our relationship."

He stared at me, a confused look on his face.

"I don't understand. What are you saying?"

"I accepted their offer. I'll be moving to San Francisco in about a month." I took a deep breath before I said the next thing to him. "And I want you to come with me. I know you can't do that right away, and it may only be for parts of the year, like winters or mud season. I know you'll need time to settle things on the ranch, and I know it's not the best solution. But I want you to be part of my life, however long it takes for you to join me. And for whatever amount of time we can steal to be together. I love you, Adam."

I twisted my hands together. I wasn't sure if I was breathing anymore.

Adam leaned forward, hands clasped between his knees, and stared at the porch floor.

Say something. Please.

He looked at me sideways. "Why didn't you just kick me in the gut? It would've been easier to take than this."

Tears streamed down my cheeks.

"Adam, you *know* how much I've wanted a job like this. You know it's my dream."

"This isn't what I planned on at all."

He stood and paced across the porch. I watched and tried to calm my nerves, which were now working overtime, leaping around like Mexican jumping beans.

"Alex," he said, stopping in front of me. "When I came here tonight, I didn't know what your news was going to be about, but I assumed it had something to do with either the paper, or maybe even moving to the ranch. I never expected this. You blindsided me."

Now it was my turn to interrupt, but he held his hand up and I pressed my lips together.

"On the drive into town tonight, I realized that I love you, more than is good for me. You can be the most pigheaded, ornery filly in the herd, and you drive me crazy most of the time, but I love you." He took another deep breath. "Marry me, Alex, please. Imagine what our lives could be like. Long horseback rides together. Nights sitting on the porch, maybe with a glass of fine bourbon or a martini or a simple lemonade. Watching little Adams and Alexes playing. Teaching them everything about ranch life, like how to ride a horse, rope a calf, herd cattle, maybe even some sheep."

I covered my face with my hands and cried in earnest now. I felt Adam's handkerchief against my cheek. I grabbed it and wiped my tears, which wouldn't stop. He sat on the arm of my chair, pulled me toward him, and rubbed my back.

"Shh, shh, it'll be fine. You just have to call that paper tomorrow and say you've changed your mind. Tell them some handsome cowboy rode into town—"

"No, Adam. That's just it. I can't. You're making it so difficult for me. The life you describe sounds wonderful. But don't you see? I can't turn this opportunity down. Not without giving it a try. I'd regret it for the rest of my life. I'd always wonder what my life would have been like if I'd accepted that job at the *Chronicle*. I don't want to spend the rest of my life thinking, what if."

Adam walked back to his chair. "Alex, what would I do in a city? I don't belong there. I belong here, on my ranch. The ranch my grandfather started from nothing. The ranch my father worked until he died. The ranch I grew up on. I belong here, Alex. I can't leave. It would be like ripping out my heart and soul."

His tortured face filled me with incredible sorrow.

"Stay, Alex. Marry me. We can have a great life here. If you go to San Francisco, you'll be a little fish in a big pond. To be honest, I don't know if your ego can take that. Don't you see?"

"I know I'll have to work my way up. But I can't pass up this chance."

He stood. "You mean you won't, because you *can* do whatever you want. But obviously, this job means more to you than I do, and there's nothing I can do to change that. I hope you'll be happy, because I won't be here waiting for you if you decide to come back. Goodbye, Alex."

I lifted my head to get a last look at his face, but all I saw was his back as he trudged to his truck. "I'll always love you, Adam," I whispered as he drove away.

An overwhelming emptiness enveloped me. I always felt a piece of me went with Adam whenever he left, but now it felt like all of me went with him. I was a shell. A body without a heart or soul.

What had I done? I had just tossed aside a man I loved with every ounce of me.

All for a job.

I sighed.

A deep sigh.

But I knew if I didn't do this, I'd spend the rest of my life asking, what if?

I walked into the house and up to my room. I didn't want to speak to anyone. I had chosen my path, and I'd stick to it.

CHAPTER 50

Sunset Valley, Montana 1955

"Afraid I have to get going," I said, checking my watch and excusing myself from my bull breeding rancher companion. It was still fairly early, but I didn't like driving at night when the deer, moose, and elk took over the roads. I just had to find Maureen and say goodbye.

It was a shame her party and my award dinner had coincided. I was glad I'd found a way to fit both into my schedule. Tomorrow I'd fly to New York to receive the Front-page Award, the annual award given by the **New York Newspaper Woman's Club** to honor journalistic achievement by women. This recognition by my colleagues gave me goose bumps every time I thought about it, but the best part of this trip would be seeing Jimmy and his wife, Carolyn, again. It'd been too long between visits. They had planned a big celebratory dinner for me at their new beach house, which Jimmy had designed, of course, complete with all their kids and grandkids. This month's *Architectural Record* did a retrospective of his work, and I must say it was impressive. I hadn't realized he had accumulated such an extensive portfolio.

It would be fun to see all of them again. They had become my adopted family, since I didn't have one of my own. I made sure I sent cards and gifts for all the birthdays and holidays, but rarely got to be there to celebrate with them. Work always seemed to get in the way. Thank goodness for phone calls, and I treasured the thank you letters from the little ones, although I often didn't get to read them until weeks after they were sent. I sometimes think I spend more time on the road chasing stories than I do in my San Francisco home. It'll be so relaxing to spend a few days on the beach with Jimmy and Carolyn. Sun, sand, and champagne.

My thoughts were interrupted when I heard someone say, "Oh good, Adam was able to make it after all."

I looked up and saw a familiar face beneath the Stetson. My heart skipped a beat. Even after all this time. There was a face I hadn't seen, in person, in decades. But a face I had seen, in my dreams, for decades. Adam. Older, more wrinkled and weather-beaten, but definitely Adam.

Damn. I felt my face flush.

Stop acting like a teenager with a crush on the high school quarterback.

I knew there was a possibility he'd be here, but as the hours passed and he didn't show up, I relaxed. I hadn't wanted to see him again. Or at least that's what I thought.

Over the years, I'd fallen in and out of love a few times, but I never fell out of love with Adam. I'd often wondered what would happen if I ran into him again. There were still so many painful memories attached to him and our last night together all those years ago.

Go say hello. Don't be such a sissy. You've been on battlefields and not felt this nervous. Just bite the bullet and get this over with. What's the worst that could happen?

I wiggled my way through the crowd, but stopped and thought better of it when he looked at me, a quizzical expression on his face. I thought I saw a glimmer of recognition, but maybe that was wishful thinking. He touched the brim of his hat and nodded slightly, then focused his attention on the two ranchers who were leading him over to the outdoor bar.

As I watched him walk away, I thought back to the last time I had seen Adam. And watched him walk away. I had only spent a short time in Sunset Valley. A time when the distant roar of ice and bombs and planes had changed my life forever.

Do I regret my decision? Sometimes.

I often wonder what life would have been like if I'd married him. Long horseback rides in the countryside, our children and grandchildren filling the house with laughter. My own family to love.

But I've traveled all over the world. Written stories covering politics, government, disasters, wars, and everything else you can think of. It's been a full life. It's said you should be careful what you wish for. I thought I had been careful.

Maybe so. Maybe not.

But one always wonders.

AUTHOR'S NOTE

First of all, I want to thank you, my readers. Without your support, this book wouldn't exist. I loved writing it and researching the time period. Although we're all familiar with the stereotypical symbols of the Roaring Twenties—the flappers, speakeasies, and roving carloads of tommy gun carrying gangsters—I didn't realize how sensationalized even small news stories could become at that time.

The nonfiction book, *Only Yesterday*, written in 1931 by Frederick Lewis Allen, was a wonderful resource, and I highly recommend it if you're curious about the 1920s. Only forty-one years old when he wrote the book in 1931, Allen's life experiences cast a different light on the era. Of course, as with all historical fiction, I consulted many books and researched heavily on the Internet before I decided the 1920s would be the ideal time period for this piece. A time when women were almost nowhere to be found in a newsroom.

This story is based in part on actual circumstances that almost wiped out a small town in eastern Montana. When a friend sent me a news clipping about this disaster, which actually took place in the 1940s, I knew it would make a great story. But when I thought about that time period, I realized it was probably quite normal to see women in newsrooms then, since so many men had been sent overseas to fight in World War II. Alex might have become just one of many women reporters. However, placing her in a 1920s newsroom put a totally different slant on her situation and gave her even more obstacles to overcome.

No book is ever written in a vacuum, and I'd like to thank my beta readers and longtime friends who went through the early versions of this story without complaint. Thank you, Karen Austin, Faith Justice, Alan Michels, Terry Scaglione, and Jill Wisoff. Your insights and guidance were much appreciated. I also owe a debt to Amy Collins, who led me to set this story in the 1920s. You have my eternal gratitude. And, of course, every author needs an editor to fine-tune their work. My thanks go to Elizabeth Buege and Melisa Hayes. Your input was invaluable.

Woodhall Press has been an amazing publisher. Dave LeGere worked closely with me from day one to bring this story to print. Thank you to Dave and his whole team.

I always love to see what my readers think of my books, so I encourage you to leave a review or your comments/questions on Goodreads or Amazon or both. I promise I do read all of them, even the one-star reviews (but I'm hoping there won't be any of those).

If you'd like to keep up with me and see what I'm working on, what tickles my fancy that day, or read some of the fascinating historical tidbits that I like to share, please consider signing up for my newsletter, *Tales from Then and Now*. I only post a few times a year (most days I'm busy working on my next book), so I won't be filling up your in-box with e-mails. Just click on this link: https://www.ejdonovan.com.

Thank you again. I hope you've enjoyed sharing Alex's journey into the world of newspaper reporting.

ABOUT THE AUTHOR

Eileen Joyce Donovan is an award-winning author whose debut historical novel, *Promises,* won the Marie M Irvine Award for Literary Excellence. She is also the author of short stories and essays for numerous anthologies, including *Chicken Soup for the Soul.* Her work in magazine publishing and advertising helped hone her writing skills. She has taught college writing classes in Arizona, North Carolina, and New Jersey. She lives in Manhattan, New York.